Chapter One

Wednesday

I n a fair and just world, he'd have looked like shit. The years would have ground him down to all but a shell of his former glory. Of course, this hadn't happened. My luck just wasn't that good.

"You made it," he said, walking barefoot down his front steps.

"Don't sound so surprised. You taught me how to drive."

Pale blue eyes gazed at me flatly. No visible gray in his dark hair. Not yet, anyway.

"Hi, Pete," I said.

Nothing.

"I come in peace."

More of the same.

I climbed out of my car, muscles protesting the

movement. My sundress was a crumpled ruin. What had looked hopeful, happy, and bright in the wee hours of the morning didn't hold up so well under the late-afternoon light. A twelve-hour drive from Sydney to South East Queensland's north coast will do that to you. I pushed my sunglasses on top of my head, ready to face my inevitable doom. A light breeze smelled of lush foliage and flowers. And the heat and humidity beat down on me, even with the sun sinking over the hills. I'd forgotten what it was like being in the subtropics during summer. Should have worn more deodorant. Should have faked a communicable disease and stayed home.

"What's it been," he asked, "seven years?"

"About that."

"Thought you were bringing a boyfriend with you."

I paused. Dad must have given him that idea. God knows where Dad, however, had gotten it from. "No. No . . . he's ah, busy."

He looked me over; I guess we were both curious. Last time we'd been in the same room was for my eighteenth birthday party. My hair had been short and my skirt even shorter. What a spectacularly awful night that was. As if he too, remembered, he suddenly frowned, his high forehead filling with lines. Victory! The man definitely had more wrinkles. Unfortunately, they kind of suited him. Enhanced him, even. Bastard.

"Better come inside," he said.

"If you're still pissed at me, then why am I staying here?"

"I am not 'pissed at you.'" His tone was light and just a bit haughty. A sure sign he was pissed. "I just was expecting your boyfriend too, that's all."

I crossed my arms.

"Look," he said, "you're staying here because we're both doing a favor to your dad. I know you haven't met her yet, but Shanti's a nice woman. She's good for him. They make a great couple and I want their wedding to be hassle free."

"I didn't come to cause trouble."

"But with you, from what I recall, it just seems to magically happen." Hands on slim hips, he gave me a grim smile. "It's just a few days, kid. Apparently, your old room is filled with bomboniere, whatever the fuck that is. So you're staying here with me."

I'd heard worse ideas in my life, but not many. Also they usually involved the risk of possible loss of limb, death, or incarceration. I'd tried to talk Dad into alternatives, but he'd stood firm, dammit. "That's kind of you, but not necessary. I'll go get a room at a hotel, this isn't—"

"They're probably booked," he said. "It's peak season so even if you could find somewhere, you'd pay through the roof. Anything nearby is going to already be busy with other wedding guests. Look, your dad wants you close so he can spend some time with you."

I said nothing.

"It's only five days," he repeated in the tone of voice he usually reserved for those dancing on his last damn nerve. "Let's just get through it."

3

Great. Awesome.

With a nod, I headed for the back of my car. All the better to hide and take a second to pull myself together.

"Did you bring much stuff?" he asked, following.

"No. I've got it."

Except, of course, I didn't. As the hatch opened, he was there, reaching for my suitcase. Muscles flexed in his arms, slightly straining the sleeves of his white T-shirt. The man had always been strong, solid. Unfortunately, he hadn't shrunk any either. I was around average height, but he still had at least half a head on me. Just perfect for looking down and putting me in my place.

"Lock up your car." He headed for the house, tugging my wheeled suitcase behind him. "We might be in the country, but things still happen."

"Yeah, I know to lock up my car," I whisper bitched.

"I heard that."

"I don't give a shit."

He laughed grimly. "Oh, kid, this is going to be fun."

Out of options, I followed. Up the stone steps and into the house. Pete had never been much of a gardener, but someone had done a wonderful job with the grounds. Not that I was willing to say as much. We were apparently at war, and I couldn't even blame him since it was all my fault. God, I hated the old familiar feeling of guilt. Life would be so much easier if I could hate him, push some of the blame his way. But the truth was, he hadn't done a damn thing wrong. Not back then. Not even really now.

My pity party almost distracted me from the house.

"You did it," I breathed, wonder pushing the no-compliment rule straight out of my head. "It's beautiful."

He stopped, blinked. "Yeah."

"Last time I was here you were still living in the shed," I said. "It was just dirt with some pipes and things sticking out of the ground. Now it's finished."

"Parts of it are still a work in progress."

I spun in a slow circle, taking everything in, from the polished wood floors to the gray quartz kitchen located off to one side. A television about the size of a football field hung on one wall, with plush-looking navy couches gathered nearby. A large dining table was made out of a solid slab of wood, the natural edges still rough enough to be decorative. I'd already seen the beginning of that work of art, so I knew he'd made it himself. And the rounded center beam was huge, standing in the middle of the room, holding up the pitched ceiling.

"What is that, two stories high?" I asked, staring up.

"Two and a half."

"Wow. You really did it."

At that, he almost smiled. Almost.

Hallways ran off opposite sides of the great room and there was a wide verandah running the whole length of the building out back. There'd be a barbeque, another dining table and lots of chairs to laze in, and stairs leading down to the pool. I knew it without looking. Just like I knew there'd be the main bedroom with a bathroom and an office off to the right. Two guest bedrooms, a reading nook, and another bathroom off to the left. A long time ago, I'd helped him design this place. We'd worked on it together, a dream house.

"It's perfect," I said quietly.

For a moment, his gaze narrowed. But then his lips returned to their former flat, unhappy state. "Glad you like it. You're in here."

I followed his back into the left wing. The house was amazing. Sadly, my gaze slipped from his wide shoulders, down the length of his spine, to find his gorgeous ass had also lost none of its impact. So unfair. But Pete in jeans always had been a sight to behold. God, his loose-limbed stride. A careless sort of confidence had always just seemed to ooze from the man.

Not that I was looking. Looking was bad.

"This okay?" he asked, throwing open a door.

"Fine. Thanks."

He tapped the top of my luggage. "Where do you want this?"

"I'll handle it."

A nod. "Your dad and Shanti will be over for dinner in a couple of hours."

"Is there anything I can do?"

"No, it's all taken care of." He scratched at his stubble. "Right. Make yourself at home. I'm going to get some work done. Be in the office if you need anything."

I nodded too. Nods were so great. Much better than words.

He stood in the hallway, staring at me for a moment. Not saying anything along the lines of how it was good to see me again. Because that would be a lie.

"Okay, Adele," he finally said, using my name, which was never a good sign. Honestly, I think I actually preferred "kid." Then, thank you baby Jesus, he left.

Carefully, I closed the bedroom door, slumping against it because excessive drama. I'd known coming back was going to be a certain level of hell, but not one quite this deep.

One hundred and twenty hours and counting.

"You looked?" Hazel hissed into my ear. "I can't believe you looked."

I lay mostly dead on the bed, my cell jammed against my ear. "I didn't mean to—it just happened."

"Rule number one was don't look."

"Yeah . . ."

She sighed. "Okay, it's done now. We just have to move past it. But out of interest, how was the view?"

"Better than ever."

"Bastard. How did you look?"

"Sweaty and crumpled."

"I told you to fly."

"Yeah, I know," I groaned. "But then he would have insisted on picking me up from the airport, and being in a contained space for the car ride to his home would not have worked. I would have just wound up having to throw myself out of a moving vehicle, and I don't think that usually ends well."

Nothing from her.

"He still hates me."

"He doesn't hate you."

"No, he really does." I stared at the ceiling. "What's going on there?"

"Hmm? Everything's fine."

"What is that weirdness in your voice?"

"What?"

"Don't 'what' me. What is it?"

My best friend groaned. "I'm not sure you need this news right now, given everything already going on."

"Just tell me."

Some swearing. "Okay. But this is not my choice. Maddie and I went to dinner last night."

"Lovely. Where?"

"The Bombay Diner and it was lovely, but that's not the point," she said. "Listen, Deacon was at the restaurant with another woman and they were very much together. Heading into serious get-a-room territory."

I exhaled. "Oh, I see. Okay."

"Okay?"

"Well, it's not completely unexpected. We had a bit of an argument last week. I don't remember what it was about, but it seemed important at the time."

Silence.

"What?"

"One of these days, you're actually going to care about one of the people you date."

"I care."

"Beyond the normal non-sociopathic 'I hope he doesn't get hit by a car and killed in the street on his way home,'" said Hazel. "Think a more advanced level of caring than that."

"Well, it's fortunate I didn't, seeing as he's cheating on me."

"I knew you'd say that."

I didn't bother answering.

"Did it ever occur to you that he started seeing someone else because you don't care?" she asked.

"You think I wasn't meeting his emotional needs?"

"That's one of my theories about your dating issues."

"See, this is why I have a therapist for a best friend," I said. "You have all the answers."

She laughed. "Only I don't get paid to listen to you."

"Sorry about that."

"Luckily, you're normally pretty boring. So I don't mind this bit of drama."

"That is fortunate," I said. "Thing is, Deacon and I had only been out like four or five times. We hadn't even had sex yet. Can I really be expected to emotionally prop up men after such a small amount of dates?"

Hazel snorted. "You're willfully misunderstanding me. I give up."

"Good. How's Maddie?"

"She's fine. We're going to her parent's place for dinner soon," she said. "Are you going to survive where you are?"

"No. I'll probably just die in a really sad and pathetic manner, slowly becoming a smell in the hallway that he eventually can't ignore. Or not. I haven't decided." More sighing from me. "God, I feel so wound up, like there's something heavy sitting on my chest. Maybe I should just have a mild panic attack and get it over and done with. Tick that box, you know?"

"Panic attacks are nothing to make jokes about," she chided. "Now go have a drink and calm down. Make peace with your situation . . . if you can't make peace with him."

"He won't make peace with *me*."

"Show him what a glorious, mature person you are these days."

"I'm a glorious, mature person?"

"Sure you are. Or at least you can pretend. Your acting skills are quite good. I believe in you." Hazel made kissing noises. "I have to go. Will you live?"

"Yeah, I'll be fine." I smiled. "Thanks for the pep talk. And the information. I promise to be a mess of tears next time a guy's cheating on me. Cross my heart. Have a nice night."

"I'll believe that when I see it. 'Bye."

I tossed my phone aside, surrendering to despair. Or just the oppressive heat and general tiredness. That's when the giant-ass spider ran up the wall directly above my head, long legs skittering as it navigated the edge of the ceiling.

"Jesus!" I scrambled off the bed, heart pounding. "Not cool."

Footsteps came running from the other end of the house, and Pete dashed into the room. "What's wrong?"

I just pointed at the wall.

His brows rose. "It's just a huntsman."

A huff of breath left his body, and with it all sense of urgency. Given my shriek, he'd probably been expecting a snake. While mostly the local populations were just harmless green tree snakes, occasionally an eastern brown would appear. Those things were aggressive and deadly poisonous.

"It's the size of my hand," I complained, trying not to sound defensive. "Ew."

"*Ew?* Seriously?" Yet again, he came dangerously close to smiling. Though this time it was more of a mockery-type thing. "You used to deal with these all the time."

"Yeah, well, I don't anymore. My spider-catching skills have lapsed," I said. "On the plus side, I've mastered Sydney's public transport system. Talk about intimidating."

He just looked at me.

"Can you please get it out of here?"

"Open the verandah door." With a heavy sigh, he disappeared back out into the hallway, reappearing shortly with a big plastic container and a piece of cardboard.

I stood by the open doorway, watching as he crept up on the ugly, hairy eight-legged monster. Realistically, I knew I'd probably scared it worse than it had me. Huntsmen weren't even very poisonous, their sting not much worse than a mosquito's. But creepy-crawlies really weren't my thing. Not anymore, at least.

Pete stepped up onto the bed, his bare feet spread wide apart as he positioned himself for the capture. The clear plastic container closed down on the creepy thing, as Pete tried for the slow and steady approach. At the last moment, its spider sense kicked in, and it leapt into a mad dash for freedom. I bit back a squeal of fright, but Pete's reflexes were up to the task. The container knocked against the bedroom wall, all eight legs and any other bits and pieces of the beast safely inside. I tried to avoid any feeling of grudging admiration. It took a fair bit of skill to nab a big, fast-moving one that smoothly.

Pete carefully slid the piece of cardboard between the wall and the container. Lots of spider jumping and scurrying ensued inside the plastic box. Continuing my display of extreme bravery, I stood back out of the way as he carried the thing outside and then took off the cardboard covering. He flicked the container so Mr. Spider went flying off into the garden, to live wild and free. Much better than copping a load of bug spray in the face.

"Happy?" he asked.

"Delirious. Thank you."

A grunt.

"Remember the first time you taught me to do that? I didn't get it right and the poor thing lost a leg under the edge of the container. Half of me was petrified, and the other half in tears." To be fair, huntsmen's legs were strangely brittle, and you had to be pretty agile to make sure they didn't lose a leg or two in the process.

Another grunt.

Great. Was this how it was going to be for my entire stay?

"Not that I don't adore the whole grouchy thing you've got going," I said. "But out of curiosity, should we just possibly talk about the issue and get it all out there? Deal with it, maybe?"

He frowned. "Hell, no."

"So we're never going to discuss it?"

"Got it in one."

I took a deep breath and gave him a thumbs-up. "Okay. Great. Good talk, Pete. Thanks again for getting rid of the spider."

Another disgruntled look and he was gone, wandering back inside. Off to hide out in his office, no doubt.

Skittering spiders and taciturn men. What the hell had I gotten myself into?

Chapter Two

Nine Years Ago . . .

I sat on the grass under a tree with my nose in a book. Day one of six weeks' worth of the endless sounds of hammers, saws, and screwdrivers was nearly over. Not that I much minded just hanging out. After all, stuff was happening in my book. Action, adventure, romance. All of the things that so never happened in the real world.

A red flatbed truck with a toolbox on the back pulled up and I prepared myself for the next round of greetings. For six weeks every summer, it was more of the same. A mixture of "hey," "how have you been," and "far out, you've grown." Most of the men had known me for years, so it was to be expected.

This guy, however, was new. And wow. I swear to God, he positively *swaggered* over to the house currently undergoing renovations. But like, not in a douchey way.

How such a thing was possible, I had no idea. Truth be told, I'd never really noticed the guys working for Dad much before. They were all fit, strong blokes—and cheerful enough to crease their sun-tanned faces with a ready smile whenever the boss's kid was around.

But Pete was something else.

One of the workers on the roof yelled out something obscene at him and the guy calmly raised his middle finger in response.

"Language!" yelled Dad, with a nod in my direction.

I hid my face in embarrassment. It sucked having to think that all the workers had to be on their best behavior because "the kid" was around.

Immediately, the guy headed my way with a broad grin. "Adele, right? Boss has been talking about your visit for weeks, getting all excited."

News to me. I mean, Dad was okay and everything, but life for him really centered on work. Which was fine and to be expected. Mom had taken me and moved to Sydney a while back, needing her space or something. Artists really are flighty. Dad needed something in his life to fill the hole, and his business played that role just fine.

"Hi," I said.

"Pete." He held out his big hand for shaking.

My hand only trembled slightly. Good going on my part.

Close up, he was even more gorgeous. The most perfect blue-gray eyes and a face that firmly qualified as dreamy. A super-strong jawline and little indent in his chin. His lips. Oh my God, his lips. And all of this finished off with shoulder-length dark hair. I could only stare.

Unfortunately, he was older than me by at least a decade.

"Forgot, you two haven't met before," said Dad, arriving just in time to totally ruin my moment. "Sweetheart, this is Pete. The new employee I told you about. He came onboard at the start of this year. Pete, this is my daughter, Adele. She just turned sixteen."

One way or another, my age was always mentioned in such cases. It was Dad's not-so-subtle way of laying down the law regarding acceptable behavior around me.

"We just met." Pete smiled.

"How'd things go at the Le's?"

"All wrapped up. They're happy."

Dad clapped him on the shoulder. "Good work."

Pete turned back to me and frowned. "Boss, you seriously making her sit around at sites?"

"What?" Dad frowned as if the thought had never occurred to him. "We'll only be another hour here. Then I've got a few things to do at the office, but they shouldn't take too long. She's fine."

"I'm fine," I confirmed.

Pete just shook his head. "Come on, you must be bored shit . . . sheetless, I mean. Yeah, sheetless."

Dad frowned some more while I laughed.

"I'm done for the day and heading to the beach," said Pete. "Why don't I take her with me?"

"You want to go?" Dad asked.

"Sure." I shrugged, slipping the book behind my back. "I'm so bored I don't have any sheets at all. Or even pillows."

Dad's frown deepened a little, but Pete nodded, pleased. "Good. Got some bathers or we need to pick 'em up?"

"Hang on." Dad fished his wallet out of his back pocket, stuffing some money into my hand. This was Dad's other thing. Shove money at the child to instantly make everything awesome. "There's shops at the beach, right? Just buy yourself some new ones, sweetheart. A towel too, okay? Oh, and sunscreen and a hat. Here, take a bit more—you might get hungry later. Got your phone on you?"

I neatly folded the cash, putting it in the pocket of my denim cutoffs. "Yes." Dad had brought me the phone last year, the plan presumably being that he could get in contact with me directly.

"Alright. Look after her." Then Dad gave Pete the look. The one that promised much fatherly rage should I be returned with a single scratch on me. "Adele, don't get sidetracked and wander off, okay?"

"I'm not four, Dad."

"Realize that."

I gave him a quick kiss on the cheek. "See you later."

"Come on," said Pete with another of those smiles that turned my stomach inside out. "Let's get out of here, kid. The waves are waiting."

Wednesday Night . . . Now

Dinner was on the back deck.

I'd showered and changed into a sleeveless, short, black linen jumpsuit that had miraculously survived the trip without too many wrinkles. Weight I'd put on in university had never really shifted. I'd long given up fighting it and instead worked with the curves. Meanwhile, the humidity was messing with my light brown hair, so I low-ponytailed it and chucked on some hoop earrings and sandals. Minimal waterproof makeup so the heat wouldn't sweat it off me. The look said mature and capable, while remaining casual. Or, I wanted it to. A girl can hope.

I carried my cell with me—given mobile phones were the god of distraction and especially useful for avoiding unwanted conversation. Forget manners; they meant nothing in a crisis. I picked up my phone, pretending to be busy. "Meant to ask, my reception here isn't great. Would you mind if I grabbed the Wi-Fi password?"

The man visibly hesitated. Obviously, I could be trusted with nothing.

"I promise not to watch too much porn," I said. "It's just that sometimes you're better off doing a job yourself, right?"

He gave me a sour look. "It's written on the fridge."

"Thank you."

"No need to be nervous," said Pete, handing me a beer.

"I'm not."

He just nodded to the fingers of my free hand. Much fidgeting was indeed happening.

"Shanti's great. I'm sure you'll get along fine," he said, sprawled out in one of the outdoor dining table chairs, still barefoot. He'd traded his T-shirt for a short-sleeved button-down shirt. Black. We matched. Maybe I'd gone overboard with the outfit. No, I looked fine. Everything was fine.

Tea lights flickered on the table, sitting alongside a platter of cheese and biscuits and stuff. A couple of citronella candles sat around us to dissuade the bugs from having us for dinner.

After getting the Wi-Fi password, I sat opposite him, keeping my gaze on the distant stars. Now that the sun had fully set, they were just visible above the hazy shadows of the mountains on the horizon.

"Something smells good."

His smile remained strained. "Rack of lamb. You still eat meat, right?"

"Yes." I took a sip of beer. "I missed your cooking."

Nothing.

Yeah, shouldn't have said that. Any alluding to the past was a big N-O.

"Hey!" my dad shouted from the front of the house. "We're here."

And then I saw it: the first real smile on Pete's face in seven years. I hadn't even known how much I'd missed it until I saw it again. Perfect lips wide and white teeth on display, his eyes alight with joy. With the people he loved, he held back nothing. I'd been on that select list once. Seeing him smile, it was similar to what I'd imagined getting punched in the gut would be like. Lots of pain, with little to no actual fun.

Dad stepped onto the deck, followed by an elegant dark-skinned woman in a sleek green maxi dress. Pete and Dad did the manly backslapping thing, even though they lived across the road from one another, worked together, and probably saw each other every damn day of their lives. He'd aged well, my dad. At fifty, the man was pretty much the definition of silver fox.

As Pete smacked a kiss on Shanti's cheek, I just kind of sat there, stupidly frozen. Guess Pete had been right: I was anxious about this moment.

"Sweetheart." Dad rounded the table, holding his arms out. "Good to see you."

"Hi, Dad." I stood, hugging him back. Only with a slight level of awkwardness, which wasn't too bad for us really. We'd never been what you'd call close.

"This is Shanti." He turned, holding a hand out to the lady. "Shanti, my daughter, Adele."

"Finally." Shanti smiled, enclosing me in her arms like I was something precious. A little like Mom did. Also, she had the most beautiful, husky voice.

Not that I'd had any real plans to, but disliking this woman would clearly not be an option, though I'd burnt through the childhood rage over my parents' divorce some time ago. All the while, Dad looked on, his usually stoic face beaming. This was a new and somewhat drastic change. He'd never been quick to smile or big on happiness. Workaholics generally weren't, in my experience. Obviously this woman had worked wonders.

"Let me get you guys some drinks," said Pete, rubbing his hands together. "What'll it be?"

"Wine for me, thank you." Shanti took the seat next to mine.

"Beer," said Dad, grabbing a seat at the head of the table. Next to his fiancée, but not quite. Face reverting to its usual serious lines, he said, "Where's the boyfriend?"

I sat back down. "I never said I was bringing him."

"Thought you did."

"No."

He cocked his head. "Huh. You mentioned you were seeing some guy; guess I just assumed. Never mind."

I could have pointed out the mistake might be care of the fact that we rarely spoke and when we did, his mind was usually elsewhere, but glorious maturity prevailed. No need to mess with the celebratory mood. Instead, I just smiled and took another sip of beer. "How are the wedding plans going?"

"Wonderful," said Shanti. "I'm so glad you agreed to come up early and spend some time with us. It's beautiful here this time of year and you had to travel a long way. So why not turn it into a holiday, yes?"

Due to being slightly nervous and therefore shit at conversation, I just nodded encouragingly.

Pete handed out drinks to my dad and Shanti, and

then we were making a toast to the about-to-be-married couple's future happiness, et cetera. After this, Dad and Pete settled down to talking about work while Shanti filled me in on her interior decorating business. Dad owned a medium-sized building company. I guessed that's how their paths had crossed. Dad's crew handled everything from architectural masterpieces tucked away in the hillsides to renovations. He liked variety.

"Adele, did I tell you I made Pete partner a few years back?" he suddenly asked, bottle of beer in hand.

"You're partners?" I asked, slightly startled. It was big news.

Pete gave me his best blank face. "Best way to expand the business, take on a few more jobs a year."

"That's great. Congratulations."

A nod.

"Not like he hadn't been with me long enough," said Dad. "When did you first come on?"

"I don't know, nine years ago?" Pete shrugged.

"You know, it seems like longer."

"Enough business talk," ordered Shanti, nodding at my phone. "Adele, show me a picture of this man you've been seeing."

"Oh. Okay." I flicked through the album to a selfie Deacon and I had taken on date two, figuring now wasn't the time to reveal he was cheating on me. "Here."

"He's handsome." She grinned, her thumb poised over the screen. "Are there more?"

"Not sure." I shrugged in attempted nonchalance.

Then I squirmed a little. "Maybe. Probably more of my friend and me taking stupid selfies than anything else."

"Oh, is this her here with the gorgeous short hair?"

"Shanti, you can't just go through someone's phone," chided Pete with a smile.

"There's nothing that interesting on there," I said, waving his concerns away. "And yes; her name is Hazel. We've been besties for years."

Dad frowned. "Sure there's nothing on there?"

"Endless nudes, Dad. Endless." I laughed. "And all the D pictures. It's just . . . a bad habit, I guess. But I can't seem to stop collecting them and so many nice men are willing to send them, so . . ."

"D pictures?"

"Dick," supplied Pete.

"Jesus." Dad gave me a dour look. "Very funny, sweetheart."

Shanti leaned closer with a sly grin. "Don't worry, Adele. If I find anything, I won't tell him."

"Thank you. I appreciate that."

"Idiots really send you pictures of their genitals?" asked Dad. "That happens?"

"Only the occasional complete stranger on social media." I shrugged. "They think it's some kind of alluring mating call, I guess. I just block them."

"Like you want to see someone's shriveled-up little penis and hairy balls," said Shanti. "Yuck."

"We need a change of conversation," announced Dad.

Pete just blinked and shook his head. "Agreed."

"Who's this?" asked Shanti, angling the phone so I could see.

"Luke. I dated him last year," I said. "He was in landscaping. Nice guy."

She scrolled through a few more photos. Mostly of Hazel and me acting drunk and crazy, making dumb faces, as you do. Thankfully, she didn't comment and kept going until she hit another couples shot. "And him?"

"Ah, Jonah. That was also last year."

"What did Jonah do?"

I smiled. "Actually, he was a sculptor and potter. He had this cool studio and did shows and gave classes."

Shanti's brows lifted. "Interesting. Who's this one?"

"Isaac. Personal trainer. Sweet person, but I couldn't handle all of the fussing about food," I explained. "Around about the time you're saying steak has too much fat content, you've lost me."

"His body does indeed look like a temple, though," said Shanti appreciatively, still swiping.

"These people are all clothed, right?" asked Dad with a slight frown.

"Of course they're clothed, Andrew. Don't be silly."

"Hmm, this one is quite handsome, Adele. And this fellow too."

Now Dad's expression turned more serious. "Sweetheart, how many men have you dated, exactly?"

As if I would answer such a question without first enduring at least some mild form of torture. Out of my peripheral vision, I caught Pete narrowing his gaze. He was really slipping into grumpy-old-man territory these days. Though it might just be the company he was keeping.

"You need to explore your options before you settle down." Now it was Shanti's turn to offer Pete some gentle chiding. "It's only sensible. Try before you buy. How do you know what you want if you don't experiment? Think of all those years it took me to find you."

Dad chose not to reply.

Thankfully Shanti put down the phone. "You know, you definitely have a type, Adele."

"Do I?"

"Oh, yes. They all have dark hair, pretty eyes, and work with their hands," said Shanti. "Isn't that interesting?"

"Hm." Yeah, I had nothing to say on that topic. For someone whose background was interior decorating, she was pretty perceptive about people too.

"I always wonder where people's tastes evolve from, don't you?"

Silence at the table.

Pete downed more of his beer. "Seems like you keep busy, kid."

And I didn't want to hate him, but for that shitty comment, I kind of did. I met his flat, unfriendly stare with one of my own. "Mostly with work and friends. But I date sometimes."

"Seems like more than sometimes."

Like hell I'd be shamed over my dating habits.

"Thing is, Pete," I said, "as I remember it, you used to

have a pretty constant stream of women coming and going. Is that still the case?"

"She's got you there." Dad shifted in his seat, plastering a smile on his face. It wasn't quite as authentic as earlier, however. "I can't even remember their names half the damn time."

"Your memory likely isn't what it used to be, dear," said Shanti helpfully. Pretty sure the woman was expert level at trolling my father. In which case, I loved her even more.

Dad just smiled. "How is work, sweetheart?"

"Fine," I said. "It's there."

"You're not enjoying it?"

I winced. The topic of work was not my favorite, but anything had to be better than further exploration of my dating history. "I have no complaints really—they pay me okay. It'll look good on my résumé. Just been a little bored lately."

"You run the office of an accounting firm, right?" asked Shanti. "How many staff members are there?"

"I assist the office manager. And around sixty."

Her eyes widened. "That's big."

"Yes, and it's right in the center of town, which is nice."

"Was hoping you might be tired of the city by now," said Dad, sitting back in his chair. The look in his eyes, I couldn't read at all. Like he was assessing me, maybe? We usually talked every few months or so. A couple of times he'd traveled down south for business and we'd had dinner. Often enough to remain mostly strangers.

"Why?" I asked, curious.

The truth was, I'd taken two weeks off instead of just the one. I might spend the second week doing a road trip along the coast, relaxing. Or I might go straight home and start looking for another job. I hadn't yet made a decision.

"Helga's been talking about retiring to spend more time with her grandkids," he said. "Thought you might like to take over the position."

Pete stiffened. "You're thinking of Adele to run our office?"

"More than that," said Dad, warming to the topic. "She could help put proposals together, take over some of the liaising work with contractors and customers. Free us up more to get the real work done."

"You've never mentioned anything about this."

"We like to think of it as a family business, right?" Dad clapped him on the shoulder. "Getting her involved just makes sense. She's a grown adult, now. Smart, capable, we can trust her, and she used to take a real interest in what was going on. Thought it would be a good idea. Don't you?"

"This isn't awkward at all." Shanti sighed, placing her hand on top of my father's. "You're too used to being the only one in charge, Andrew. Decisions need to be shared now. Let alone just announcing this at dinner."

Dad just shrugged. "He'll be onboard once he thinks it over. It's a great idea."

Meanwhile, Pete's lips had slammed shut.

Damn. "Dad, I appreciate the vote of confidence, but . . . I just wasn't expecting . . ."

"You always loved it up here," he said.

"You do?" Gaze narrowed, Shanti gave me a questioning look. "But it's been such a long time since you visited. I've been waiting to meet you for years, ever since Andrew and I first started seeing one another."

"Busy," I said, and swallowed hard. God, I needed something much stronger than beer. "Like Pete said, just . . . really busy."

Dad huffed out a breath and looked to heaven. "Come on, I know we were all a bit upset when that nonsense first happened. But it's ancient history now. There's no reason you couldn't come back."

"Since what happened?" asked Shanti slowly.

No one answered.

"She's seeing someone down there. Sounds settled." Pete's grip on his bottle of beer was just about white knuckled. "Probably has no interest in moving."

"If they were serious, she'd have brought him," said Dad. Pretty damn accurately.

"What about Mom?" I asked.

"You told me she's away painting, at her artist retreats a lot." Dad shrugged. "She's had you close for years and anyway, the woman likes to travel. No reason she can't come visit you up here for a change."

"I don't know . . ."

"Why?" Dad pressed. "What don't you know about? Tell me your concerns and we can sort them out one by one."

And I didn't look at Pete and Pete didn't look at me. If I'd thought climbing under the table would have helped, I'd already have been on my knees. Pretty sure there was no escape hatch down there, however.

"Enough," Shanti said in a stern voice. "Stop pushing her. But also, I hate not knowing what's going on, and something is definitely going on here. What happened years ago? Somebody explain it to me, please."

Jaw tensed, Pete kept his head determinedly turned away.

Dad sighed. "It was nothing really. A storm in a teacup."

No one else said a thing.

Shanti's eyes drilled into Dad, and he shrugged, acquiescing. "But I guess you may as well know. Adele started coming up for the summer when she was sixteen. I was usually too busy climbing over half-built houses to spend time with her. So Pete did. He started taking her to the beach with him, going to a movie now and then, stuff like that."

"He was just being kind," I said.

"Yes, he was. The business was growing fast and took up all of my time back then," said Dad. "I wasn't around as much as I should have been."

"But you're going to make up for that now." Shanti squeezed his hand and Dad meshed their fingers together. God, they were so in love. So good together. Deacon didn't even particularly like holding hands. No wonder I'd been about to dump him.

"You want to tell the rest, sweetheart?" asked Dad. "It's kind of your story."

Shanti turned her head, all the better to see me.

To think, I'd actually been trying to create a good image. The attempt at glorious maturity was shot to shit now. Across the table, Pete raised his bottle of beer to his lips, his cheekbones standing out in stark relief. Not a happy boy.

Better just to blurt it out and be done with it. It was so stupid, really. But even after all these years, I still felt incredibly embarrassed about the whole thing. "I had a crush on Pete and attempted to seduce him on my eighteenth birthday by flashing my tits at him. He'd refused to see me as an adult, so I decided to press the issue. Dad walked in and assumed Pete had been fooling around with his teenage daughter or something, punched him in the face, and told him he was fired. Dad threatened to call the cops, my mother, and God knows who else. There was a lot of yelling. A fair bit of blood. Lots of people heard it all go down. It wasn't good."

Pete snorted. "It wasn't good? I spent the fucking night in the emergency room getting my nose set."

"I always wondered how it was broken," said Shanti calmly. "There's that intriguing bump on the bridge."

"I overreacted," said Dad. "Honestly, I think I feel worse about the whole thing than anyone else."

But given the sweat pouring down the back of my dress, and Pete's squirming in his seat, I was pretty sure this was not true. Though it was cute of him to think so. I kept my eyes down, it seemed safest. "Eventually Dad calmed down. I got him to understand it was all on me and he un-fired Pete."

"Yes, well, I didn't get a chance to thank you for that, what with being in the emergency room and all," the man bit out.

"As I've said before, I'm sorry."

Pete continued to glare at me like I considered kicking kittens and pinching puppies a good time. Maybe I could just sleep in my car for the next few days. If I put the passenger seat down, it should be okay. More comfortable than staying with him, at least.

"Oh for goodness sake, Peter." Shanti grinned. "Accept her apology. We all did things we regret when we were young and stupid. Honestly, I think that's one of the funniest stories I've heard in a long time," she said, turning to me. I can't believe you actually flashed him."

I raised one shoulder. "I'd had a few drinks. It seemed like a good idea at the time."

"And you haven't been back here since?"

"No. I haven't really been welcome."

"Well . . ." said Dad. "It wasn't quite like that."

"Sure it was, Dad."

He almost smiled. "You did cause a hell of a mess. Pete's fifteen years older than you, for Christ's sake."

"No wonder you freaked out for a moment, Peter, when I asked if she could stay with you," said Shanti. "Why, you went as white as a sheet. I was worried you were ill."

"I think you're overexaggerating there." Pushing back his chair, Pete stood. Tension radiated from every strong line of his body. "I'm going to get us some more drinks. Get dinner on the table."

"I'll help," said Dad, following him back inside.

Shanti turned to me and smiled. "Sorry about asking you to stay here, by the way. I got a little carried away with all of the wedding things. I've practically filled the whole house. Next time you visit, the guest room will be waiting for you. I promise."

"Thanks."

She stared out at the view for a moment, obviously thinking deep thoughts. "Adele, I think you and Peter must have been very good friends for him to still be so angry about it all."

"Seriously, he didn't do anything wrong or inappropriate. Please don't think badly of him—it was all me."

"I know that," she soothed. "He's an honorable man, a good one. That's why it's not like him to hold a grudge."

"No, normally if anyone messed with him like that, broke his trust, they'd just be out of his life. That's not quite possible, here." I fiddled with the label on the beer, rubbing the condensation around. "Makes things complicated."

She made a humming noise. "Well, I have no children of my own and I want you around more. If you truly do love being here, like your father says, and you're bored with your job, then joining the business might not be such a bad idea. I know he'd like to see you more. He talks about you often."

"He does?"

"Yes."

I didn't know what to say.

"I think you need to fix things with Peter," she said, as if it were that easy.

"I've been trying."

"He is a stubborn man, as most are. They always think they know best until we show them otherwise." She smiled. "Try harder."

Chapter Three

Nine Years Ago

"What's her name again?" I whispered, sipping on the straw of a monster-size slushie. One of the true benefits of going to the movies. Along with popcorn and air-conditioning, of course. Saturday had turned grossly hot, and all the ceiling fans at home could do was push around the hot air. Dad was at home, working on a quote for a job. When Pete called and suggested a film, I jumped at the chance. There'd been no mention, though, of him bringing someone. Not that I was jealous exactly, because that would be dumb.

"Already told you her name twice, kid."

"Yeah, but she's like the third one in as many weeks," I said. "It gets confusing trying to remember them all."

He did a one-shoulder shrug. "I have a lot of friends."

"Sure. You're a friendly guy."

"Yes, I am."

"It's been fifteen minutes," I said. "What do you think she's doing, full hair and makeup? A spray tan? What?"

A faint smile curved Pete's lips. "Shut up and watch the movie."

"I think the vampires freaked her out."

"Are you going to talk the whole way through?"

"Maybe."

"Christ. You chose this one just to mess with me, didn't you?" he asked, forehead all bunched up at the sight of Bella and Edward exchanging fervent, heated looks onscreen.

"Should you really be letting a sixteen-year-old decide what movies you take your dates to, though?" I asked back, voice low. Though there weren't many people in the cinema. The film had already been out for a few weeks. "I think that's the real question here."

"It's not a date. We're just friends."

"What did you say her name was again?"

"Shh. I'm trying to concentrate."

"Want me to tell you what happens next?" I asked. "I already read the books like a dozen times."

He just threw popcorn at me.

"How rude." I brushed it off my lap. "You know, I have a theory."

"And what might that be?"

"That you're basically using me as a chaperone."

He blinked. "I'm *what*?"

"With these women," I said, shaking my head because *duh.* "I mean, with me along, they can't get all serious on you or anything. No chance for a 'where are we headed, let's discuss our commitment level' type talk. You're totally using me as a chaperone. It's diabolical, really. I mean, you get the good-guy points for taking pity on me. But you also have a reason to keep your latest friend at a distance. Given the amount of friends and the rate at which you go through them, it makes sense. Admit it."

"I admit nothing." He snorted. "Maybe I just like your company. I mean, you're funny sometimes. You don't *completely* suck."

"Thanks."

"Now you compliment me."

"Nah," I said. "Pretty sure your ego is big enough as it is."

More popcorn flew my way.

"For a thirty-one-year-old, you can be quite immature at times, Peter."

"For a sixteen-year-old, you can be quite a brat, Adele."

Then he smiled, easy as that. I couldn't help but smile back.

Unfortunately, his date returned at that point. We sat in silence, eyes on the screen. Movies weren't nearly as much fun when Pete and I weren't whispering crap at each other.

Wednesday Night . . . Now

Sleep just hadn't come after that dinner. I'd lain awake for an hour or so, staring out into the dark, my mind racing in circles. Heat pressed down on me, my pillow damp from the sweat on the back of my neck. I could turn on the air-conditioning, but I'd kind of missed the weird little night noises and the scent of the frangipani outside.

Eventually, I gave up and got up.

There was enough ambient light for me not to need to turn a light on. I changed into my bathing suit, grabbed a towel, and made my way out onto the deck, then down the back stairs. Overhead hung an almost full moon, everything perfectly, peacefully quiet. Almost.

"Shit!" I yelped at the sight of someone in the water. "I didn't see you there."

"Assumed that," he mumbled.

My heart beat double time. Fear in general, or fear of him, I wasn't sure. "Would you rather be alone or am I allowed to swim?"

"You're an adult. You're allowed to do whatever the hell you want."

"And yet it's your house," I pointed out. "I'm just the unwelcome guest."

"You're not unwelcome, exactly."

"Yeah . . . not convincing."

Great. I dumped my towel on a wooden bench and made my way over to test the water temperature with my toes. A little cool, but not cold. Butt on the edge, I eased myself into the pool. I quietly gasped when the water slid over my chest and up to my neck. Perky nipples, but never mind. What the bikini didn't cover, the low lighting would. God, it felt good to evade the heat for a while.

"You never would just jump," he said.

"I like to know what I'm getting into."

He swam to the side, where a glass and a bottle of scotch waited. "Only got the one glass, but I'll share if you want."

"Scotch tastes like ass."

A chuckle.

"Is that really safe, swimming and drinking on your own?"

"I know what I can handle," said Pete. "And desperate times, desperate measures."

And I was welcome, my butt. People always make young love seem like this wonderful thing. Something to be treasured. But the truth is, it sucks. Because of that first love, you just might get to spend the rest of your life looking for that person in others . . .

After Shanti's reaction and Dad's words, however, I was pretty much over the self-flagellation aspect of mine and Pete's relationship. Same went for his bad-tempered bullshit and unwillingness to move on. I was done. Seriously. Full on. Done. "Oh, go fuck yourself."

"What did you say?"

"You know, Pete, it was seven long years ago," I said. Ranted. Whatever. "I behaved like a dumb kid and I've acknowledged that. I've apologized many, many times."

He wiped a hand over his wet face. "Did you actually just tell me to go fuck myself?"

"This is ridiculous. If you really can't make even a small attempt at forgiving, or at least pretending to forget, I'll go sleep on Dad's couch or something." I turned, making for the stairs.

"You can't just wake up your dad and Shanti in the middle of the night."

"So I'll sleep in my car."

"You're serious?"

"Yes." I climbed to the top of the pool steps, stopping to wring out the back of my hair. "Life is too short. And just for record, it's not like I got out of that situation unscathed. I lost my best friend and got banished from a place I loved. Not exactly my idea of a good time."

"Kid, wait." He stood at the bottom of the steps, still almost waist deep in water. And I could have done without an updated visual of how good he looked half-naked. The pecs and the flat stomach and the start of the vee of his hips leading into his board shorts. God help me, he even had a happy trail. My sex dreams of him were lurid enough without all the detail, thank you very much. You'd have thought after so long my imagination would have moved on to different fodder. But no such luck. Guess my imagination lacked imagination. It's like my brain and vagina had gotten stuck way back when. He'd imprinted on me. It was beyond my control.

"I think this is a big part of the problem," I said. "You

see, I'm not a kid anymore."

"No shit."

"What? Was I not supposed to grow up?"

Then he glared at my body as if it personally offended him. Jesus. The bikini wasn't that skimpy.

"God, you're right." I sighed. "I should have left my breasts at home. How thoughtless. I'm so sorry. My bad, Pete."

He snorted. "You're not funny."

Huh. "Was that a sort of laugh? I'm glad to see that you're able to get in touch with your own crazy regarding this particular situation."

"My own crazy?" He scrunched up his face. "I don't even know what you're on about. Get back in the water."

"No."

"Adele, please. If you want, we'll talk about it," he said, looking off into the darkness. "Get back in the water."

"My body offends you?"

"Give me strength," he muttered, before climbing the steps toward me. "No, your body does not offend me. But I think I saw enough of your breasts on your eighteenth birthday to last a lifetime."

I held out a hand. "Hey, respect my personal space. Back up."

"No."

Next thing I knew, he'd lifted me up in his arms and thrown my ass out into the middle of the pool. I surfaced, gasping and spluttering. "You asshole!"

He gracefully dived back in and the second he surfaced, I splashed water in his face. Thus began a war I was probably always destined to lose on account of his superior muscle mass, and the size of his big-ass hands. But obviously I had to start it, because a splash-fight is the only reasonable way to respond to one's maturity being brought into question.

"Stop it. Stop!" I turned to the side, trying to shield my thoroughly soaked self. Hell, trying to get my wet hair out of my eyes so I could see. "I hate you."

He sighed, relaxing back in the water. "Yeah. I hate you too."

I paused. "Do you really?"

"No." More sighing. "Stay, please."

"You'll stop giving me shit?"

"I don't know. I'll try." He headed back to his scotch glass. "You going to keep your shirt on?"

"I'd planned to. Swimwear's exempt, of course."

Some grumbling. No idea what he said.

I took the opportunity to catch my breath, floating on my back, watching the night sky. And I could feel his gaze on me, but whatever. My breasts were in no way responsible for his moody disposition. He and his pretty face could own his attitude flaws without my help. Temporarily at least, perhaps this could work. Long enough to see Shanti and Dad married. I hoped.

Pete said something, but the words were muffled with my ears underwater. I resurfaced, swimming closer. "What?"

He watched me from the side of the pool, blue-gray eyes mysterious in the shadows. "Your best friend, huh?"

"You were." I shrugged.

"What about people your own age down south?" he asked. "Thought you had friends at school."

"I had a couple. Sure." My hands gripped the stone siding, keeping me afloat. "No one I could talk to like I did with you. You didn't judge me or anything. I could just . . . I felt more comfortable with you."

Silence.

"Probably drove you nuts listening to me prattle on."

"No," he said. "Not that you didn't come out with some crazy shit, sometimes. God, some of your brilliant ideas . . . but I always liked listening to you talk."

"Nobody made you attend the Star Wars marathon twice with me."

"It was just those first three—"

I held up a hand. "I'll admit, my pubescent affection for Hayden Christensen may have led me astray, somewhat."

"Kid, you thought Jar Jar Binks was funny."

"Hey," I snapped. "Take that back. I never said that. No one in their right mind thinks that."

He took a sip of whisky. Pretty sure he was using the cut crystal glass to hide a small smile.

Lazily, I kicked my feet in the water. Not being a puddle of sweat felt seriously good. "Are you really going to keep calling me 'kid'?"

"Yep."

"Okay, old man."

"You always were a brat. No idea why I put up with you." He splashed some water my way. But his heart wasn't in it, you could tell. "If you don't drink scotch, what do you drink?"

"Gin."

A nod. "What'd you think of Shanti? She's nice, isn't she?"

"Yeah, I really liked her."

"What about you and this guy your dad thought you were coming up with?" he asked. "What's going on there?"

Hmm. I turned to face the side of the pool, resting my chin on my hands. "Do you want the truth or a pretty lie which may aid in making the next five days go more smoothly? Your choice. I honestly don't mind."

The wary look returned. "Thanks for options. Why don't we stick with the truth for now?"

"He cheated on me."

"What?" he asked, outraged. "You're joking. What an asshole."

"Yeah. My friend just told me earlier that she saw him out with someone else getting handsy in the corner of a restaurant." I gave him a half-smile. "I think it's safe to say that one's over."

"I'm sorry."

"We weren't that well suited. I mean, I was attracted to him, but something was just missing," I admitted. "To be honest, I'm not that cut up about it."

His brows remained drawn tight. "That's good, I

43

guess. Anyway . . . I'm sorry about my comments about your dating life over dinner."

"Ah, okay. Thanks."

A grunt.

"Sorry I called you a manwhore."

He blinked. "You didn't call me a manwhore."

"No? Must have just thought it," I said. "But I'm sure I was wrong and that you've had deep and abiding feelings for each and every one of your numerous girlfriends over the many long years. Just out of interest, can you even remember all of their names?"

His shoulders lifted as he exhaled hard. "Yeah, alright. I take back my apology."

"Okay."

"You know, kid, you almost sound jealous."

"I don't think so, old man. Just pointing out the hypocrisy there," I said, laughing.

While I'd like to pretend it was the romance of the moon on the water, I'm pretty sure his dark, searching gaze was to blame for the sudden pounding of my heart. I was out of my depth. I was wet in a way that had nothing to do with the water. Grumpy and intense shouldn't be so hot. Teenage crushes aside, I liked guys who were fun and easy to be with. Single people who liked girls and had a penis but weren't Pete. Those were really my main points of focus when it came to dating. I don't know what Shanti had been on about. And they said women didn't know what they wanted. Yeah. Go, me. "Jealous, as if. I like them younger and faster than you."

He shook his head. "No, you don't."

"I most certainly do."

"No. Don't get me wrong—fast can be fun sometimes. But more often than not, it's all about taking it slow. Taking the time to do the job right and making sure everybody gets what they need," he said calmly, casually. As if we weren't talking about sex at all. "Don't let any idiot tell you otherwise."

I had nothing.

"Anyway, I'm going to bed." With ease, he pulled himself out of the water. The muscles in his arms and back were truly something else. "You okay here on your own?"

"Of course. 'Night."

He grabbed a towel, along with his bottle of scotch and glass, and wandered up the back steps. While the front view was nice, the back view was also kind of breathtaking. Rule one had basically been cremated and buried in the backyard. I hoped it could rest in peace. Because no way could I stop looking.

Not packing my personal massager for this trip had been a mistake.

Chapter Four

Eight Years Ago

"**B**ut it's not safe to leave children or animals alone in hot cars."

Pete scowled, arms full of gaudily wrapped Christmas presents. "Kid, I'll only be a minute."

"No."

"Adele, stay in the vehicle."

"*No.*"

"Come on, just—"

"Your air-conditioning is broken and it's like forty degrees today." Squinting into the midday sun, I joined him on the driveway of a large beige brick home. My green cotton dress was already stuck to my back with sweat. "There's not even a bottle of water in the car. I'll wait on the patio in the shade, where I won't die of heat exhaustion, thank you very much."

He swore under his breath.

"Oh, relax," I huffed. "You won't even know I'm there."

God knows what look he was giving me through the dark glass of his shades. But I bet it wasn't pleasant. Today was not working out how I'd planned.

"Who lives here, anyway?" I asked. "Is it some new girlfriend you don't want me to meet? You didn't actually finally get serious about one, did you?"

"It's not a girlfriend."

"Then who?"

Not only did he not answer, but the muscle in his jaw jumped. Not good.

"I've been waiting all year to hang out with you and now you don't even want me around." My shoulders slumped. "Why did you call?"

He lowered his chin, looking at me over the top of his shades. "Calm down. I said I wanted to spend today together catching up and we will."

I said nothing.

"I've just got to get this out of the way first, okay?"

The lawn in front of the house was neat. Precise even. But there were no flowers, bushes, decorative plants, or indeed any type of attempt at a garden. Who did that? There was minimalism and then there was bland to the point of ugly. This property fell into the latter.

Pete stepped closer. "This is my dad's place."

"Your parents?" I asked with a smile.

Almost wearily, he shook his head. "Yeah. But we're

not really on the best of terms."

"Oh."

"Peter?" a voice called from the front door, safely hidden behind a security screen.

"Do you want me to go back to the car?" I whispered.

"Too late," he said. "Come on."

I followed him up the drive. With the click of a lock, the door opened. An older man stood waiting. His expression was far from welcoming. Despite it being the weekend, he wore shiny shoes and gray slacks, and a business shirt with the buttons done up all the way to the top. Not a single wrinkle in sight.

"Just wanted to drop these off for Christina and the kids," said Pete, hovering on the doorstep.

"Come in," said the man. "Who's this?"

"Adele. My boss's daughter. I'm looking after her today."

And that made me sound about eight years old, but I chose not to comment.

A grunt from the man.

"Adele, this is my father, Carl."

"Hello, Mr. Gallagher." I attempted a smile. It didn't quite work.

Carl looked me over with a frown. "I see."

What he saw exactly, I had no clue. Nor did I care to ask. At first, there'd been a little surge of excitement in my gut at meeting Pete's family, and a sudden desire to make a good impression. But Pete was right; the sooner we got out of this place, the better. The weather might be hot, but this man seemed stone cold.

The inside of the house matched the outside. White carpet and an ivory leather couch. Everything seemed pristine and expensive, but entirely uninviting. As if no one ever sat on the couch and used the big screen. As if no one really lived here at all. A couple of family photos sat on a teak sideboard, the only color to be found. A happy, newly married couple. A laughing young family of four at the beach. And an older photo of an elegant woman with dark hair who reminded me of Pete.

"I didn't bother with a Christmas tree," he said, tone of voice suggesting he was well beyond such festive nonsense. "Just leave them in the corner."

"Alright."

"There's more than I thought there'd be," said Carl. "I'm going to have to take an extra suitcase."

"That's why I offered to mail them," said Pete.

Carl didn't look appeased.

"Right." Pete gave his best fake smile. "Work's going well. I'm buying a piece of land just outside Palmwoods. Settling next week, actually."

Nothing from his father.

"Going to take my time, plan the house and work on it myself."

A nod.

"Well, it's been nice to see you, Dad," said Pete, taking my elbow and ushering me toward the door. "Hope you have a good trip. Tell Christina I'll call."

"Don't forget, Perth is two hours behind."

"I won't," said Pete. Then, prodding me forward, he urged, "Let's go."

I didn't talk until we were back in the car and halfway down the street. Far, far away from the horrible man he had to call a father. Yes, I was curious. But since Pete hadn't wanted me to go in his family home, I was pretty sure he wouldn't want to talk about their history. So instead, I just said, "I'm sorry."

"That you didn't stay in the car?" he asked, a wry smile on his face. "I bet you are."

"No. I'm sorry that you have to put up with him being like that."

Pete sighed, reached over, and patted my hand.

"You're great and he shouldn't treat you that way."

"Thanks, kid." The lines in his face and stiffness in his shoulders gradually eased. "What can you do? Family's complicated. Let's forget about him. It's just you and me now. What do you want to do today? Hell, what do you want to do this summer?"

I grinned. "Actually, I have an idea."

Thursday . . . Now

When I woke the next morning at around ten, the house was empty. No surprise; builders started work early. I, however, was on vacation and deserved a sleep-in. Pete had left directions for working the coffee machine along with an almond croissant in a brown bag from the local bakery. I'd bet any amount of money he still went jogging into town before work. But given our midnight swim and the scotch, I'd have thought he'd be in need of a sleep-in too.

I had a text from Shanti telling me to give her a call when I was up and about. Instead, I put on some denim cutoffs and a T-shirt and walked across the street. After eating the croissant and downing lots of coffee, of course. The door to their house was open, a coolish breeze blowing through the big old Queenslander house.

"Hello?" I called out.

Shanti stuck her head out of Dad's office, a phone attached to her ear. She smiled and whispered, "Help yourself to coffee, Adele. I shouldn't be long. Your father is out back."

I nodded and she returned to her conversation.

The outside of my part-time childhood home hadn't changed any. But the inside was drastically altered. In a good way. All of Dad's crappy furniture had been replaced. A peacock-blue velvet love seat sat beside a long white couch. Dark wood lamp tables and a low, long coffee table were nearby. Large, interesting, minimalistic paintings in monochrome colors hung on the walls. Touches of silver and splashes of the peacock blue and a harmonious emerald green were scattered about via ornaments and throw cushions. It probably never would have occurred to me to try putting those colors together.

There was a cool fifties retro vibe to certain pieces of furniture. All in all, the place looked like something out of a magazine. Shanti knew her stuff.

In the back of the house, the wraparound verandah had been widened since my last visit. My favorite big old jacaranda tree still stood in the yard, however, providing some shade and making a pretty mess. The beautiful little purple flowers were everywhere.

"You used to tell me you were going to bed, then climb down that tree and run off to hang out with Pete," said Dad, on his knees in the new section of decking, paintbrush in hand.

"I didn't know you knew that."

"I knew." Dad smiled. "He told me so I wouldn't worry if I found you gone."

"And I thought I was so clever sneaking about. We were usually just stargazing."

A nod. "Coffee in the kitchen if you want some."

"Yes, Shanti told me. I've had my requisite three cups, though. I'm good," I said. "You got another brush?"

One brow rose. "You want to help?"

"Sure."

"Over on the table."

I grabbed a paintbrush and squatted down near enough to reach the tin of decking oil, but far enough to be out of Dad's way. Thank God I'd worn sunglasses; the day was hot and bright. The smell of oil and wood conjured all sorts of old memories of hanging out around Dad's jobs. Underneath those, the scent of rich red earth and lush foliage. It was good to be back after so long in the city.

"Pretty sure Shanti has plans for you two today," he said. "Consider yourself warned."

"Got it."

A few minutes of silence.

"Are you being careful of splinters?" he asked. "I should get you some gloves and something to rest your knees on."

"You're not wearing gloves."

"I'm covered in calluses. My skin isn't soft like yours."

"It'll be fine."

"Do you want a coverall? The oil won't come off your clothes if you get a splash, you know."

I laughed. "I'm fine, Dad. Relax."

"Well, it's on you if you spend the rest of your day smelling of turps. I can tell you from much experience that it isn't Shanti's favorite scent."

I nodded wearily. This wasn't my first rodeo with a paintbrush and decking. For a little while longer, we worked in silence.

"You still up for the Buck's Party/Hen's Night combo thing tonight?" he asked. "It won't be anything big, just getting together with a few friends at the pub. Neither of us feel the need for tequila shots and strippers."

"Sure. Sounds good."

"You can meet Pete's girlfriend." He shot me a look out of the corner of his eye.

I kept my face good and blank. "Yeah? What's she

like?"

"Seems nice enough. She's a lawyer, I think," he said. "All of the women he brings around seem nice enough. None of them tend to last long, though. Think you might have picked up on that."

"As I recall, it took you a while to find Shanti and you weren't exactly dying of loneliness in the meantime."

"Fair call," he acknowledged with a nod.

"I really like her, by the way."

"Good." Dad beamed. "She likes you too. Wouldn't stop talking about you last night."

A kookaburra started up somewhere close, its laughter filling the air. Some miner birds screeched in protest, and all the while, insects hummed. The sound was like a continual wave, rising and falling, but never quite disappearing. Nature, the whole world, seemed especially vivid and alive.

"How's your mother?" asked Dad.

"Good," I said. "She's been selling a few paintings and her classes are always popular. She seems happy."

"Good."

I grinned. "She thinks I should throw it all in and go travel around Europe. Go sit on a Greek island for a while or something."

"This does not surprise me," he muttered. "Your mother's answer to everything was to run away."

"You two were badly suited."

"Very. Is that what you want to do, go travel?"

"I wouldn't mind doing some traveling, but my savings aren't really up to it," I said. "Sydney's expensive."

"You come work with us, we can sort out time off for you to go places."

"Claims of nepotism don't concern you?"

He sat back on his heels, wiping the sweat off his face. "Sweetheart, either you'll flourish in the job or you'll fail. That's on you. I can only offer you the opportunity."

"Only you and Pete can offer me the opportunity, you mean."

"Right." He shrugged. "For all his bitching, he'd be fine with you coming onboard."

"Hm. What if I leave my life in Sydney and move all this way only to find that I suck at the job and you fire me?"

He grimaced. "Well, on the bright side, Shanti should have the guest room ready by then, so you'll have somewhere to stay if you're down and out."

"Great," I said drily.

"Sweetheart, you were always interested in the business. Enjoyed looking over the jobs and being part of it in small ways, talking to people." His gaze was dead serious. "I think you could be good at this. Helga's been great, but she was never interested in developing the role beyond admin support. We need more. You work with us, take over some things, eventually we'll look at bringing in other admin assistance if needed."

"Have you talked about these things with Pete?"

"Yeah, 'course," said Dad.

I just looked at him.

"Just thought maybe he'd react better to the idea of it being you if he had less time to think about it."

"That's so wrong. He's your partner now."

"Nuh." Dad smirked. "It's just good strategy."

"Adele, what on earth are you doing there?" Shanti emerged from the house, dressed in a gorgeous sheath dress. "Not only are you on vacation, but it's our spa day. You're supposed to be relaxing."

"Spa day?"

She put a hand to her head. "Did I forget to tell you? I've had so much on my mind. But, yes, we need to get going. Facials, massages, nails, you name it, head to toe. My treat."

"Wow. Thank you."

"You're very welcome, but we need to get a move on."

"Okay." I rose, dusting off my knees. "Am I dressed too casually?"

"No," said Shanti with a smile. "You'll be fine."

Dad took back the dirty brush with a wink. "Have fun."

The location for the Buck's Party/Hen's Night was the over-a-century-old Palmwoods Tavern. It had a great beer garden, which made it ideal for the night's events. Open and airy, with lots of bromeliads growing in pots scattered around and twinkling fairy lights strung from a mango tree. I'd imagined Shanti would be used to less humble surroundings. But the woman pulled up a stool at one of the tall tables in our party's area and started knocking back a beer, no worries. The crowd seemed to be a mix of people from the happy couple's jobs, along with a few other friends. Dad and Shanti had given me a lift after I had a quick shower and got changed.

Pete was apparently busy. Which was a shame, since I felt like a new woman. I'm not sure if my glorious maturity was showing as Hazel had suggested, but the spa day had been magnificent. Lavish in all the ways. I'd been waxed, buffed, and blow-dried to within an inch of my life. I'd offered to pay for my half, but Shanti wouldn't hear of it. She didn't mess around when it came to luxuries.

I'd decided to show off my shiny French manicure with tan open-toe wedges, skinny jeans that lifted my butt and made the most of my long legs, and a flowy white cotton top. It happily skimmed my belly. The spa day included full makeup and hair, so I was pretty damn sure I looked shiny with my long, flowing locks. Confident enough to face anything, up to and including Pete's latest girlfriend. Hopefully.

I was sipping a Coopers Pale Ale when Pete and his date walked in. And of course she looked like a model who'd decided to try slumming it with us normal folk. Way beyond your basic nightmare. Long red hair and an amazing face. Every inch of her precise perfection.

Shit.

Not that I was ugly. I was okay looking. Generally

pretty. But Nicole Kidman's doppelganger had just turned up on the arm of my first love.

Pete, meanwhile, had worn black sneakers, black jeans, and a fitted gray T-shirt. Damn. He looked relaxed, yet hot as hell. As much as I might joke about his good looks to Hazel, the fact remained that it was frustrating to be so seriously affected by a guy so far out of reach. My gaze roamed the bar, searching for superior eye candy. Someone to momentarily distract my raging hormones with. But no luck. No one else even came close to comparing.

It had been seven years, but my libido did not seem to have lost any of the teenage lust for Pete. Summoning up all my maturity and self-respect, I made a point of not noticing his arms, which were of the nicely lean muscular variety, and not at all worthy of odes. He'd gone and gotten a new haircut, shorter on the sides, longer and slicked back on top, which I also did not notice. All of that tanned skin and beautiful crinkly steel-blue eyes were entirely wasted on me. Or at least, I wish they were.

He met my gaze and I was the first to look away. While some would have described him as breathtaking, panty-wetting goodness, I just quietly despaired.

No, forget that—I was over him. Had been for years. I dated. I had sex. Some of it was even good. Simply because a few old misplaced feelings lingered didn't mean a thing. A silly schoolgirl's crush, nothing more. Any thoughts to the contrary were reckless and wrong. Nonsense best ignored. Honestly, this sort of heartache and confusion were exactly why I'd been in no rush to return. No matter how much I missed the area.

"Adele?" Shanti slipped an arm around my waist. "I want you to meet a friend of mine, Jeremy. He makes bespoke furniture and home accents here on the coast using only local recycled woods. Incredibly talented. Already, he's selling into Europe."

"Shanti, you're too kind. But I'm really just a humble woodworker." Jeremy was around my age, with long dark hair tied back and a friendly smile. A classic Greek god kind of face. Definitely marble worthy from an artistic point of view. Yet he lacked the idiosyncrasies that so endeared Pete to me. Dammit. "Nice to meet you, Adele."

"Yes. Hi," I said, shaking his hand. His skin was warm.

Shanti patted him on the shoulder before turning to me with a grin. "Adele, doesn't he have pretty eyes?"

Oh God.

The man just laughed.

"Jeremy, this is Andrew's daughter, Adele," said Shanti. "A beautiful, bright young woman."

Beneath all of the expertly applied makeup, my face flamed.

"It's all true. You know, Jeremy, she's considering moving up from Sydney to join the family business and helping to expand the office," Shanti continued. "If so, you'll be talking to her about any jobs from now on."

Jeremy's brows rose. "Is that so?"

"It is indeed," said Shanti. "But it's all very hush-hush. She hasn't made up her mind yet. I'm trusting you to help us persuade her."

"We'll see," I said, trying to get my embarrassment levels under control. "For now, I'm just visiting for the wedding."

"She doesn't have a date for that either," said Shanti in a low voice. "Something to think about."

Give me strength. "Shanti . . ."

"What?" She batted her eyelashes. "A new stepmother can't help her darling stepdaughter along with meeting people?"

I laughed. Much awkward. Overflowing with it, in fact. "Okay. I think you've helped enough now. Thank you."

Jeremy gave me a look. Something along the lines of, *what can you do?*

With a parting wave, Shanti thankfully glided off to join my father.

"Sorry about that," I mumbled.

Jeremy just smiled. "I've never seen anyone bulldoze people as gracefully as Shanti. You're too busy pleasing her to stop and think. She's remarkable."

"That she is. She's like Tinder on steroids."

He grinned. "Adele, would you like another drink?"

"That's a splendid idea."

"Excuse me. You're Jeremy Karas, right?"

With a small smile, the redhead sidled on up to

where Jeremy and I had been sitting and drinking for a couple of hours. He was a nice guy and a great distraction from the whole Pete-with-a-drop-dead-gorgeous-woman-hanging-off-of-him thing. Well, he *had* been a great distraction, until the drop-dead-gorgeous woman appeared at his side. We turned politely to her.

Pete stood next to her, of course. His eyes flitted up to mine as I turned to face them. *Whoa.* Flitted up from *where*? If it had been any other guy in the universe, I could have sworn he was checking me out. But that was impossible, of course. Pete was far above such things at the best of times, especially when he had a supermodel beside him. Also, I was me. And he'd made his not entirely favorable opinion regarding me more than well known.

Meanwhile, the redhead was simpering at Jeremy. Or she might have been just being friendly. I don't know; my mood had been a little off for a decade or so.

"Leona Addams. I have one of your side tables," she said. "Absolutely exquisite."

"Thank you very much." Jeremy gave her a welcoming professional face. I bet he sold lots and lots with those sleepy, seductive green eyes. "I'm delighted to hear you're enjoying it."

She twirled a glass of white wine in her hand, allowing the men to make their introductions.

"Pete." He nodded at the younger man. "Good to see you."

They shook hands. "Liked your work on the Johnson place."

"Thanks," said Jeremy. "Things you can do when there's no limit, huh?"

"Exactly." Pete laughed. "Adele. You look nice."

I raised my gin and tonic. "Thank you. So do you."

"You didn't say *I* look nice," said the woman.

Pete gave her a slow smile. "That's because you always look amazing. 'Nice' would be a gross understatement."

Kill me now.

"Leona, this is Andrew's daughter, Adele," said Pete.

I held out my hand for shaking. Her slender fingers were limp, dismissive. Fine with me. Down within my shallow depths, I wanted to dislike the woman anyway. I'd have to take off my shoes to count all the ways in which she and I were different, and I'd still run out of fingers and toes. She looked like the type who was sleek and slender and shiny on a day-to-day basis. It took me a whole fucking six-hours in the spa to look this put together. Talk about unfair.

"You're staying with Peter?" she asked me.

"Yes. Just for a few days."

"Lovely." Curious eyes looked me over. Then she downed the last of her drink, depositing the glass on the table. "I have an early start."

"You need to go?" asked Pete.

Thank God she wasn't staying for a sleepover. The last thing I needed was to lie in bed listening to squeaking bed frames, imagined or otherwise. An axe to the head would be kinder.

"Call me." She placed her hand on his chest, leaning in to give him a kiss. Pete's hand sat at her waist. At least there wasn't tongue. I might have had to gouge my eyes out if there were. Then, with a heated look, she wiped away a trace of her pink lipstick. "I heard about this amazing seafood restaurant we should try. Apparently the mud crabs are the best on the coast. Maybe tomorrow night?"

"What a wonderful idea." I gave her my best fake smile. "Isn't it, Pete?"

He shot me an irritable glance. "I'm allergic to shellfish. As you might remember, Adele."

"Oh." Leona frowned, fingers tightening around her designer handbag. "Jeremy, so wonderful to meet you. Adele, I'm sure I'll be seeing you again."

"I'll walk you out." Jeremy stood. "I have an early start too."

"It was nice talking to you." I smiled.

He gave my hand a quick squeeze, and said, "You realize within a minute of me leaving, Shanti will be texting me making sure I have your number."

"I do realize that. Here, put yours in my phone." I passed it to him. "No promises either of us will use it, but at least we'll be covered for Shanti's inevitable interrogation."

There was some more nodding and handshaking and good nights. Then Pete sat beside me, stealing my drink and taking a mouthful.

"You've been seeing her for how long and she doesn't even know that shellfish could kill you?" I asked sweetly.

"What do you talk about with these women?"

"I don't know. Stuff."

"What stuff?"

"Stuff," he repeated. "Are you giving me relationship advice now? Should I have candlelit dinners where we exchange allergy lists? I can see why your relationships didn't last."

"Very funny. But I thought at least you'd have hit her with the story about when you ate prawns as a teenager and blew up like the Michelin Man. That cracked me up every time."

He smiled for a moment, either at the memory of it happening or the memory of me laughing at the story. Then his gaze darkened, and he stared into the gin and tonic. "I don't talk to everyone like I do with you. *Did*. Like I *did* with you."

An old Aussie Crawl song started and some of the boys from my dad's office cheered at the next table. Apparently they were making the most of the open bar. Beer glasses were piling up.

"I don't know," I said. "I think there was a lot we didn't talk about."

"I had to keep it age appropriate." He took another sip of my drink, and then handed it back to me with a smile. "And you say scotch tastes like ass."

"Bombay Sapphire is a gift from God and I won't hear a word otherwise."

We sat in silence for a minute, taking in the scene, listening to the music. A couple was passionately kissing in a dark corner; loud conversations were happening all around. Even Shanti was laughing, head thrown back, delighted grin. Dad stood beside her chair like a sentinel, just watching her enjoy herself. It was sweet.

"Sorry I was difficult, with your girlfriend," I said eventually.

He sat back in the chair, ankle propped on one knee. "I don't know if I'd call her my girlfriend exactly. We're friends."

Huh.

"Jeremy Karas, huh?"

I shrugged. "Shanti introduced us. He seems okay."

"Sure." His fingers tapped out a beat against the metal armrest. "Talented guy. He's an artist, really. I wouldn't have minded buying a piece myself, but the fucking prices he charges."

"Well, you're getting older," I said. "You can't just go wasting money. Need to save up for all that Viagra."

"That is a gross and ageist generalization, young lady," Pete said sternly. "And not applicable in this particular instance, as it happens."

"Confidence is important. I understand."

"You really weren't spanked enough as a child, you know that?"

I laughed.

"Also, you talk about sex stuff when you're nervous."

"No, I don't." I scrunched up my face. "Now you're just imagining things. Early onset dementia. So sad."

He just shook his head.

"The thing is, I find it hard to care too much about what I say around you." I shrugged. "I'm pretty sure I burned all the best-friend bridges with you all those years ago. It's liberating in a way. I can say whatever I think."

"Hadn't noticed you holding back. Ever." The low lighting cast mesmerizing shadows on his cheeks, the harsh line of his jaw. Even the slight cleft in his chin. "You liked him, then?"

"Jeremy? Sure." With one finger, I played with the lemon slice in my drink, pushing it under the surface.

"Not sure he's really your type."

"Why's that?"

He shrugged. "I don't know, just a feeling."

"You know, this is what I missed out on when I was younger," I said. "Getting dating advice from you. Though you're going to need to be more specific than just a feeling. But I could ask you all the questions I've always wanted to ask a guy and you'll give me the information."

The little line between his brows deepened. "About what?"

"About sex!"

"I am not talking with you about sex."

"But it's age appropriate now," I said.

"To the contrary, we are now far too old for such frivolities." One corner of his mouth lifted a little. At least I could still make him smile when I wanted to.

"So last time I was here I was too young, and now I'm too old?"

"Precisely." He nodded. "There was a four-minute

window about three years ago where such a discussion might have been appropriate. Too bad you missed it."

The music changed to Cold Chisel and the table next to us cheered yet again. Someone growled, "Barnesie."

"God, I haven't heard this in years," I said. "They're playing all the classics."

"What, you only go to hipster cafés?"

"I have to get my smashed avocado on sourdough somewhere." I grinned, sucking the gin off the end of my finger, because ladylike.

Pete's hand stilled, his gaze intensified. "You know, in some ways you've changed. But in others, you're exactly the same."

"What were you expecting?"

"I don't know."

I cleared my throat. "I have a theory."

"What's your theory?"

"That people grow more into themselves over time."

Slowly, he nodded. "Makes sense."

"Actually, that probably came from my best friend, Hazel," I said. "She's a therapist. Sometimes our conversations wander into areas of philosophy and general emotional growth and well-being. Or K-pop. But then BTS is important to everyone."

"What the hell is K-pop and . . . BTS?"

With a groan, I looked to heaven. "How out of touch are you?"

"Apparently a lot." He laughed. "Thank God you're here to tell me what's what. Why don't I fetch us another round, and then you can catch me up?"

I watched his tall form wend its way through the crowd, and into the thick throng of people milling around the bar. The workers from Dad's business were definitely taking advantage of the free drinks, and good luck to them.

"Hey." A thick, heavy voice dragged my attention back to the here and now. A young man stood before me, his eyes bloodshot with pure alcoholic joy. His wiry arm was wrapped around the neck of his somewhat older yet similarly inebriated friend, though it was hard to tell who was holding up whom.

"I'm Fitzy," he said. "This's my mate, Larry. Can you settle a bet for us?"

"I don't know," I said, just a little wary.

"Larry says that you were the one who booby-trapped Pete, all those years ago when Andrew slugged him." The guy gesticulated toward me with his half-empty beer.

"Booby-trapped." Larry smirked. Who knows how many beers it had taken them to manufacture that pun?

"Wildly original and hilarious," I muttered. My shoulders sagged. Maybe it was too much to expect the scandal to have disappeared over the years. Probably I could come back to town in fifty years and there would still be young building-industry types regaling each other with stories of the boss's daughter who flashed her tits on her eighteenth birthday.

It was the stuff of legend.

"But I say it can't be you, because you have an awesome rack, and no one could complain about copping an eyeful of that." Beside him, Larry nodded soberly at his friend's logic, in the way that only the totally wasted can manage. "It's only natural."

"Anyway," Fitzy continued. "We were figuring that, if they're good enough to flash for Pete, maybe— Ow!"

Fitzy's head bent violently to one side, arching upward to expose his right ear. Standing behind him was Pete, his face thunder. He had the smaller man's earlobe in his fist, twisting it hard around and upward. Fitzy jolted upright, his drunken legs straining as he tried to raise himself high enough to relieve the pain. But all it did was bring him face-to-face with Pete, his brow creased with anger.

All of the laughter stopped dead.

"I think you've had enough, Matthew," Pete growled. Apparently "Fitzy" was just for friends, and Pete did not look friendly.

Even on his tiptoes, the younger man barely made it to Pete's height. Beside him, Larry made a run for it, apparently deciding that discretion was the better part of mate-ship.

"Yes, boss," Fitzy squeaked, sounding suddenly much soberer. "Sorry, boss."

"Apologize to the lady." Pete swiveled him around by the ear to face me, like a puppet held on a single string.

"Sorry, miss," he stammered. "Ma'am."

Pete pivoted him back around, so they were once again eye-to-eye. "You do not speak to her again," he said.

"You don't even fucking look at her. Is that understood?"

"Yes, boss."

"Maybe if you get out of here fast enough, the whole thing will have slipped my mind by Monday morning." Pete released him, and he stumbled off into Larry's arms, one hand nursing his ear.

"Sorry about that," Pete said to me.

"It's fine." I could really quite happily go about my night (and life) away from this oh so humorous scene. Bound to happen, but I didn't need to be a part of it. I rose to my feet, finishing off the remains of my drink. "You do realize I could have handled the situation myself?"

"He's an employee and this is a work gathering, to a degree. I'm unfortunately responsible for his behavior."

I wasn't entirely convinced.

"I know you can look after yourself, Adele."

Shit. Even Dad was looking over now. What a prime example for why me being here amongst these people again was such a wondrously bad idea. Even the ones who hadn't been at my eighteenth had obviously heard about what went down. I was just an embarrassment.

Pete pressed his hand against the small of my back. "Why don't we go? We don't need to be around this."

"Might as well."

We wove our way through the crowd and over to Dad. "Something happen?" he asked.

"No. I think the drive has caught up with me," I said, kissing him on the cheek. "I'm ready for bed. 'Night, Shan-ti. Thanks again for today."

She gripped my hand, giving it a squeeze. "Are you sure you're alright?"

"Absolutely."

"You're driving her home?" Dad asked Pete, standing behind me.

"Yeah," he said.

"Adele, tomorrow I want to hear all of your thoughts on Jeremy," ordered Shanti.

I just smiled.

Dad gave me another probing look. He wasn't falling for my bullshit at all. Next his gaze shifted to the men at the table. "Time to cut them off, I think. They've had more than enough for one night."

"Good idea," said Pete. "See you tomorrow."

Via the hand still sitting just above my butt, he directed me toward the exit. He shouldn't have been touching me. The warmth of his skin sinking through the thin cotton of my top was much too comforting. Thoughts of how his touch would feel in other places came far too easily. Such as his fingers stroking down my arm, sliding between my own fingers to hold tight. Along with more pornographic scenarios that we won't go into. My imagination could go from sweet to explicit in no time at all when it came to Pete.

Away from the noise and lights, the night was quiet. A fruit bat flew overhead, a darker shape against the dark sky. The parking lot was still half full at ten o'clock.

We parted at the back of his vehicle, a reasonably new big double-cab ute. My skin wasn't tingling because it was where his hand had been. Most likely, it was due to a rash or something. The jeans were helpful for climbing into the passenger seat. In the backseat lay a mess of papers, some tools, and a couple of items of clothing. It smelled of sawdust, a little earth, and a hint of cologne. Maybe coffee too.

The engine purred to life and Vance Joy was playing on the stereo. I stared out into the night. "I like this song."

"Yeah?" he sounded pleased.

There was something intimate about being in the dark together in such a small enclosed space. Something old and familiar, comfortable and special. Not that the drive home took long. Past a gift shop, a news agency, a chemist, and other such places. Farther out of town, on the way to the highway, there were a couple of pineapple farms. Some paddocks of fruit trees and dams. A lot of the large properties had been sold, however, broken up, and developed into housing estates in the last decade or so. It was sad to see. Dad had bought his block of land about fifteen years ago, off the main road, tucked away from the rush and noise. When Pete started working for Dad, he talked the lady who owned the land nearby into selling since she wasn't doing anything with it anyway and he loved the area.

"They'll forget about it," he said, pulling into the driveway. "It's not like all of them haven't done stuff they regret over the years."

"I'm not really worried about it."

He parked the car in the garage attached to the side

of the house. "Careful getting down."

"I'll be careful getting down." I smiled. "You don't need to baby me."

"I'm not babying you; I'm looking after you."

I didn't know what to say to that.

"You dad would kill me if you got a hair out of place on my watch."

"Right," I said. "Well, considering the man actively encouraged me to climb trees and play football, I don't think he's all that worried."

A low laugh. "If you think I won't be proving to your father that you're safe with me until the end of time, you've misread the situation."

"I seem to do that a lot." I followed him up the front stairs. "Though I doubt I'll be around much, so don't feel you need to dedicate your life to the cause."

Keys jangled and he unlocked the door, turning on a light. "You're really not interested in the job?"

"Do you want me to be?"

"Huh." A wallet and the keys were tossed onto the dining room table. "For all your talk of burnt bridges, you sure do seem to care about what I think."

"I wouldn't even consider it if you don't want me there—I'm trying to do less of the aggressively inflicting myself upon you these days," I said. "As a general rule."

He leaned his ass against the table, watching me with interest.

"It just makes sense, right?" I held up my hands. "If having me in your place of work would be an issue for you, make you uncomfortable, then that's the last thing I want to do. Neither of us would be having a good time in that situation."

"True. But I'm out on site most of the time."

"Still . . ."

He crossed his arms, cocked his head. "What if I didn't have a problem with you coming onboard?"

"Then I guess I would need to think it over."

Nothing from him.

"Anyway . . . thanks for the lift back. And everything." Hesitantly, I took a step toward my temporary end of the house. I used to be able to read him much better than this. Figure out his moods, have a vague idea of what was going on inside his head. These days, I had nothing.

"Right," he said. "'Night."

"Good night."

Only he didn't move and neither did I. Then he grabbed the back of his neck, turned away, and asked, "Feel like a swim?"

"Ah, sure. Why not?"

"Great," he said. "See you down there."

Chapter Five

Eight Years Ago . . .

"You drove Pete's truck into a pole?"

"Reversed it, actually."

Apparently the distinction didn't help. Dad's face remained heavily lined and unhappy.

"We were practicing reverse parking and Pete thought it might be better not to do it near other vehicles," I said. "So we had a trashcan up one end and the pole down the other."

"And you hit the pole."

"Yes."

"Not the trashcan, which would have just fallen over and made a mess, but not damaged anything."

"Dad, I didn't plan this. It was an accident."

"She was actually doing pretty well there for a while," said Pete, sitting on the couch with a bottle of beer. "Then her foot slipped off the clutch and . . . yeah."

Dad turned the unhappy look on him.

"How's your neck feeling?" I asked.

Pete just shrugged. "I'll live. The truck's tailgate is a fair bit fucked, though."

"Language," grunted Dad.

"Sorry."

I held up my hands. "I need the practice if I'm going to pass the test. I'm seventeen now, you know."

"And ready to hit things with vehicles, apparently."

Pete snickered and threw back some beer, rubbing at one of his shoulders. He had nice shoulders, thick and strong. I hoped I hadn't permanently damaged them.

"You know, that's really harsh. I feel very unsupported right now," I said. "Need I remind you, we called and you said it was okay for Pete to give me driving lessons?"

"I didn't expect you to hit something and damage his truck on your first lesson." Dad started to pace. Never a good sign. "Jesus Christ, is this what it's like to have a teenager?"

"Been a teenager for a while now—thought you might have noticed," I said, sitting curled up in the corner of the couch. Not getting teary, because that would be stupid.

Dad didn't need to know there had been a sudden mess of crying straight after the crash. The impact probably wouldn't have seemed like much to an onlooker, but it had jerked our bodies about fiercely. Pete, of course, had been infuriatingly relaxed about the whole thing, though it had been quite a shock to me. But damned if I would show Dad any glimpse of that.

"Look on the bright side," I said. "You only have to put up with me for six weeks a year. How many vehicles can I possibly damage in such a short amount of time?"

"Let's not find out," muttered Pete.

"Sweetheart, you know I don't mean it like that."

"I'm sorry I messed up and interrupted your work," I said.

Hands on hips, Dad hung his head, taking several deep breaths. "Okay, I deserved that."

Silence.

"Let me make something very clear to you," he said, gaze glued to me. "Adele, you are my daughter and I love you. When you called me to say there'd been an accident, you scared the absolute crap out of me."

I was not convinced.

"The thought that I can't protect you . . . that there are things out in the world that might hurt you." He sighed. "I'm just glad you're okay."

I swallowed hard. "Okay."

"And this idiot's probably due a company vehicle anyway."

Pete's sudden smile was beatific. He lifted the beer to me in toast. "Way to go, kid. I knew you'd come through for me in the end."

Dad laughed. "If she dents that one, at least the insurance claim will be handled through the business."

Funnily enough, Pete stopped smiling at that.

Thursday Night . . . Now

By the time I got down to the pool, he was already in the water, happily drifting in the deep end. My eyes took a minute to adjust to the dark, since the lighting was dim. Just enough to be able to get down the steps and everything without falling on your face.

"Hey," I said quietly.

"Hey."

I felt more than saw his gaze drift across my face, down the length of my body. My nipples of course loved the attention. Goddamn them.

This was new and unexpected, even after his maybe checking them out at the bar. Wildly different from the way he used to look at me. Back then, his gaze was more along the lines of pat-on-the-head-cute-puppy fondness. I don't know. Then again, maybe I was just imagining it all.

"Jump," he said.

"No."

His laugh was low and rough and perfect. Maybe this hadn't been such a good idea.

"Pete, you of all people should know better than to encourage me to go jumping into things."

He made a humming noise. Then strong arms stroked through the water until he reached the edge. "But this isn't making decisions without thinking them through. This is just for fun. Jump, Adele."

Carefully, I stepped into the water, down the stairs.

"Not going to happen."

"That's a nice bikini," he said.

"Thanks." I went up to my shoulders. All of the lovely wavy hairdo had been carefully rolled up into a bun. "Don't splash me. I don't want to get my hair wet tonight."

"Whatever you say."

On the edge, he had his bottle of scotch, a bucket of ice, a bottle of gin, and a bottle of tonic water. The man had even sliced up a lemon. Talk about hospitality. "I don't know if I chose right. Guy at the shop told me this one was the best."

I joined him at the side, examining the gin bottle. "Hendrick's is great. Thank you."

"It is? Good."

"My liver is never going to survive this trip."

He laughed. "I don't normally drink this much either."

"Am I driving you to drink?" I joked.

"A little, maybe." He glanced at me, then got busy pouring in the gin and topping it off with tonic water. Last but not least, the slice of lemon. A gin and tonic without a slice of lemon is rubbish and never let anyone tell you differently.

"I don't know whether to be honored or offended."

"Kid, why don't we just be?" He exhaled, handing over the drink. "For you."

"Thank you."

Once he'd poured his very minimal two to three fingers of scotch, no ice, he tapped his glass against mine.

"Cheers."

"To just being," I said.

We both drank, side by side, floating at the edge of the pool. He looked spectacular with his wet hair slicked back, the muscles in his shoulders and arms right there. I could feel my heart hammering against my ribs, overexcited over nothing. Because nothing was going on and nothing was going to happen. I mean, of course it wasn't. Maybe, though, if I was really lucky we'd eventually be sort of friends again. I'd no longer have lost him from my life completely.

That would be so great.

"How are things really going with your mom?" he asked.

"Good. But, you know, she and I are always good." I shrugged. "She has her life and I have mine. Mostly, she just wants to hang out in her studio or go on the painting trips, hold her classes. That's her whole world."

"Thought you might have followed her into art for a while there."

"Me?" I laughed. "No. I can sketch okay, but nothing like what she does. I always preferred books to paintbrushes."

"What about writing? You always kept a diary."

"Yeah, it's full of salacious details about you."

"Great," he said drily. "But you did see the journalism through?"

"I did a couple of classes and honestly . . ." I shook my head. "They were scarily hardcore and competitive. That's when I realized, if I wasn't willing to share that cutthroat attitude, then I didn't want it badly enough."

"Hm."

"It just wasn't for me."

He took a sip of scotch. "What about all of the traveling you talked about doing?"

"Funny thing about flitting all over the globe," I said. "It costs serious money. Plus, my current workplace isn't keen on us taking all our leave at one time. Makes it difficult to plan a decent trip. But I'll get there."

He nodded, just watching me.

"What about you?"

"What about me?"

"Leona, huh?"

"We already covered that ground. Tell me about your friends."

"No, it's my turn," I said, downing some of the gin and tonic. Ah, the essence of life. "What about your father? Did he ever get over you not working behind a desk?"

His laughter was short and somewhat pained. "I really did used to talk to you about all sorts of shit, didn't I? He's pretty much written me off as a lost cause. My sister keeps him happy. She has two small kids and runs the branch of a bank. She's basically Superwoman."

"Wow. Good for her."

"Yeah," he said. "Meanwhile, as far as he's concerned, I still just bang shit with hammers. Makes for interesting dinner conversation at Christmas."

"If only you'd followed in your father's footsteps and gone into finance too . . ."

"Exactly."

I snorted. "Not that you wouldn't look pretty in a suit, but it's absolute bullshit. You build homes for people. You help create these amazing art-like buildings all over the coast. If he can't see that, forget him."

He smiled. "Thanks."

"It's the truth."

"Maybe I should take you as my date next Christmas, let you defend poor little old me," he joked.

"I'm interested."

"I'll keep you in mind." He laughed. "You got lots of friends down south?"

"I've got my roommates, Hazel and her girlfriend, Maddie. They're good people."

"Good."

"Honestly though, it's hard to find kindred spirits you can really let loose with," I said. "I don't know if you ever noticed, but my sense of humor can be a little strange. Some of the things I come out with . . . people don't always get me. So not really a whole bunch of people, just a couple of close friends."

He nodded.

"People you can be yourself with are rare."

"You're right, they are." His gaze turned serious.

"What's that look?"

"Not to interrupt our just being," he started, "but I am still sort of curious about a few things . . ."

"Such as?" I asked.

He groaned, shoving back his hair. "I almost don't want to ask, but I've got to know. What did you honestly see happening in your eighteen-year-old mind that night?"

I winced. "Really?"

"Yeah. Sorry."

Maybe I could just drown myself. That might work.

"I just, I can't square it in my head. Did I make you think there was something more?"

"Shit. Okay." I downed a goodly amount of the drink because emergency. "It wasn't care of anything you did outside of breathing, and I don't know . . . science says you can't exactly stop that and stay alive. So not your fault."

"Alright."

I grimaced. "I suppose I thought that if I could declare my desire and undying affection for you in such a grand manner then you would be hit by the stunning realization of my flourishing womanhood."

"That was the baring-your-breasts part?"

"Right," I said. "But you can't forget the words, Pete. There were words. I practiced that speech a lot, you know. Though I then forgot most of it due to internal panic and alcohol. But they were weighty poetic words that were supposed to sway you as to both the determination and righteousness of my cause."

"The righteousness of your cause?" His brows rose and he too, drank. "Jesus. So what was I meant to be doing during all of this?"

"I don't know. Swoon?"

"No, come on. How did you honestly think I would react?"

"How did I think you would react?" I sighed. "Upon reflection, the smart money was probably on you telling me to stop being an idiot and put my clothes back on."

He snorted. "Sounds about right."

"But there was of course a small, timid flame of hope burning inside my chest that you'd be shocked and stunned into admitting that you felt exactly the same way," I said. "Next would have come the passionate kissing and deflowering segment of the evening."

"I was supposed to take your virginity in the hallway of your dad's house?" he asked, expression somewhat appalled. "You must think I have balls of steel."

I laughed. "The fantasy went more toward us moving things over to your place. Or maybe your truck. Less chance of getting busted."

"Right. And you thought your dad's reaction to all of this would be what?"

"Hey now." I held up a hand. "I was finally, at long last, eighteen. His opinion didn't really much matter to me. But I guess ideally we would have gone to him hand-in-hand the next morning and told him of our love and how we were destined to be together. Possible engagement ring involved. I don't know . . . details were sketchy by that part."

"Fuck," he said, shaking his head.

"You already said that."

"It bears repeating." He swiped the water off his face. "Knew I shouldn't have asked."

"Yeah, but you did. Too late to go back now. I was young, dumb, and in love," I explained. "Reality, consequences, things like that didn't particularly factor into it. Add a few drinks, and that was that."

He mumbled something under his breath.

"What?"

"You weren't in love with me. You just thought you were."

And yeah, no. "Pete, there's a lot about what happened back then that I'll readily admit was ill-judged, outright wrong, and even possibly plain stupid. But don't tell me how I felt. I know how I felt."

"You do, huh?" he said, his tone dripping with sarcasm.

"Yes. Just because I was a teenager doesn't negate it."

"I'm not so sure about that."

"Oh come on," I said. "Look at the facts. Plenty of people meet their significant others when they're young."

"Maybe," he said. "But let's look at your feelings in a larger context."

"Alright."

He stopped to taste the scotch, obviously thinking it all over. "So, am I to understand that in none of the years since then have you met someone and been with them in a more . . . what shall we say, a more intimate, real, and involved way than our platonic friendship, and realized that you felt more for them than you ever did for me?"

"No," I said simply.

"No?"

"No."

His forehead creased, then he shook his head. "Maybe you just haven't fallen for anyone yet."

"I fell. It hurt like hell. Eventually, I picked myself up and moved on."

A grunt.

"I'd also like to point out that sex doesn't necessarily equal true intimacy. It's physically baring, that's true," I said. "But sharing your innermost thoughts, your heart and soul, being who you really are with someone—that's a whole other level."

"You were a teenager. You didn't even know who you were yet." He sighed. "And apparently you didn't know a thing about sex, either."

"Don't be so condescending. I was getting there."

Another adamant shake of the head.

"Hey, you asked. I'm sorry you don't like the answer I gave you, but it's the truth. By all means, however, continue to believe what you like." I shrugged, taking a sip of my drink. "You've been in love, right?"

"Once or twice."

"And at what age did you first fall in love?"

He exhaled, dunking his head under the water and coming back up before answering. Keeping the single malt out of the water, of course. "I don't know. About your age. A few years younger, maybe."

"Who was she?"

"A girl I worked with. She was one of the salespeople at a building supplies place." He smiled. "Bought a shit-load of stuff I didn't need just to get to see her each day. Nearly left me broke."

I laughed.

"We lived together for a year or so." The smile faded from his face. "But she was ready for marriage and kids. I wasn't."

"Think you'll ever want that?"

"Don't know." His gaze narrowed on me. "What about you? You want the whole marriage and kids, kid?"

I smiled. "Cute. Honestly, I don't know either. No one I've dated has made me think we might be headed anywhere near that direction."

"You've got plenty of time."

"It's such a huge commitment, being with someone day in and day out." I waved my hand across the surface of the water, watching the ripples. "You agree to spend the rest of your life with them, but there's lots of things that could go wrong. I don't want to choose the wrong person and wind up divorced like my parents."

"Hm."

"They wound up hating each other. It wasn't pretty," I said. "I mean, they're fine now, not that they really have anything to do with each other."

"I get what you're saying. It's a risk."

"Yes, it is." I moaned. "God, this is getting maudlin."

He finished off his scotch. "I'd better be off to bed.

Not all of us are on vacation, sleeping in till all hours."

"Please," I said, likewise finishing off my drink and setting the glass on the side of the pool. "You'd be up with the sun anyway. You're just one of those unnatural morning-people weirdos."

He smiled.

I held out my arms.

Brow furrowed, the man stopped and looked at me.

"You can't have it both ways, Pete," I said. "Either in your platonic eyes I'm still basically a kid, in which case we do hugs. Or I'm this tempting thing, in which case you're absolutely entitled to keep your distance."

His gaze narrowed, then he swallowed. "A hug would be fine, I guess."

I stepped into him, wrapping my arms around his neck and resting my head on his shoulder. Fuck, he felt good. His warm skin and hard body pressed against mine. Though, yes, I was doing the bulk, if not all, of the pressing. Most of it gratuitous. Meanwhile, his big hands kind of patted my back a couple of times uncertainly. But he didn't move away. Beneath the salt of his skin, the scent of him, of his cologne, was only just detectable. The man made my mouth water. I didn't even really feel bad about putting him in this position.

"See, isn't this nice?" I asked.

He took a deep breath. "Yeah."

I sighed happily.

"Okay, we're done." Strong hands gripped my hips, setting me back from him. His smile had returned to being of the strained variety. "Time to get to bed. I ah, yeah . . ."

"Good talk." I headed for the steps. "Can I carry some of the bar gear up?"

"No. You just go on ahead," he said. "I've got it. 'Night."

Chapter Six

Eight Years Ago . . .

"What about him?"

"Hmm. No." I took a sip of my iced coffee, scanning the passersby. "She's pretty."

Eyes hidden behind his shades, Pete sat slumped back in the café chair, totally at his ease. "Think you might like girls?"

I thought I might like *him*. Actually, I knew I did. But I might as well wish for the moon for all the good it would do me. "I figure it comes down to the person, not what's in their pants, you know?"

"Sounds a bit more mature than I can manage." He shrugged, then nodded. "But sure."

It was Boxing Day. We'd decided to avoid the crowded shopping malls and equally crowded beaches by finding a nice, relaxing café. Due to his shit family situation and no current serious girlfriend, I'd convinced Dad yesterday to invite Pete to go to lunch with us at the Palmwoods Tavern. Pete claimed he could cook, but Dad sure as hell couldn't. Also, he'd been too busy to get groceries. We'd been living on takeout for a week or more. Eating out was the way to go.

Fine with me.

"Did you call your sister for Christmas?" I asked. "Christina, isn't it?"

"Yeah." A shadow passed across his face. "She's a few years younger than me. We got on okay, but we're not really close. She's on the other side of the country, for one thing. Probably to avoid having to spend too much time with Dad."

"You said she had kids?"

He shrugged. "Primary-school age. They're pretty cute. She puts pictures up on Facebook."

I nodded.

"Honestly, I talk more to you than I do her. Maybe I should just adopt you as my little sister? Put pictures of you up on Facebook." He smiled. "What do you think?"

"I am *not* your little sister."

Pete took off his sunglasses, a heavy scowl suddenly in place. But not directed at me.

"What?"

"That idiot checking you out over there," he said. "Yeah, I see you. Put your eyes back in your head, asshole."

Sure enough, a surfer dude stood at the counter, waiting on his coffee. Cute smile. Hot body. Not as hot as Pete's, but we couldn't all be walking perfection.

"Aren't we sitting here checking people out?" I asked.

He ignored me, ranting on . . . "Put on a fucking shirt, why don't you? You're not on the beach now. Dickhead." Obviously, we were not worrying about language. Pete followed the guy's progress out of the café, his mouth a thin, unamused line, body on high alert. "To answer your question, he's got to be at least in his twenties. Way too old for you; you're just a kid."

I frowned. "I won't always be."

"But you are for now."

Friday . . . Now

My head was a little sore the next morning, care of the gin and tonics. I put the bikini back on along with some shorts and a T-shirt, took some painkillers, then got moving. Caloundra, a beach town, was only about a fifteen-to-twenty-minute drive. Took me a little while to find a parking spot at Kings Beach, then into the ocean pool I went. The surf looked a bit rough and I wasn't sure my body was up to dealing with actual waves.

I kept my sunglasses on, rather than lose my retinas to the sun. There were lots of happy families and children screaming in delight. Coffee and eggs Benedict further helped revive me. I managed to find a café by the beach where I could sit pondering the pandanus palms, white sand, and crystal-blue water stretching out to the horizon. Beautiful.

As far as I knew, the only thing scheduled for today was the barbeque tonight with Shanti's family. Happily, this gave me hours to pull myself together. Between the long-haul drive up here and the frequent boozing, I was feeling a little delicate. This relaxation time was necessary.

With the car windows down and fresh air blowing in my face during the drive home, I almost felt human upon my return. Surprisingly, it was the middle of the day and Pete's vehicle sat in the driveway.

The man himself stood on the front steps, hands on hips. Cargo pants and a polo shirt with the company logo on it seriously shouldn't look so good. But, of course, on him they did. "Where the hell have you been?"

My brows jumped. "The beach. Why?"

"You couldn't let anyone know where you were going or answer your phone maybe?"

Huh. "I forgot to check it."

"You forgot to check it?"

"Yes," I said. "What dire emergency has occurred to warrant this response, pray tell?"

He cocked his head and looked at me, jaw working back and forth. Lots of frowning, but his gaze actually seemed a little torn. Then he turned and stomped into the house.

Wow. Okay.

I smacked the remaining sand off my Birkenstocks and gathered up my damp towel and stuff, taking my time. Because no sane person would rush to follow a cranky-ass bear into its den. I did have some small amount of survival instincts. They just didn't tend to kick in. But honestly, what the ever-loving fuck? I PMS'd with fewer mood swings than this man.

"Thought you didn't want to get your hair wet," he said accusingly as I stepped inside. He sat slumped on one of the dining chairs, palm bouncing off the long wooden table.

"I changed my mind."

A grunt.

"Seriously, what is your problem?" I asked, more than a little upset myself.

Despite the outdoor shower at the beach, my long hair was loaded down with salt and tangled to shit. I wound it up, getting it off my sweaty neck. The day was already promising to be sweltering. "You always recommended hitting the beach to cure a hangover. Thought I'd give it a try."

Another grunt.

"Are we communicating entirely in caveman language now?" I asked. "Because I'm not sure that's going to work."

"Not really in the mood for your sarcasm."

"I wasn't really in the mood to get yelled at in the front yard like a naughty child," I said. "So I guess that makes us even."

The pale blue of his eyes turned arctic.

"Pete." I held tight to the strap of my handbag. "What's going on?"

"Your dad asked me to drop by and pick you up," he told the far wall. "He wants you to sit in on a business meeting. Get a feel for things. See what you think."

"He never mentioned anything about that last night."

"I tried to call to let you know, but you weren't answering your phone."

"No, I was swimming at the beach," I reported in a calm voice. Not beating him over the head with my bag, no matter how much I might have liked to. Out of interest, I pulled my cell out of the bag. Five missed messages. That was quite a lot. "Then I grabbed some breakfast. I left my phone in the car and didn't think to check my messages when I got back to it."

His jaw tensed. "I got worried."

"You did?"

"What if you'd been in a car accident or something and I had no idea where you were?"

"Okay." I took a deep breath. Now we were getting somewhere. It wasn't like people didn't care about me, but this was a little intense. "What if in the future I make sure to leave you a note?"

"And check your messages."

"I'll do that."

The tension in his shoulders eased some. "Good."

"Now you apologize to me for reaming me a new one instead of talking to me about your concerns like an adult."

His gaze shot to my face.

I just waited.

Then, eventually, he sighed. "Sorry. I shouldn't have spoken to you like that. I just . . ."

"You were worried. I get it," I said.

"You good to go?"

"No." I scratched at my salt-filled scalp. "I'll need a quick shower and change of clothes."

A jerk of the chin. "Please don't take long—people are waiting."

The meeting included Dad, Pete, and the seconds in charge from each of the two building crews. They talked about the progress of current jobs (though things were pretty quiet this time of year with people on holiday plus Dad's wedding coming up), how things were coming together with upcoming ones, and shared industry gossip. All while I sat in the corner with a cup of coffee, making a few notes on my phone. Until the other guys left, I was pretty much ignored. Which was fine.

"You playing a game on there?" asked Pete. "Are we disturbing you?"

"Doing some research and taking a few notes, actually." I gave him my best professional smile. "Sounds like the business is running as smoothly as ever. If I come onboard, Helga can clue me into all the admin details. But if you want me taking over some of the liaising between customers et cetera, then I'm going to need to expand on the bare-bones knowledge of the process I've currently got."

"It'd be a steep learning curve for you," he said flatly.

Dad's brows drew in slightly. "Said it wouldn't be easy, sweetheart. But we'll of course be there supporting you every step of the way."

"So I'm guessing you also want me to think about ways to grow?" I asked.

"Among other things."

"Is this the room where you talk to prospective customers?"

"Yeah," said Dad. "If they come in. Usually, it's just to sign papers. Initially we go to them, check out the site."

I nodded. "Okay. The office as a whole could do with a little work and there's no computer in here. A lot of your suppliers keep stock lists and photos solely online now."

"That's what the tablets are for." Dad waved a hand at the one lying on the table in front of him.

"You might want to think about getting a screen in here just the same," I said. "I take it you've been mostly getting jobs by word of mouth?"

"Right," said Dad, "referrals from contractors and customers."

"That's probably partly because your website sucks. I mean, has it been updated in the last fifteen years?" I asked. "If you want to reach business farther afield then you'll want to look at updating it. The information on there is scarce, for starters. You might want to consider getting some professional pictures taken of previous work for the site. Some framed and hung up in here might be nice too."

Pete just blinked. "So your contribution is that we make things prettier?"

"How about updated to this century and more easily accessible to potential new clients?"

"She's got a point." Dad scratched his head, thinking things over.

"You don't rate high in online searches either. Might be worth looking into."

"Sounds like a lot of money," grumbled Pete.

"You talk about growth, but you don't want to invest in marketing?" I shot back.

"Hey, what's going on between you two?" asked Dad, voice slightly raised. "I thought you'd sorted things out."

Pete said nothing. But the bad vibes kept right on coming.

"That's all I've got for now." Gathering my stuff, I rose to my feet. "Don't get stressed, Dad. You're getting married tomorrow. Happy thoughts."

He sighed, also standing. "We done here, then?"

"Yeah." Pen tapping against the desk, Pete nodded.

"Sweetheart, want to spend the afternoon helping me get the backyard set up for tonight?" asked Dad. "It involves climbing ladders and trees to hang up fairy lights."

"Sounds great. Can I visit with Helga for a bit first, though?"

"Of course."

The Friday-night barbeque mostly consisted of Shanti's extended family who'd flown in from Darwin. Nice people. Very chatty. Good thing, since I was feeling a little overwhelmed by everything. Yes, I talked to people at work and socialized some outside of it. But this was intense. A family barbeque now meant about two dozen people and an over-the-top exotic feast. The array of food was amazing. Turkish breads and dips, giant mezze platters, a variety of salads, and mouthwatering grilled meats. Pretty soon, I'd stuffed myself so much, I couldn't eat another thing.

Also, my plan to give my liver a night off wasn't working out so well. Every time I put a glass down, someone seemed to hand me another. Shanti's cousin owned a small winery and the grape juice was flowing like nobody's business. And it was damn good.

Meanwhile, Pete was still communicating with me in mostly grunts and glares. An intricate language. So rich and varied and full of nuances. Not. We'd largely managed to avoid each other.

"Adele, how are you, my darling?" asked Shanti in a loud voice. I think she'd had a couple of drinks too. Pre-wedding jitters, maybe?

"Good, good. And you?"

"Fantastic. Isn't it a gorgeous night?" She wrapped an arm around my waist, pressing herself to my side. "And you look magnificent."

"You are so good for my ego."

"What? I merely state the truth."

We laughed.

I'd settled on a chambray fitted midi dress I was particularly fond of. Had a nicely cut vee neckline that stopped just low enough to rule out wearing a normal bra, but still looked tailored and classy. Same wedges as the night before, and I'd tied my hair up to get it off my neck.

Shanti clucked her tongue. "Your nose is pink from the sun."

"Damn."

Dad then joined in to inspect my minor sunburn. "Told you to put on a hat."

"I was wearing sunscreen."

Pete stood nearby. He'd been cornered early on in the evening by two of Shanti's sisters. I really couldn't fault their taste in men. Even if he currently was ever so slightly annoying the living shit out of me. There'd really been no need for his attitude in the meeting. If he didn't want me near the business, the man needed to brave up and say so.

I smiled. "I also went for a swim at the beach this morning. Might have been then."

"You need to be more careful," said Shanti.

"It won't happen again. Promise."

"Andrew, her glass is almost empty." Shanti took my

still half-filled wineglass, handing it over to Dad.

"What are you drinking, sweetheart?"

"The Sémillon, thank you."

Once Dad disappeared, Shanti whispered in my ear, "How odd that Leona isn't here."

"She was invited?"

"Pete usually brings her to things. I wonder if they've had a falling out. His mood is more down than I might have hoped for." Her gaze roamed over the couple of dozen barbeque invitees. "You really do look lovely tonight, darling."

"So do you."

She gave me a squeeze, her glamorous silk caftan swirling about her in a riot of colors. "Peter will come to his senses eventually, and I'm sure you'll be great friends once again."

"We're doing okay," I said. "I just seem to have a gift for irritating him, unfortunately."

"Yes, your father mentioned . . ." Shanti turned toward where Pete was still penned in by Shanti's equally gorgeous sisters. Maybe that's why he hadn't brought Leona. Scoring at weddings was a fine old tradition dating back many a year. Of course, he looked dazzling. He'd gone with black pants and a white button-down shirt tonight. The sleeves were rolled up to his elbows and a couple of buttons undone at his neck. Damn him and his raw male beauty getting all up in my face from across the room. The truth was, sober or otherwise, he went straight to my head.

"It must be very strange for him to know you as a teenage girl and now suddenly here you are all grown up and so beautiful," said Shanti. "He seems very intent on keeping an eye on you this evening."

I licked my lips. "Maybe he thinks I'm going to start dancing on a table."

Shanti laughed. "That would be quite the sight to see."

"Here you go." Dad handed me a full wineglass. And given the things were about goblet size, this could easily turn messy.

"Thank you."

"How did the office visit go today?" asked Shanti.

"Helga loves the idea of her taking over," said Dad. "Sooner the better, as far as she's concerned."

"The woman definitely has better places to be." I smiled. "She showed me lots of pictures of her garden and grandchildren. She also has grand plans of staging a coup and taking over as president at the local croquet club."

"Good on her. It's all down to you now, sweetheart."

Shanti clapped her hands. "I'm very hopeful this will all work out and we'll have you much closer, Adele."

"Me too. Your aunty would like a word when you're ready." Dad offered Shanti his arm and off they went.

As if Pete felt my gaze on him, he looked up. A very grown-up and civilized staring competition commenced. Like hell I'd look away first, no matter how twisted up inside he made me feel. He was probably plotting my death. Might be best for me to sleep with the door locked tonight. A chair wedged under the knob or something. It was important to plan ahead.

Eventually, he made his excuses and came my way.

"Adele."

"If me considering the job is a problem for you, I really wish you'd just tell me."

His brows rose. "Straight into it, huh?"

"I think that's best, don't you?"

He said nothing.

"Yes or no, Pete. It's really that simple," I said, keeping my voice low. "Don't worry about Dad. I'll just say I wasn't interested. But I want your honest opinion this time."

"My honest opinion." His smile was all sharp teeth. "Alright. I think if you come back and take this job, you'll be bored in no time, and take off leaving a fucking mess again."

"That's what you think?"

He jerked his chin. "That is what I think."

"Wow. Okay." I was honestly kind of shocked. My shoulders slumped. It felt like all of the air had been let out of me. To think, I'd imagined we were getting along better. How quickly things changed. "Thank you for being honest with me. Brutally so."

"You're welcome."

I downed about half of the wine. It was necessary.

"See, when I went home today and you weren't there," he said, "I thought, for just a moment, that you might have packed up and gone back down south."

I froze. "Wait, what?"

"Yeah. Thought you'd left without a word."

"But all of my things were still there," I said, sun-burned nose scrunched up in disbelief. "I only went to the beach."

"Right. I soon figured that out." He nodded. "But, can you see how me thinking that maybe you'd gone, finding that idea so believable even for just a second, is really damn telling?"

"Yes, Pete. It demonstrates your neurosis quite well."

"Can't resist being a smart-ass, can you?" He grinned, then swallowed. "But here's the thing. I don't trust you, kid. That's what it comes down to."

"You don't *want* to trust me."

"Maybe. Is there a difference?"

My smile wavered. "So it doesn't actually matter what I say or do. You're never going to forgive me."

He saluted me with his glass. "Have a nice night."

Hazel: *If you're awake we need to talk. If you're not awake we should still talk anyway.*

Me: *Wide the fuck awake.*

Hazel: *Calling.*

"I need an update," said Hazel the second I picked up the phone.

"Hello to you too."

"What's going on up there in the sunshine state?"

I groaned. "You're sure you want to know?"

"Oh my God, I know that tone of voice. What did you do?"

"Okay." I took a deep breath. "So we talked and I hugged him."

"You hugged him or you humped him? Tell the truth."

"Hugged only, honestly," I said. "I kept my pelvis mostly to myself."

"Huh. That's it?"

"Apparently that was enough. The man has been less than happy all day."

"Jerk."

"Oh yeah," I said. "I'm untrustworthy and basically the worst."

"I don't know. Must have been one hell of a hug."

"I didn't even grope. It was all rather restrained." I flopped back on the bed. "How's Maddie and everything?"

"Good, great," she said. "We're the boring old farts. We have to live vicariously through you now. What else have you got?"

"Um, I met the girlfriend. Though he says she's more a friend."

"Ooh."

"Lawyer. Gorgeous. Thin."

"Damn her."

"Yep."

"Are you going to try to hug him again?"

"I really don't think such behavior would be welcome," I said. "What do you want me to do? Attack him in dark hallways? Sneak up on him when he's asleep?"

"Pretty sure both of those options would count as assault."

"Maybe not, then. I'd rather kick him right now, anyway."

"Hm."

"We were getting on so well," I said. "Sharing of thoughts and feelings, even."

"Feelings are scary."

I said nothing.

"Especially for someone like you who generally avoids them."

"Is that your professional opinion?"

"My professional opinion is that between your parents' messy divorce and this guy rejecting you so spectacularly when you were eighteen, you decided no emotional entanglements," she said. "For the most part at least. It was safer, right?"

"I'm not saying emotions are the enemy, because that would sound crazy. But we all know they are."

"Yeah, but now you've turned them back on and things are happening."

"Not anymore they're not—he shut me down completely," I said.

She made a noise in her throat. "Sorry it all went south."

"I'll survive. Thanks for listening and providing the diagnosis."

"You're very welcome," she said. "Call me if you're about to do anything too insane and need talking down from the edge."

"Ha. Sure. You got it."

"'Night."

Chapter Seven

Eight Years Ago . . .

"Adele Margaret Reid, did you sneak out?"

"Maybe." I smiled. "And where on earth did you hear my full name?"

Pete shrugged. "I don't know, must have been when your dad was pissed at you sometime."

"You have a good memory."

He sat on a log in front of a small campfire, a glass of scotch in his hand. Behind him sprawled his brand-new humble abode, a shed with a small kitchen-and-bathroom setup. There was just enough room left over for his futon and a TV. I'd have gone a little crazy in such cramped quarters. But Pete deemed it sufficient to live in while he saved his money and built his dream home.

"Speaking of which, better tell your father you're over here," he said.

"It's only across the road." I sat down beside him, trying to get comfortable without getting any splinters. Maybe coming over in my sleep shorts and tank top was a bad idea. "Besides, when I left, he was snoring so loud the roof was rattling. If he does wake up, I've got my phone on me. It's fine."

"Hm."

"It's the middle of summer—why do you need a fire?"

"Atmosphere." His smile, there was something almost dopey about it. Same went for the relaxed set of his face and hazy eyes.

"How drunk are you?" I asked with no small amount of wonder.

"I've had a couple."

"You know, I don't think I've ever seen you actually under the influence."

He snorted. "You've seen me have a drink before."

"Yeah, but you're seriously drunk."

"Am not."

"Then why is your ass about to slide back off the log?"

He shuffled forward, giving me a stern look. Like I'd gone and moved the log on him or something. Idiot.

I turned away so he wouldn't see my smile. "So, neighbor."

"We are neighbors," he said with a grin. "That's great, isn't it?"

"It is."

"I always liked fires, going camping," he said, switching back to the earlier topic in the way the inebriated do.

"We went a couple of times before Mom got sick. Dad would actually take the stick out of his ass and relax for a change. Do a little fishing. Go on some hikes."

"Sounds nice. But fishing is gross."

"I'll cross that off our list of stuff to do."

"Good." I watched the flames, letting them mesmerize me. "No idea how you could stick a big hook in a poor, innocent little worm."

"Oh, no. They love it. Feels like a massage to them."

"I don't think so." I laughed. "You know, if I was here in winter we could toast marshmallows and cook sausages and do stuff like that."

"We can do that in the summer too. I'll pick up some stuff tomorrow."

"Awesome," I said. "Guess how I escaped."

"Shit. What did you do?"

"I climbed down the tree outside my bedroom window. Just like a ninja."

"You fall and break something, your dad's going to kill me."

"Don't be silly." I ruffled his dark hair. Thick and silky. Very nice. "He'd be too busy putting bars on my window."

"True." He swatted my hand away. "Don't mess with my style, kid."

I laughed some more. "Please. You have no style."

Some grumbling.

"So, no girls who are just friends to hang around the campfire with you?" I asked.

He sighed. "Went to a party earlier, but I'd rather just have some quiet time on my own."

"You want me to leave?"

"No, no. You're fine." He patted my knee. Then seemed to realize he was patting my knee and retracted his hand at the speed of light. Sheesh. It'd been in a comradely fashion, not a come-hither one. Talk about being overly cautious.

"You didn't drive in this condition, did you?" I asked.

"No, 'course not. Friend gave me a lift."

I pondered this. "You know, I've met some of your girls who are friends. But I haven't really met any of your *friends* who are friends."

"The fuck did you just say?"

"You know what I mean."

He downed some more scotch. Johnnie Walker. It smelled awful. "That's because, Adele, you're a seventeen-year-old young lady and they're mostly a pack of much older assholes. Highly unsuitable for you to be around."

"That's ridiculous. I'm sure they'd be fine."

"I'm not risking it," he said.

"I suppose you need some time away from me outside of work and sleep."

"That's true too." He laughed.

I elbowed him in the ribs, making him almost fall off the log again. His balance was way gone. The man had obviously done some serious drinking.

"They're okay guys, really," he said. "Some of them are great. But you're—"

"Just a kid?"

"I was going to say young and pretty. Not that I think they'd hit on you or anything . . ." His brows descended. "But put a few beers in them and you might stop looking like the boss's daughter."

"Well, that's not fair," I said. "Drunk or sober, they're responsible for their actions and how they treat people. Not me."

"I know. But let's not borrow trouble, okay?"

I didn't answer.

"You can go drinking at home with friends your own age. In a year or two. No rush. Though you know you can have a really good time without getting inebriated," he rattled on. "Might be better just to stay sober and have fun that way, you know?"

"Pete, you really think I'm pretty?"

But he just frowned some more. "Huh? Yeah, of course you are. That's my point."

"Thank you. I think you're pretty too," I said. Oh my God. My heart. Such explosions. "Can I have a drink? I haven't tried scotch before."

"Not a chance."

"Okay."

Saturday ... Now

"'Morning."

"Yes," I said.

Along with this word, I gave him my most dubious look. He'd earned it. After last night's insults he had no business standing in the kitchen wearing only a pair of soft gray sleeping pants, a blue-and-white-striped oven mitt on one hand, and a smile. I don't care who the house belonged to, the smile had to go. The man could also put a shirt on if he was so inclined. Like I needed to see any more of his flat stomach, pecs, and the rest. For fuck's sake. Exposing me to this man's nipples before midday was asking a lot. Also, armpit hair probably shouldn't be considered sexy.

There was something seriously wrong with me.

"You have a weird look on your face," he said.

"No I don't."

"Okay. Ah, grab a seat." He pointed a spatula at the stools drawn up along one side of the kitchen counter. "Coffee?"

"No, thanks."

"Milk no sugar, right?"

"It's fine, really. Shanti will be waiting for me."

The smile finally faded. "Kid—"

"Lots going on today." I turned away. "I'd better get going."

"You're going to need to eat and you're useless without coffee."

Hmm. He had a point.

"Sit. Please."

Saying no to him was harder than it looked. "Alright."

Much taking of deep breaths. Then I lay my dress over the dining room table, dumping my shoes, bag, and makeup kit alongside it. I climbed up onto the stool and he slid a cup full of caffeinated goodness in front of me.

"Pancakes okay?" he asked.

"Pancakes are great. Thanks."

A nod. "What are the plans for the day?"

I sucked down a goodly amount of coffee first, because coffee. "Shanti's got hair and makeup people arriving soon. A small, intimate group of us are going to all get ready together. Girls only, apparently."

"Right." He smiled before turning back to the stove. "Intimate for Shanti can mean any amount up to a hundred or so. Be prepared."

Soon enough, a plate of pancakes along with a berry compote and ricotta were placed in front of me. Along with cutlery wrapped up in a napkin. The man knew how to lay it on; I just had no idea why he was bothering. He'd made his thoughts regarding me quite clear last night.

"You should have been a chef," I said, digging in.

He shook his head. "Too stressful. Notice how they're always screaming at each other and having meltdowns on those shows?"

"And your current job is low key?"

"It's not so bad," he said. "More involved since I became a partner, but I enjoy it. And it's what I'm good at."

"You never thought about going solo, starting your own business?"

"Yeah, but . . . I like working with your dad and being a part of something bigger," he said. "Feeling like I belong somewhere, you know?"

I nodded, shoveling food into my mouth. Anything to stop me from making conversation, because I was angry at him, dammit. This was the problem with me and Pete. I cared. I wanted to know what he thought about things, how he felt. It just came naturally. Made expressing my rage by ignoring him tremendously difficult. Also, I was starved for him. Seven years' worth of nothing had made me ravenous for the man. Best to keep my eyes on the food, my mouth busy with chewing.

"Good?" he asked.

I downed a mouthful of coffee. "You know I like your cooking."

"Just checking."

Silence.

He didn't grab the stool beside me, instead choosing to stand opposite to eat. I needed blinders or something. A privacy screen. Anything to distract me from his half-naked state of being. First thing I was going to do when I got back home was sleep with someone. Anyone. Just because it hadn't ever worked before didn't mean it wouldn't now. I mean, statistically it was unlikely to help. But I might as well try anyway. One friend from university swore by random penis. Used to say it cured her blues every time, and she'd gone into medicine, so really she should know.

"What are you thinking about?" he asked.

"Nothing."

"Bullshit, your head's never quiet." A fork full of pancake and ricotta went into his mouth. Even the way he ate was manly, jaw moving with intention, lips closed. Not that I'd imagine there were many different versions of the process. But for some reason when he did it, I wanted to watch. So weird. Don't even get me started on the eye porn of his strong neck.

"You look like you're in pain," he said.

"Headache," I lied. "Probably just the wine from last night."

Without another word, he fetched me a glass of water and some aspirin. I downed two with a vague smile of appreciation. Really should have just made a dash for the door the moment I saw him. It would have been the smart thing to do. I'd thought coming back, seeing him again, might resolve some issues for me. But mostly I just felt mildly depressed. Tomorrow morning, I'd get up early, pack up the car, and be gone before he was even awake. It wasn't possibly cowardly and rude, it was smart. There, I had a plan.

"Slow down," he said. "Keep eating that fast, you're going to make yourself sick."

"I'm not a child. I can set my own eating speed, thank you."

"I realize that."

"Do you?" I asked, genuinely interested. Given the way he acted, the man had not a single fucking clue. I might as well still be sixteen, with him warning me off this boy and that. Reminding me to wear a hat and to not read and walk at the same time or I'd hit a pole. As if that had happened more than a couple of times at most.

"Yes," he said, voice subdued. "I can call Shanti and tell her I've held you up if that'll calm you down."

"No. It's fine."

"I see." He set down his cutlery, jaw tensed. "You're eating fast because you don't want to be around me."

I said nothing.

"Adele . . ." He sighed.

"I've really got a lot on my mind today," I said, cutting to the chase. "Can we please not?"

His gaze was seriously unhappy. I almost felt bad for him. Almost.

"Please," I repeated.

"We're going to have to talk about it sometime." And the man could tell himself that all he liked. Wasn't going to happen. "What I said last night...Look, I just don't want you leaving again thinking I hate you."

"I don't think that." Though I sort of did. I also sort of thought he was at least 51 percent raging asshole. But those were the breaks. So he and his grumpy ass and moody mouth obviously wouldn't be a part of my life in the future. So be it.

"We'll talk later. After the wedding is over." He rubbed at the back of his neck like maybe he had a headache too. Only his was real.

"Okay." I nodded to back up the lie. "After the wedding. Sounds good."

The ceremony was beautiful. Dad looking so proud and happy in his tuxedo. Shanti in an off the shoulder floor-length white gown that draped like a dream. They'd bought out a restaurant up in the hills, the back deck with views stretching out to the ocean. Vows were said as the sun set. All of the photos had been taken earlier, so we were free to relax and enjoy the celebrations. Golden-red light gradually faded to violet and blue. Lanterns were lit as the first star appeared. Kookaburras and other birdlife going crazy.

Pete looked fucking awful in his slick black suit. If "awful" could possibly be misconstrued to mean masculine perfection itself. The bastard. I half wanted to hump his leg as Hazel had once suggested. His hair was slicked back in a baby pompadour-type style. It suited him far too well. No stubble; his face was all smooth sharp edges and an amused smile. You could tell he was genuinely delighted for Dad along with being a little entertained by the old man's dopey lovesick grin.

As much as I didn't mean to look at Pete, my gaze kept wandering in his direction.

"Here you go," said Jeremy, the not-so-surprise guest. Shanti would have her way. He smiled, handing me the drink. "Gin and tonic?"

"Perfect, thank you."

"Do you mind if I . . ." He nodded at the crowd.

"Of course, I'm fine."

"Back in a minute, then." The dapper man headed off into the crowd to greet someone he knew. Shanti had probably asked him to babysit me. Told him I knew no one and God knows what other sob stories in an attempt to keep him tied to my side. And I liked him, but I wasn't looking for a date.

Waiters circulated with trays of appetizers. Goat cheese wrapped in prosciutto being my personal favorite. Though, really, any finger food was good finger food. Olive tartlets, rice-paper rolls, you name it.

"Nice ceremony," said Leona.

"Yes." I smiled, not eating and talking at all. How vulgar.

Leona, meanwhile, was turning heads in a beige slip. Talk about red-carpet ready, not that I'd gone dowdy. The forties-style navy-and-white floral fit-and-flare dress made the most of my figure. While Shanti's brigade of miracle workers had piled my hair up on top of my head in elegant curls and my lip gloss could outshine the best. I'd even blown my Christmas fund savings on a pair of black Havana Forties Louboutin sandals. As confidence enhancers went, they worked wonders. In the store, I'd been channeling Ava Gardner at her finest. Standing beside Leona's effortless glamor, however, I felt more like a dumb kid playing dress-up.

"How are you enjoying your visit?" she asked.

"Good, thank you."

"Pete said you've graduated?"

"Yes, I completed a bachelor of arts."

"Ah." She didn't turn away fast enough to hide a smirk. "Have you found it useful?"

"Incredibly so, yes."

Doubt filled her gaze. "Great."

Nothing from me.

"I was hoping I'd catch you alone for some girl talk."

This did not sound good.

"I suppose you've known Pete for quite some time," she said with a smile I didn't trust one iota. Her teeth were so shiny. Had to be veneers. "What with him working with your father and everything. He mentioned you used to be close."

Used to be. Ouch. "Hm."

She nodded, taking a sip of champagne. "We've been dating for a while now, but he can be a bit of a closed book, as I'm sure you're aware. When I called him on it, he of course disagreed. He said that he talks to you and your father."

"Oh?"

"Yes. So I was wondering if you could help me. It's just that I'm very fond of him. But there are so many topics that are off the table and I have no idea why." She leaned closer, her smile widening. Trust levels plummeted to below zero. She flipped her glossy red hair over one shoulder. "He rarely mentions his family, for instance. Do you know much about them?"

"Leona—"

"It's not that I'm unhappy with our relationship exactly," she continued, sounding oh so casual despite the content. "He's wonderful company and very good at, how should I say, meeting a woman's needs. You know what I mean."

"Right." Fuck's sake. It's not like she was being subtle.

"I'd like to get to know him better, though, you know?"

"Please, stop. Just stop."

Her mouth moved, but no words came out.

"Leona, whatever your relationship is," I said, "what he chooses to tell you is up to him."

"Oh, of course." She licked her lips, cheeks pinked with embarrassment. "I'd never suggest you betray his confidence."

Girl talk, my ass. It was amazing, really. To think he could reduce a woman to such underhanded bullshit maneuvers. She seemed so confident and in control. Men sucked. Matters of the heart sucked even worse.

"Excuse me, I need to . . . yeah." I made my unsubtle escape, hiding out inside the restaurant. White linen tablecloths were bedecked with shiny silver cutlery, potted orchid centerpieces. No name cards, which was a relief. The last thing I needed would be getting placed next to Leona for more girl talk. There'd been enough awkwardness for one night.

A quiet kind of rage burned inside me. As sad as losing his mother at a young age and having his dad be such a dick was, Pete needed to take some of the credit for being so damn emotionally stunted. For being so shut down. Then again, who was I to talk? My relationships weren't exactly success stories. For years, Mom had refused to discuss my father. Any questions had been met with a blank wall followed by a change of subject. And Dad had either said her name in a tone dripping with condemnation or gotten an angry look on his face and stomped off. Neither had been a great role model for love and forgiveness. But didn't you eventually get to an age where you had to own your own shit?

Everyone had their emotional baggage. The bulk of the time, though, I think I managed to store it away. To not let it interfere with my life. I just hadn't met the right man yet, obviously. My Prince Charming would come along one day and I'd forget Pete ever existed. The way just a glance from him made my heart race and thighs clench would be completely forgotten. Charming and I would have amazing sex and thoughts of another man would never even cross my mind. We'd have the kind of conversations that lasted into the early hours. Where time lost all meaning, the outside world faded away, and there would just be us baring our souls to one another. Also, any and all occasional arguments would be resolved swiftly and to each party's satisfaction. They wouldn't even really be arguments, more like small nonsensical disagreements. Like who-left-the-lid-off-the-toothpaste-type cute shit. Not about leaving the toilet seat up, because that's gross.

Holy cow. This really was starting to sound like a fairy tale. I should probably have Hazel check me out in case I really had become delusional. Meanwhile, I stood there taking deep, calming breaths yet still sort of wanting to hit something. This was not how I'd intended to celebrate my dad's wedding. Fucking Pete.

"You alright?" asked the man himself, emerging from the back hallway leading to the bathrooms. Boy did he looked hot as sin in that suit. I wanted to grab him by the tie and do bad things. Angry things, to work off my foul mood and heavy heart.

"Just had a little talk with your girl who's a friend," I said.

He scrunched up his forehead. "What?"

"Leona. Duh."

"What about her?"

"You told her you talk to Dad and me about things."

He looked away. "I might have."

"Way to throw me in the middle of your half-assed relationship."

He gazed at me like I was the lunatic. It only fed my rage.

"Actually, what she said made some things clear to me, interestingly enough." I rested my hand on the back of a chair, gin and tonic still at the ready. "I was safe back then, wasn't I? That's why you talked to me about things, because there was no real emotional investment in opening up to me. I was just a kid, after all."

He cocked his head. "Am I meant to be following this?"

"Oh, I think you can work it out if you try." I smiled. "Though I won't keep you hanging. Leona was curious about you and thought I'd answer some questions about your background and so on."

Good Lord, the frown on the man's face. He'd turned it all the way up to eleven.

"How lonely," I said. "I mean, you spend time with these women, but you don't open up to any of them."

"Adele—"

"That's why you freaked out over our chat the other night."

"I don't know what you're talking about."

"And why you acted like such an asshole to me yesterday and then were all pancakes of remorse this morning." I narrowed my eyes on him, putting all of the pieces together. "You just can't make up your mind, can you? You're all kinds of mixed signals. On the one hand, a grown woman got behind your walls and you didn't like it. It might actually mean something, being real with me now."

"Bullshit."

"But on the other hand, you missed me, just like I missed you." I tilted my head from side to side. "Boy, did I write you some bad poetry."

"Are you finished?" He turned to the windows, straightening the knot of the black tie at his neck. "We should be getting back out there."

"I used to be safe and now I'm not."

He stood tall, shoulders back, gaze set.

"The connection between us is still there, though," I said with a smile. "Oh no. This breaks all of your no-emotional connection rules. Alarm bells must be going off inside your head. What are you going to do, Pete?"

"I'm going to go back to the fucking party," he rumbled. "You do what you want."

"Okay."

He strode out of there quick smart. It was kind of thrilling, having him on the run, figuring him out. A little, at least. And maybe I should have been less joyous about putting him in a bad mood. Though generally speaking, the man seemed to live in that emotional state when I was around. I certainly had no issues about selling out Leona, however. The woman shouldn't have put me in that position in the first place.

"I hate you."

"In all honesty, you're not my favorite person either," I said.

There was happy drunk, sloppy drunk, crying drunk, and then, apparently, there was Leona drunk. Morose and resentful, mostly. Definitely no tearful "I love you, mate" coming from her. She sat wilting in the corner, a glass of chardonnay in hand. Makeup still perfect. God knows how she managed that.

"He told me he doesn't want to see me anymore," she slurred.

I kept my mouth shut.

"You just told him I was prying in order to drive a wedge between us. Admit it."

"Leona, you did that all on your own," I said. "Maybe try not pumping veritable strangers for personal information about your boyfriend next time. It's dodgy as hell."

Mostly, I felt not guilty. Mostly.

I stood in front of her, blocking the view of the rest of the room. No one else needed to see what a mess the woman was making of herself. Not that I particularly blamed her. I knew firsthand what being relegated to the void by Pete felt like. It hurt.

Dinner and all of the speeches were finished. Along with most of the other guests, Shanti and Dad were on the dance floor getting down to some vintage disco. Pete was dancing with one of Shanti's sisters. Meanwhile, my date and some other business types were drinking and chatting at one of the tables. Pretty sure Jeremy was more interested in attending the wedding to network than in getting into my pants. Fine with me.

Leona made a good show of sitting up straight and acting sober. "That was a private conversation. You had no business repeating what I said."

"Oh, please. You were way out of bounds and you know it," I said. "You invaded his privacy and put me in a deeply shitty position." I met her scowl with one of my own. "You wanted inside information on him? Well, here it is: he's a moody son of a bitch who refuses to open up to anyone and holds a grudge like nobody's business."

She pouted at nobody in particular. "I want to go home."

"Fair enough." This was undoubtedly a good thing. Nobody wanted Dad and Shanti's wedding to be forever remembered for a drunken showdown shouting-match debacle on the dance floor. Their day should stay perfect. Full of all the happy and love. "Do you want me to call you a cab?"

"I drove here." She frowned. "Guess I'm in a slight predicament."

Dammit. I should just make Pete deal with her. That would be fair and just. But the chances of me extracting him from the dance floor without alerting Dad and Shanti to what was going on were nil to none. And I wanted to avoid any further harsh recriminations between them.

"Okay," I announced. "I'll drive you home."

"You're not driving my Lexus!"

"Well, it's either that or cab it home, and then cab back tomorrow and pick up your car."

"How will you get back home?"

I sighed. "I'll call a cab from your place."

She stared out the floor-to-ceiling windows at the darkness beyond. "Well, I suppose it's the least you can do, considering."

I bit my tongue. She was right, even though there were a hundred reasons why she was out of line by prying, and I was entirely within my rights complaining to Pete about it. But the truth was, I would have kept my stupid mouth firmly shut if I had known the jerk would just up and dump her.

"Are we doing this, or what?" The sooner I put this whole thing behind me, the better.

"Yes. Alright," she said, unsteadily rising to her feet. She held her head high. "I'll talk to Pete when I'm good and ready to."

"Mm."

"He'll come to his senses. We make a great couple," she continued as I escorted her drunken ass oh so subtly out of the restaurant.

Hopefully, the happy couple would be too busy to notice my absence. I didn't want to leave, but I sure as hell didn't want to risk Leona causing a scene either. Later, I'd text Dad and Shanti, make up some excuse. Jeremy probably didn't care and Pete certainly wouldn't. If he was furious at Leona, there was a definite side order of irate just for me. And I was over the emotional confusion of dealing with him in general. Done. It'd been good to spend some time with my father and to meet Shanti. But the fact was, the sooner I got in my car and left tomorrow morning, the better things would probably be for everyone.

Chapter Eight

Seven Years Ago . . .

"Queen Adele?" I asked, brows raised.

"What? You don't like it? I made it myself. I even drew little stars on there, see?" Pete wrapped one solid arm around me, lowering the embarrassing cardboard sign he had been holding up. Thank God. "Good to see you, kid."

"Good to see you too."

"Happy belated eighteenth." He smacked a kiss on my cheek. I'd have preferred some on-the-mouth action, but beggars couldn't be choosers.

"Thanks." I smiled. "Dad's at work?"

"Ah, yeah. He got tied up with something, so I said I'd pick you up. That okay?"

"Of course."

People pushed past us, the arrivals lounge at the airport busy as hell, what with universities and schools all going on summer break. I tugged at the bottom of my T-shirt self-consciously, covering my small belly. So my first year at university had involved a small-to-medium amount of partying with the occasional bout of overeating. It was a pretty damn common circumstance. Didn't keep me from being annoyingly overly self-conscious in front of him, however. At least now I could fill out a bikini. There had to be a bright spot to everything, even thigh dimples.

A woman walked by, checking out Pete and then some. Kind of amazed she didn't give herself whiplash. Sheesh. I linked my arm with his, gave him my warmest smile. Hopefully we looked like lovers reunited. Like the man was all mine. I could dream.

"Let's go get your bag," he said, leading me through the crowd toward the luggage carousels. "How much did you pack this year? I hope you don't break my back."

"You look sturdy to me."

The show pony flexed his biceps with a grin. "What, these guns? Do I pass muster?"

"Oh God, don't call them guns."

"Not cool?"

"Not even a little."

He laughed.

"So," I cuddled up to him. "I'm eighteen now. Legal. You can't dump me on Saturday nights when you go out drinking anymore."

His eyes widened. "Yes I can."

"Nope. I'm coming with."

"Absolutely not," he said. "Forget it."

"Why not?"

"Because your father would kill me, for starters." He ran his gaze over me from head to toe. My chest area got a definite frown, followed by a shake of his head. "It's not happening. I'd have to spend the whole damn night stopping idiots from cracking onto you."

Oh, please. "You would not."

"I would," he said. "You stay home, spend time with your dad. That's what you're here for."

"Oh, come on. You know he works twenty-four seven."

"Answer's still no."

"Fight it all you want, Pete." I grinned. "But things are going to be different this year."

Saturday Night . . . Now

Dad and Shanti's place was alive with light and music when I got back at around midnight. Guess the restaurant eventually kicked them out. Meanwhile, I was not only mostly broke, but dead tired. Leona lived in some fancy high-rise in Noosa, nearly an hour up the coast. What a not-so-delightful surprise that had been. The wait for a cab on a Saturday night had been long. Followed by probably the most expensive car ride of my life.

I'd done my penance. Any residual guilt I had over telling Pete about her snooping was long gone, eroded minute by minute on the cab ride back with every uptick in the meter's fare.

Pete had to be across the road with the wedding party, because his house sat in darkness. Suited me just fine. I could go to bed without having to see him and set my alarm for bright and early, before he'd be awake. Surely even he'd want to sleep-in the day after a wedding. With a little luck, we could go another seven years without seeing each other. An ideal situation for everyone involved. I'd sent Dad a message apologizing for missing the end of the night, saying I had a headache and was going to bed. They were leaving on their honeymoon in the morning. Now that we'd reconnected, hopefully we'd be better at keeping in touch in the future.

On the off-chance Pete was home, I kept the lights off and removed my shoes at the door. As pretty as the heels were, my feet were about ready for a massage or at least a good soak. Sadly for them, and the rest of me, there'd be neither. Just me in my lonely bed with an aching heart.

Inside, there was enough ambient light with the moon shining in through the kitchen windows. Enough to get me to the guest room without walking into anything. Especially if I used the kitchen counter as a guide.

"Look at you creeping in," said a voice out of the darkness.

I actually jumped, almost dropping my shoes and

purse in the process. "Shit. I didn't see you there."

"Obviously." He sat at the dining table, the good old glass and bottle of scotch in front of him. The white of his dress shirt stood out, the rest of him little more than a shadow. "Did you get Leona home okay?"

"Yes."

"Thanks," he said. "Saw you walking her out. I would have looked after her, but it's probably better this way."

"She was pretty drunk. And I don't think anybody wanted a scene."

"Hm." He said nothing more.

Now was my chance. "Well, it's been a long night . . ."

"Been thinking about what you said earlier."

"Oh?"

The scotch bottle clinked against the glass as he poured. "I still think you're wrong."

"Of course you do."

The bottle went down on the table, and he stood, scooping up the glass and walking toward me. The closer he came, the more I could see. Like the disarray of his hair and the top three or so buttons undone on his shirt, offering a glimpse of his gorgeous chest. How he'd rolled up the sleeves to his elbows and taken off his shoes and socks. It did something to me, seeing him a little undone. I started breathing a bit faster, my thighs tensing. My heart and loins were nothing if not predictable. Even after all of tonight's resolutions regarding leaving posthaste, avoiding him, moving on with my life, meeting Prince Charming, and all the other stuff I had resolved as the taxi meter ticked off the last of my savings.

"Did you enjoy the wedding?" he asked.

"W-what?"

The man stood much closer than necessary. "The wedding. It was nice, right?"

"Sure."

Faint strains of music carried from across the road. It seemed worlds away. He downed a mouthful of scotch, gaze never leaving my face. All I could smell was the single malt, his cologne, and the slight scent of salt on his skin. After all, it'd been a hot night and he'd been dancing in the suit. He wasn't happy; I knew the signs well enough. The tension in his jawline and the look in his eyes. All heated and intense.

"So you've been sitting in the dark, drinking and brooding, huh?" I asked. "That sounds constructive."

"What did Leona have to say?"

I laughed. "Oh, hell no. I'm not getting caught in the middle of you two again. Why don't you try settling your issues like normal people and actually talk to one another?"

"You have such a clever mouth, Adele." He cocked his head. "Always got an answer, don't you?"

"Enjoy your scotch, Pete." I turned away. "I'm going to bed."

"What's the rush?" Strong fingers wrapped around my arm, not gripping me hard, just enough to hold me in place.

"I've spent enough time tonight in the company of a

drunken asshole, thank you." I smiled.

His return smile was lopsided. "You're angry."

"I'm tired."

"You're angry and tired. Me too," he said. "Less so on the tired, though. Actually, I'm wide the fuck awake."

"Good for you."

He finished off his drink, then reached past me, setting the empty glass on the kitchen counter. "Keep me company."

"I don't think that's a good idea."

"Why not?" he asked, expression full of false interest. "Thought you'd love the chance to tell me off some more."

I looked away. "We're done here."

"No, we're not."

"Yes, we are." I pulled my arm out of his grasp. "We're finished, Pete. Our friendship or whatever the hell it is these days . . . It's over, kaput, the end. Took me seven years, but tonight I finally wised up."

"That so?"

"Yep," I said. "I refuse to keep feeling this way about you. It's such a stupid waste."

His gaze narrowed.

"You know, I even have a plan."

"What might that be?"

"In the morning, I'm going to go home and fuck every available man I meet until one of them does it for me." My smile felt jagged and horrible. It couldn't have been pretty so see. "And then I won't think about you anymore."

His fingers curled into tight fists. Nice to know I

wasn't the only one affected. I put my hand on his chest, getting up in his face. Two could play the invading-personal-space game, for fun and intimidation. As if I would back down.

"It works for you, right?" I asked. Maybe I should have been a little wary of the hard set of his face, the fury in his eyes. But I couldn't stop now. "Why shouldn't it work for me?"

"Sounds like you've got it all figured out."

"I'll be heading out early. Doubt we'll be seeing each other again anytime soon." Leaning into him, I went up on tippy-toes. This was it, the end. Later, it would hurt. Right now, though, I couldn't even say I was sorry. He'd been a storm inside me for so long, messing with my head and my heart. Unrequited love was a bitch. "'Bye, Pete."

It was meant to be a soft kiss. A chaste one, even.

The minute my lips touched his, however, everything changed. Callused hands grabbed the sides of my face and my mouth opened on a gasp. His tongue swept inside, taking me over. *Holy hell.* Shoes and purse hit the floor, forgotten. Nothing about this kiss was slow or easy. The man devoured me. Every ounce of emotion poured into that kiss, all of the anger and frustration between us. His tongue was teasing and tasting, driving me wild. Then he drew back to suck and nip at my bottom lip. One hand slid around the back of my neck, the other over my hip to grab at my ass. His hold was firm, a little rough even. He treated my body like it belonged to him and I wasn't gentle either.

Apparently, experience mattered. Because all I could do was try to keep up.

I held on tight to his open shirt, straining against him, needing to get closer. I'd have crawled inside the man if I could. Turned out that under certain circumstances, the taste of scotch worked for me in a big way. Against my hip, his cock hardened, digging into me. And oh my God, I'd done that to him. Me. How amazing! Meanwhile, my body felt liquid, core aching and empty. I needed him inside of me and it seemed like I'd already been waiting forever.

"Pete. Please."

"Fuck," he muttered, breath hot against my ear.

I fumbled at the remaining buttons on his shirt. My damn fingers didn't seem to be working. Easier to just push the whole thing upward. Luckily, the man decided to help, tearing the shirt off over his head. More skin was good. And he was so hot and smooth, a thrill to the touch. The solid flesh of his pecs and the flat plane of his stomach.

He tore at the zipper on the back of my dress, dragging fabric down over my shoulders. A growl came from deep in his throat, a noise of frustration, impatience. I'm reasonably certain I heard the silk rip. I didn't care. His hands and mouth seemed to cover every bit of skin revealed, touching and tasting me everywhere. The dress got stuck on my hips. Out of the way enough for now.

He didn't even bother undoing my bra, simply peeling down one of the lace cups to free my flesh. My breast filled his hot palm as it took the weight. Fingers plumped me, his thumb flicking over my hard nipple. The sting of pain followed by the heat of his kiss made my head spin and my body ache. There was no room for thought as he fed me deep, wet kisses. Slowly, he took us to the floor. No time for anything else. Just the urgent need to have him inside me.

The hardness of the polished wood was cool against my back. My legs were spread, his body between them. And with his broad chest above me, his weight taken on one arm, he was all I could see. I swear even the insides of my thighs were wet, I was so ready. It would have been embarrassing with anybody else. But this man, he had to know, he had to understand. It had always been him.

"Pete, I need—"

"I know," he said, voice harsh and low.

His absolute focus on me, right here, right now, made me weak. So many times, I'd imagined him like this, I'd dreamed about it. Now here he was, gaze stark with need. His skin seemed to be stretched tight over his sharp cheekbones and striking face. As if he was every bit as out of control and overexcited as I was. Like I wasn't alone in feeling all this.

His hands bunched up my dress before going to his belt buckle, then the button and zip below. "Hard and fast."

I nodded.

In one quick move, his pants and boxer briefs were shoved down. Immediately, I got an elbow beneath me because like hell I'd be missing this.

Holy shit, the sight of his cock. The size of his cock.

If need hadn't been beating through me with such a beat, dark and heavy, I might have hesitated for a moment. But his fingers wrapped around the thick length, squeezing. My mouth watered, everything low in my belly tightening. Both of us were panting, desperate. But he took a breath, seeming to try and calm himself. To slow for a moment.

With one hand, he drew a line from my belly button, down through the small tangle of pubic hair to my sex. The pad of his thumb lightly circled my clit, getting me wetter, making me even more swollen. Fingers slid inside of me, pushing in deep, pumping slowly in and out of me. First two and then three. His gaze never shifted from between my legs. Everything there felt swollen and hypersensitive. Better than ever before and we'd barely gotten started.

"You're very wet." Then he took hold of himself again, dragging the wide crown between my labia. "And so damn beautiful."

My insides clenched, so damn empty. His mouth covered mine, hungry and demanding, forcing me down, flat on my back. Then he pulled my underwear aside and pushed in, hard and fast as promised. My breath stuck in my throat, my heart seizing. Christ, the feel of his cock stretching me, the thick length buried deep. One hand lay beside my head, the other keeping a punishing grip on my hip, holding my body in place to receive him. There'd be bruises tomorrow. Evidence of this moment. I wanted that so badly, for him to bite me and fuck me. To take me hard and leave me hurting.

He pulled back, pushing in even faster this time. Such perfect friction. It was electric. Lighting me up inside. I moaned and the look in his eyes . . . it was hard to describe. I held on to his shoulders, skin slick and slippery. Hot as fire and all so real. His gaze bore into mine and I couldn't have looked away if I tried. This man had me completely.

Skin slapped against skin with the force of his thrusts, sweat dripping off his body and onto mine. It was brutal, animalistic, the way he grunted every time he slammed into me. The heavy scent of sex and sweat filling the hot night air. I don't know if he loved me or hated me. Right then, it didn't even matter.

The tension in me coiled higher and higher. Blood surging, hammering behind my ears. Every muscle in me seemed strung out, my body begging for release. When it hit, it hit hard. A wave of pleasure igniting every nerve ending. My back bowed, pushing against him, my whole body shaking. It just kept rolling through me, dragging me under. I was lost and found, made and undone. Then he shouted, hips bucking against me, driving his cock so deep I thought he was a part of me. I wished he was.

The weight of his body pressed down on me, the heat of his breath against my neck. My hands slid over his back, up into his damp hair. I held on tight in a state of pure bliss.

"I'm crushing you," he mumbled, pulling out of me.

I tried to demur, but it did no good.

He moved slowly, like he'd been hit. By a car, maybe, or a bolt of lightning. I don't know. But his big body collapsed on the floor at my side. We both lay there on our backs, staring up at the dark ceiling, trying to catch our breath. Eventually, there came the rustle of fabric as he pulled up his pants and got at least half dressed. The zipper seemed alarmingly loud. Accusing, even. Though that might have just been my imagination.

"You alright?" he asked in the same quiet voice.

"I think you broke me. In a good way."

He said nothing, climbing to his feet.

I took the opportunity to stick my breast back into the bra. To straighten myself up a little. Pretty sure my dress was ruined. So, that was angry sex. With Pete, it was shockingly good. My insides were still fluttering and quaking. They really needed to settle down, because I had a feeling the good times were over.

"Come on," he said, offering a hand.

I let him pull me to my feet, not sure if my legs would hold me. Every muscle felt weak and a little wobbly. Support would have been good. But he dropped my hand and awkwardness settled in the space between us.

"I ruined your hair," he said.

"Never mind."

He pointed toward his room. "I'm gonna . . ."

And it wasn't an invitation. More like official notification of his plan to make an escape. I tried to smile but could barely meet his eyes. Not when I knew what I'd see. "I, um . . . shower."

He nodded. "Okay."

The thud, thud, thudding woke me at around five. Outside, the world was gray, just coming to life. Birds everywhere were making a racket. But that wasn't what woke me. Barefoot, I padded out onto the back deck, down toward his end of the house. My hair hung in tangles, thin sleep shorts and a tank top probably insufficient coverage for the cooler morning.

A punching bag hung down the end of the verandah. Dressed in only a pair of joggers, shorts, and some gloves, Pete was pounding his fists into it mercilessly. Sweat gleamed on his skin, dark hair hanging in damp tendrils. God only knew if he'd slept at all.

To think the sex had been angry and intense.

I just watched him in silence, his muscles bunching and straining. The dedicated fury and focus on his face. He was beautiful, a work of art. *Irate Man the Morning After Regrettably Incredibly Hot Sex*, that's what they'd call it, the painting or sculpture or whatever. Everyone would rush to see him with his nostrils flaring and thick neck. The hard planes of his back and trim waist.

Eventually, he caught sight of me out of the corner of his eyes. One glove went to the bag, to stop it from swinging. He just looked at me, thick shoulders rising and falling with each breath. His gaze nothing less than tortured. Tormented. It was staggering, the self-loathing in his eyes, the pain.

I felt like I'd been slapped to the point where I almost took a step back. My face was burning, mind reeling. Fuck him for this. I didn't make him kiss me hard enough to bruise my lips. Nor had I compelled him to have sex with me on the floor. All of that, he'd initiated. Not to say I hadn't been a willing participant, but I hadn't forced the man to do shit. And he had the gall to look at me like this. I swallowed hard, holding back the tears. I would not cry. At least, not yet.

"Don't worry, Pete," I said. "It can just be our dirty little secret."

Then I turned and walked away.

Chapter Nine

Seven Years Ago

"I'm envisioning a yurt."

Pete scrunched up his face. "A yurt? This is your great idea that kept you up half the night, seriously?"

"Yes! Think about it," I said. "A main central room with a big pole in the middle and the roof goes up to a skylight at the top. It'll be awesome."

In the daylight, his block of land was a green haven with towering gums and a bunya pine. Below them were some banksia. Down the back, where the ground was more shadowy and moist, grew some more tropical plants like swamp lilies, bird of paradise, and bromeliads.

He scratched at his stubble. "I'm not sure I want to live in a yurt. Aren't they made out of goatskins or something?"

"We'll use wood," I said. "No goats will be harmed in the making of this building."

"That's good news. Trees are much easier to catch."

"Kitchen, dining, and lounge there in the open-space room in the middle." I waved an arm around in demonstration. "Then off to either side, wings with the bedrooms, bathrooms, and whatever. A verandah running along the back of the house for hanging out on."

"And we're building this out of wood?" He cocked his head, staring out at the land too. Obviously not yet sold on my complete winner of an idea. The fool.

"Yes."

He picked up a stick, drawing a rough diagram in the dirt beside the ashes of last night's campfire. On days like this, it was way too hot to hang out in his living shed. Especially when there was a breeze blowing outside. We'd already been to the beach and had lunch with his latest. Monica, Melissa, something like that. But I could easily see us heading back there if the heat kept up. Damn my father for not putting in a pool. Just because he didn't want to look after it all year round solely so I could use it for six weeks. Such a selfish man.

"You're going to put in a pool down the back, right?" I asked.

A nod.

"Good."

"I was thinking of maybe bringing in an old Queenslander," he said. "Renovate it like your dad did. Probably be a hell of a lot easier."

"But my idea's better."

He blinked. "But I'm the one that has to do all the work."

"But it's our dream."

"It's *your* dream, kid. I just want to get out of this shed."

I gave him my best sad face with just a dash of disappointment thrown in.

He sighed. "I'll think about it. No promises."

"Okay." I grinned. "I'll do some sketches of it for you."

"I mean it. No promises."

Sunday Morning . . . Now

When I wheeled out my suitcase, he was seated at the kitchen counter, brooding over a cup of coffee this time. *Give me strength.* Heathcliff had carried on less. I wished Pete had stayed in his room. It would have been the nice thing to do, to not drag this out any further.

But no.

He'd apparently just showered, his hair wet and slicked back. Wearing fresh cargo shorts and a T-shirt. Some old band-tour thing. The soft old cotton fit him far too well. No matter; I could do this. I'd even put on a happy sundress with grass and ladybugs on it, because that was how little he affected my moods, life, and everything in general. Shanti and Dad would already be on their way to the airport for their early-morning flight to Bali. There was nothing else I needed to do. Nothing slowing me down.

Straight out the door, into my car, and on the road. That was the plan. Hell. I intended to set new land-speed records for a woman dragging a loaded suitcase. Someone should time me.

Still, first things first. I cleared my throat, going for dignified, but probably failing. "I was going to text you," I said, nodding to him as he sat with his coffee. "We forgot to use protection last night."

His eyes widened.

"I'm on the pill and get tested regularly. I assume you do too?"

"Ah, yeah," he said, looking a little shocked. "I do."

Good to know.

"Shit." He shook his head. "I didn't even think . . ."

"Me neither. Didn't occur to me until it was running down my leg."

His brows drew in to form one unimpressed line. "You were going to *text* me about that?"

"What? You'd prefer a telegram?"

"I'd prefer an adult conversation."

"So would I, but apparently we're past that," I said, hand tightening on the handle of my suitcase. "If we were ever there to begin with, which I highly doubt."

He lifted his coffee cup to his mouth, but for some reason thumped it back down on the counter before taking a drop. His seat was pushed back and he walked toward me. Out of pure survival instinct, I held up my hand, took a step back. The man didn't stop, however. Instead, he walked straight into my hand, my palm pressing against this chest.

"You've been crying."

"No, I haven't."

"Adele," he said, voice horribly gentle.

"Alright, maybe I have. But it's none of your business."

"I think it is."

"Let's agree to disagree." I straightened my shoulders. "Time for me to go."

"No."

"See you next time, Pete. It's been real." And I tried to step around him, but the bastard grabbed my shoulders. Built like he was, pushing against his chest didn't achieve shit, even with two hands. I'd have kicked him in the shins if the case hadn't been in the way.

"We need to talk," he said.

"Not happening."

"Listen to me—"

"Go fuck yourself, Pete." My hands beat against his chest, refusing to surrender. It was all building up again, not that it had ever really gone away. The pain and rage and hurt he caused. All of the dumb-ass feelings I should have let go of years ago. They crowded the tip of my tongue, ready to spill, out of my control. "Honestly, I'm so sick of all your bullshit. Your existential angst or whatever the fuck your problem is. You're such a cunt, do you know that? You wanted me last night. You started it. But I wind up feeling like shit and I'm done, do you hear me?"

He kicked the suitcase out of the way, pulling me in closer. Not stopping until he held me against him. I just ignored the tears, hoping they'd go away. Too upset to care either way. The idiot could think what he liked.

"I'm fucking done," I repeated, choking up just a little, dammit. "I'm going home and—"

"Please don't tell me the 'every available man' thing again," he said, face against the top of my head, voice rumbling in his chest. "I'm not sure I can take it."

"I don't give a shit what you can handle, you dickhead. And stop rocking me—I'm not a fucking baby."

"Whatever you say."

"Don't pacify me, asshole."

He didn't bother to answer and I didn't bother to speak again. Guess I'd run out of insults for now and my throat hurt. I huddled against him, crying my heart out. No matter how I tried to calm down and get a handle on things it just kept rising inside of me. More sobs, hiccups, and pain. I wanted to just be angry, but it kept coming out as tears.

At some stage during my meltdown, he picked me up and carried me over to the couch, sitting me on his lap. Still holding on tight. And slowly, finally, the tears stopped and all was silent.

Wow. That'd been . . . extreme.

I knew someone should say something, but I didn't

know who should talk first. Pretty sure he was faster than me, so crawling away and making a run for the door was in all likelihood out of the question. I fished a tissue out of my pocket and blew my nose. Such an attractive sound. Also, his shirt had a big wet patch on the front. Feelings were such an inconvenience. Maybe I should get a lobotomy. I don't think I'd ever been so angry and miserable at the same time. Now that the storm was spent, however, I wasn't quite sure what to do.

"I don't think I've ever actually been called a cunt by a woman before," he said.

"No? It was probably time."

"Hm."

I shifted in his lap, giving all of the signals to be let go. But the arms around me didn't move an inch. "Pete?"

"Yeah?"

"Um. I need water."

Easy as pie, he lifted me up, heading toward the kitchen.

"Or I could walk."

He didn't bother to answer. Instead, sitting me on the counter while he filled a glass with water and presented it to me.

"Thanks," I said, proceeding to down the whole thing.

The man leaned back against the stainless-steel fridge, arms crossed. "I don't usually stick around for the fights."

"You could have just let me leave."

"I don't want you to leave," he said, gaze stuck to my

face.

I just waited.

"Adele, I wasn't hitting the bag because I regretted having sex with you."

"Why, then?"

"My existential angst, as you put it, was due to me *not* feeling bad about what happened between us."

I blinked. "Please explain."

"There are a lot of very good reasons why we shouldn't be doing this," he said, gaze hooded. "Problem is, I don't really seem to care."

"You don't?"

"No."

"Huh." Weird. "Let me see if I've got this right. You hated yourself for not hating yourself?"

"Yeah, you could say that," he said. "I want you to stay a bit longer. Can you?"

My mouth opened, but nothing came out.

He pushed off from the fridge, coming toward me. Not good. Things felt much safer, more in control, with him on his side of the kitchen. "We need to figure this thing out between us. That's not going to happen if you get in your car and leave now."

My grip tightened on the glass.

"What can I do to convince you?"

"I don't know . . ."

He took the glass out of my hand, setting it aside. Then his hands curved over my knees, fingers touching me so softly, caressing. I watched it all with open suspicion, legs kept firmly shut. If only my skin didn't like him so much. A mild allergy to him right now would be quite helpful. Nothing overly itchy or ugly, just enough to make me want to keep away from him. Give me time to think.

"Did I hurt you?" he asked, thumbs slipping beneath the skirt of my dress to skim my thighs. "I was pretty rough with you last night. A lot rougher than I normally am."

"I'm fine."

"Good."

And those fingers beneath my skirt, they were sneaking steadily upward. It was strange, watching him put the moves on me. I'd seen him do some subtle stuff to girlfriends over the years. Like taking forever to put sunscreen on their backs. The occasional kiss on the neck or resting a hand on the leg while driving. Light foreplay. Tender stuff. Touches suitable for public spaces and prying eyes such as mine.

"Talk to me," he said. "Terrifies me when you go quiet and I have no idea what's going on inside your head."

I sighed. "Pete."

His hands stopped their adventuring beneath my skirt and one slipped behind my neck, drawing me down for a kiss on the forehead. "Please, stay."

"Why?"

He stared into my eyes for so long it made me wonder what was going on inside of his head too.

"Why should I stay, Pete?"

"So we can figure out what this is. Because you're important to me and I don't want to lose you for another seven years." His grip on my legs firmed. "That's why, Adele."

"It's not just about sex?"

"Look . . . what we did last night? That was unprecedented," he said. "I'd be lying if I said I didn't want more."

"You were a virgin? Should have said something, I would have tried to be more gentle."

"Ha-ha."

While I did have another week of holidays, I didn't know what to do. Pete wasn't safe. Not in my current apparently fragile state. Sex shouldn't be so complicated, and feelings had never been involved to this degree. It made things dangerous.

"Adele?"

"You know what you did hurt? My heart."

He winced. "I know. I'm sorry."

"Are you?"

At this, he seemed lost. Guess I'd never doubted his words before, not about something this important. He held my hands in his, expression thoughtful. "You said you were tired when you came in late last night and it's only six in the morning now, so I don't imagine you got much sleep."

"Not much," I agreed.

"No. Me neither." His hands gripped my hips, setting me down in front of him. "How about if you come and have a nap with me. That way at least, if you do go later, you won't be falling asleep at the wheel and have an accident."

"I don't know."

"Let me look after you. Please."

I gave a short nod.

He took my hand, leading me toward the hallway to his bedroom. I guess the man had a point. I was on the verge of the mightiest of yawns. Even my bones felt tired and hung over. Despite only having the one drink the night before at the wedding. Apparently, the Norse have a word for uneasiness after debauchery. Perhaps I had that. Even with no alcohol to speak of, I had definitely been debauched. Frankly, last night I'd been so debauched I'd be surprised if I had a single bauch left to speak of. The lingering ache between my legs said no.

Also, maybe I was emotionally wrung out after the crying jag. It made sense.

His bedroom was spacious, with a high ceiling and the walls painted a dark green. A king-size bed sat un-made, white sheets in disarray. Looked like I hadn't been the only one tossing and turning. A painting of ibis birds and strangler figs hung on the wall. It was nice.

"Come on," he said, leading me onto the mattress. He moved into the middle and lay down, pulling me down beside him. Close beside him. Pillows were carefully ar-ranged, then his arms slid beneath my head and over my middle.

I was spooning with Pete in his bed. How unex-pected.

"This okay?" he asked.

"Yes."

He pressed his mouth to the bare skin of my shoulder. "Sleep, Adele. We'll sort it out later."

I'd like to say I couldn't settle, that having him holding me just felt wrong. But, of course, it didn't. Even with daylight streaming in the open French doors, I was asleep in no time.

I woke up alone, the bedroom door closed. The alarm clock on the bedside table said it was four in the afternoon. Bloody hell, I'd slept for ten whole hours. Must have been exhausted. Pete's scent lingered on the sheets and it was tempting to just lie there a while longer. My dress was of course a crumpled ruin. The ladybugs nowhere near as cheerful as they had been. Not that it had helped my mood this morning. Some things were beyond being fixed, even by a dress with pockets.

I followed the scent of food out into the main room. Pete stood in the kitchen, washing off a wooden cutting board in the sink. Things were definitely happening in the oven. Good things.

"Smells like a Sunday roast," I said.

"And it should be ready soon."

"Did you sleep?"

"Yeah," he said, wiping off his hands on a tea towel. "Only woke up a couple of hours ago. Figured you'd need to eat before you leave."

I stopped.

"*If* you leave."

"I'm hungry. Good thinking."

He nodded. "Not that I want you to go—let me make that clear. But I also checked your car for oil and water, just in case. Easy to overheat in summer out here. Plus, you might want someone to look at the tires when you get back. The front ones are looking a little worn."

"Thanks," I said. "I will."

I wrapped my arms around myself, not really sure what to do with my limbs. The way he watched me brought my nerves straight back to the surface. God, I could do with just chilling out. Relaxing. This situation and all of the uncertainties were doing my head in. When the man you've been in love with for pretty much forever finally starts paying attention to you in the way you want, apparently it can be both good and bad. I was only used to there being unresolved sexual tension on my part. But being on the receiving end of this do-me vibe . . . it was something else.

Flattering, distracting, overwhelming. I don't know.

"What do you really want here, Pete?"

"I already told you." He stepped closer, and then closer still. Until he was gently undoing the barrier of my crossed arms and holding my hands. "Stay a bit longer, Adele."

I didn't usually have this much trouble breathing.

"We'll see what happens."

"You know what'll happen," I said, voice most dubious. "We'll wind up having sex again. You'll freak out and maybe decide this time that trading bodily fluids with me was the worst mistake of your life. Then I'll have to abuse you again and make a run for it. Honestly, it's exhausting."

"It does sound involved."

"Don't mock me."

"I wouldn't dare." He tried to hold back a smile. Jerk. "What if we try putting the existential angst and you abusing me on hold, and just enjoy each other's company?"

"You're really hung up on the existential angst thing, aren't you?"

"I've never been accused of having it before. I think it makes me sound deep, don't you?"

He leaned in, lips soft against my cheek. And being this close to him made me a little dizzy. The feel of his breath on my face, his body right there. It got me high. Thinking in a straight line was next to impossible.

"You're being very nice," I said.

"I'm not allowed to be nice?"

"Depends. Is it the kind of nice where you're hoping it leads to sex?"

He snorted. "It's the kind of nice where I realize I've been an ass to you since you arrived and I need to make that up to you."

I said nothing.

"You don't have a very high opinion of me right now, do you?"

"I know how you operate, buddy. I know what you're like with women." I moved back a little, all the better to look him in the eye. Mostly, his expression still read amused, the curve of his mouth and all. But there just might have been a hint of worry in his gaze. Good. "You're very, very nice to them. It's a balancing act, the way you keep them physically close, but still keep them mentally and emotionally at arm's length. Then slap the label 'casual' on the whole thing to keep things safe."

His gaze narrowed. "That's what I do, huh?"

"You know you do. If you can't even be honest with me, then we have nothing to talk about."

"Hang on." He tightened his hold on my hands, bringing them to his mouth, then holding them against his chest. Face serious, he stared me down. "Okay, Adele, let's say you're right. That shit wouldn't work with you anyway. Apparently you know me too damn well."

"So what's your plan?"

"That we take some time and get to know each other as adults."

I thought it over. "My feelings for you aren't casual. They never have been."

"I know," he said, voice subdued. "But I don't know where this is going either."

Fair enough. We might have known each other a long time, but adding sex to the relationship was new. No one could give guarantees at this stage. Not if they were being honest. But the fear and worry kept on churning inside of me.

It was a lot to think over. "Feed me and we'll see."

Our early dinner was served on the back deck in the shade. With the sun still high in the sky, sunglasses were a must. Roast pork with homemade apple sauce, potatoes, carrots, and bok choy. I ate with the single-minded determination of someone not only avoiding conversation but also starving.

"What did you think?" he asked when I took the last bite.

"You'll make someone a fine wife one day," I said, saluting him with my glass of iced water.

He smiled. "I resent you trying to label me with your gender norms."

"Remember when you were living in the shed and all you had was that crappy old barbeque?" I said. "You'd still be grilling fish and pineapple kebabs and corn on the cob and . . . God, I don't know what else. It was gourmet something every other night of the week."

"I like good food."

"And Dad wondered why I hardly ever ate at home."

"Sorry, beautiful," he said. "But your father can't cook for shit."

We both went quiet for a moment. A mixture of shock over his use of such an endearment combined with the mention of Dad, perhaps.

"He thought picking up a vegetarian pizza constituted me eating my vegetables," I said. "Pretty sure it was just so I could say yes when Mom called to inquire as to my general well-being."

"Might have worked if you hadn't picked off half the toppings."

I made a face. "Only the capsicum and mushrooms. That stuff is awful."

"I remember trying to teach you to cook."

"I'm not too bad," I said. "Not as good as you, but I manage."

"Or do you still eat breakfast cereal for dinner?" The side of his mouth curled up and I kind of wished I could see his eyes behind the sunglasses. "Tell the truth."

I laughed. "Sometimes."

He just shook his head.

"Who taught you?" I asked him. Not his father, I'd bet.

"Ah. Well . . ." He turned away, looking out at the view. "When Mom got diagnosed with cancer, she was sick for a long time, and we were pretty much living on frozen meals. Horrible shit. Tough meat and sloppy vegetables. Microwaved pies and sausage rolls was another of Dad's favorites. They were atrocious. Chrissie and I pretty much lived on cheese slices and tomato sauce."

"Together?"

"Not saying it wasn't messy." He grinned. "Anyway, next door to us lived this Italian *nonna*. She was always baking, cooking up these amazing things. So of course Chrissie and I start hanging around, begging for scraps like orphans. I don't think there's a *nonna* alive who can resist feeding children."

"She sounds nice."

"Yeah."

"And she taught you?"

He lifted one shoulder. "When I kept hanging around, she put me to work. After Mom passed, Dad didn't give a shit where we were as long as we stayed out of his way. Chrissie would just read or go to her friend's place across the road. But I was hopeless at sitting still. Some days, I'd go off on my bike. But other times, I'd help out in her kitchen. Found that I liked it. Not that Dad would let me cook at home—too much hassle, I'd make a mess. Probably didn't even know what I was doing, and I'd burn the house down. But I swore that when I was older, no way was I ever eating shit like that again."

"Your dad's a jerk."

"That he is."

A whipbird called from a nearby tree and we shared a smile. A little more of the old intimacy and easiness sneaking back in. If only it didn't feel like home here with him. It would make resisting so much easier. And while my brain was pretty sure I should resist him, my vagina was all down with having lots more sex with the man. Lots and lots. Of course, the wisest course of action would be to protect my heart and get out of town. Go home to the city and my boring job. Not that I hadn't missed my friends. Hazel in particular would be waiting for an update. But leaving the Sunshine Coast had always torn at my heartstrings. For weeks, I'd sit around all mopey and glum. It used to drive Mom nuts. Sydney had its perks, but here there was just more room to breathe, less traffic and chaos. And more Pete.

"You cooked, I'll clean." I rose, starting to gather the plates. Happily, he hadn't asked me about leaving again. A good thing, since I still didn't have an answer.

"We can both do it."

All of the dishes and utensils were carried back into the kitchen. Pete found a container for the leftovers while I rinsed off the plates ready for the dishwasher. It was scarily close to domestic bliss. Like old times when we'd hang out together, not talking about anything of particularly great importance. Just enjoying each other's company, as he'd said. Every now and then, we'd brush against each other. About what you'd expect working in a confined space. Yet those touches seemed loaded. A little thrilling and a lot important, somehow.

"There's some ice cream if you'd like," he said when we were finished. "I think I've got burnt fig or honey and almond."

"Sounds fancy. But I'm full."

"Well, you want to watch some TV for a while or go for a swim? What do you feel like?" He stood all casual like, thick arms crossed over his chest. "I mean, traffic would probably still be bad on the highway now. Everyone heading home from the beach after the weekend. You might as well wait a little longer."

"I guess so."

His brow furrowed and he scratched at his cheek. "Of course, then there's driving at night . . ."

"What wrong with driving at night?"

"It's just, you know, if anything happens and you're alone out there in the dark somewhere."

"I do have a phone."

"Right. Sure. But are you going down the coastal road or inland?"

"Inland," I said.

He winced. "Some of those country areas. Who knows if you'd even get service?"

I gave him a look most dubious.

"It's your decision, of course."

"Thanks," I said drily.

"I just want you to be safe."

"And naked?"

"What? No, no, no." He shook his head. "I didn't say that, did I?"

I tipped my chin in doubt.

"It's the truth. Any thoughts of nakedness are owed to your dirty mind, Adele. Not mine," he said. "I'm just standing here, respectfully being concerned for your welfare while you're fully clothed, because that's the kind of man I am."

"It is, huh?"

I wandered out of the kitchen, trying to think things through. While being thoroughly distracted by the way he was watching me, walking behind me. He hung back, but he followed. It was like there was a connection stretching between us, keeping us linked. Neither one of us wanted to break it. Yet there my suitcase sat, waiting by the door. Still waiting.

Shit. *Dammit.* I couldn't do it. The thought of leaving just seemed cowardly and wrong. Truth was, I wanted the sex and the complications and everything. Who was I kidding? I wanted it all with him. Always had, probably always would.

"Alright, I'll stay," I said. "Just for another day or two, though."

"Yeah?"

"Only because you're being so pathetic and needy. It's sad, really."

"Whatever works." He shrugged. "I'm willing to squeeze out a tear for a few days extra."

"Hmm. Let's just take it slow."

His easy smile spread heat through me from top to toe. I was so screwed.

Chapter Ten

Seven Years Ago

"What are you doing here?"

"Playing some pool, having a drink." I tapped my bottle of beer against his. "Nice to see you, Pete."

He nodded hello to the couple of guys from work I was playing with. And I'd been smashing them. We weren't betting on the games or anything. Victory, however, was sweet and it was most definitely mine.

"All of those hours I spend in the university bar are finally paying off." I smiled. "Here's to higher education."

He did not smile back.

"Oh, relax."

"Does your father know you're here?"

"Yep," I said. "Not that it would matter if he didn't because eighteen now, remember?"

So much scowling. It couldn't be good for him. He eyed my navy shorts, white blousy top, and wedges askance before downing some beer. I thought I looked nice, but apparently not according to the expression on his face.

"Finish that one up, then I'll drive you home," he said. Ordered, actually.

"Are you kidding? I'm on a winning streak."

He leaned in. "Yeah, they're letting you win hoping they can get into your pants. Wise up, kid."

I turned my back on the pool table and the two young guys keeping me company. They were apprentice electricians who worked for one of Dad's subcontractor buddies. Nice enough, one of them was damn cute and he knew it. Not that I was interested. It was all just friendly and would remain that way. Unfortunately, my affections were all tied up by the oblivious man at my side.

"Wow." I slid an arm around his shoulders and he gave it a dubious look. "Listen to me very carefully, Pete. I'm currently enjoying myself in a way that is entirely suitable and indeed expected for a person my age. If you can't handle that . . . I love you, I do. You're my best friend. But you need to stop overreacting and being a dick about this."

"I'm being a dick?"

"Yes, you are." I stepped back, returning to the game. Doing my best to ignore him and his words. Like I couldn't win a game of pool on my own.

He returned to the men from Dad's crew whom he'd

come in with. But I could feel his eyes on me, all pissed off and ranty. Probably wishing he could drag me out of here by the hair and give me a doll or some blocks to play with. I smacked the pool stick into the white ball, screwing up my next shot entirely. All his fault.

"My turn," one of the dudes said.

Craig, I think his name was. Yeah, Craig and Brandon.

And I'd busted Brandon checking out my ass a couple of times when I went to take a shot. But I could ignore him easily. The whole death-glare thing from Pete, however, was putting me off. I really wanted to beat him over the head with a pool cue. Sadly, it was illegal.

Balls kerplunked and Powderfinger's "On My Mind" played loud and proud. A good-size crowd filled the room for a Friday afternoon, celebrating the end of the workweek.

My happiness, however, was gone.

One of the barmaids stopped by Pete's table and gave him a long, overly familiar hug. So they'd banged. What a surprise. I'd be insanely jealous, but what was the point? As he'd just demonstrated, I'd always be a child in his eyes.

"Adele," said Craig, clapping me on the shoulder. "You lost!"

"Damn. Must be my turn to buy a round, anyway."

Brandon grinned. "You take care of the beers and I'll thrash him for you."

"Sounds good."

The next hour or so passed in much the same way. I

played twice more, winning one and losing one. By the time Pete, aka the Fun Reaper, returned, I had a nice buzz going and had almost started to relax again.

"How's it going?" he asked.

"Fine."

"You're right, I'm sorry." He sighed. "I was out of line. Can you forgive me?"

I stopped. "Really? Yes."

"I'm sure you're a demon with a pool stick. You going to play me?"

"If you like."

I gave him a tentative smile and he pulled me in for a hug. The idiot even patted me on the head. And I didn't win that game. My concentration was crap because I was too busy checking out his ass when he went to take a shot.

Sunday Night . . . Now

"Why are you whispering?"

"Because I'm hiding in the bathroom," I said. "This is a secret call."

Hazel sighed. "Jesus. You finally get what you want and you're hiding in the bathroom freaking out?"

"Yes."

"Look," she said, "from what you've told me, the man is being reasonable. You need time to reassess your relationship and determine if it can work with you both being adults and intimate with one another."

"Okay. Yeah. That makes sense."

"So ask yourself, 'Why am I panicking?'"

"I don't know, but I'm terrified."

"Actually, it does make sense if you think about it," she said.

"Can't think—my brain's going too fast."

"Right, because you're finally on the verge of getting what you've always wanted. What if it all goes wrong?"

"Exactly," I said, shoulders slumping.

"You've had a lot of time to work him up as something almost godlike. Maybe you're also worried about him living up to those expectations, Adele. Or you being good enough for him."

"Please. I barely even consider him worthy to kiss my feet."

She laughed. "Good, I like your attitude. Keep telling yourself that. Or at least that you both deserve happiness. But the only way you're going to sort out all these things is if you stop hiding in the bathroom and go and confront the situation."

"Yes. But I think if we keep talking about the situation I'm just going to get more anxious and confused about the situation."

"So stop talking and take action," she said. "A couple's physical relationship can be every bit as important a method of communicating as using actual words."

I nodded, not that she could see. "Right. So I should

just go bang him. I'd be lost without you, Hazel."

"I know."

"I can do this."

"Sure you can," she said. "Go jump that man, ride him into the ground."

"Thanks. Will do."

"I have to go—Maddie wants an update on your soap opera life."

I frowned. "It's not quite that bad."

She just laughed and hung up on me. Friends. What could you do?

At any rate, I took her advice and stopped hiding. The house was quiet, still. I wandered out onto the back deck. In the distance, the sun was sinking lower, giving the air that twilight softness and haze. Pete was swimming laps, strong arms powering through the water. I didn't want to ever become inured to the sight of this man. Especially seeing him half-naked. I wanted all of the butterflies, the pleasure. Forever and ever, or however long I could keep it.

He stopped and smiled at me, treading water in the deep. "Hey, you coming in?"

My hands gripped the skirt of my dress.

And I was so done with worrying. My thoughts had been chasing themselves in circles all day, wearing me thin. What was even the point when it only took you away from where you wanted to be?

"The temperature's good," he said, moving to the side of the pool. "Why don't you go get your bikini?"

"No." I shook my head.

No more delays or excuses. No more scared and alone. I jumped. Cool water shocked my skin, surrounding me, closing over my head. The skirt of my dress billowed out, hair floating around me. Some weird surge of joy filled me, a feeling of freedom. I exhaled hard when I reached the surface, a smile on my face.

"You jumped."

I nodded, making for the side. All the better to wrap my arms around his neck, my legs around his body. His arm anchored us to the edge, the other hand sliding beneath my ass. Up close, he was exquisite, dark wet hair slicked back, gaze hooded. No one had ever looked at me the way he did now. Like I was more than just some riddle to be solved or a body to be conquered. But as if I held some integral part of him, maybe. The man looked at me like I truly mattered, as if he really saw me, and I hadn't even realized just how much that had been missing from the others.

"Hello," he said.

"Hi."

I pushed back my hair, tightening my thighs around him. He was so solid and real. Not that I'd been fooling around with blow-up dolls previously. But the others had been boys, guys, dudes, while he was a man. The difference was definitely there in all sorts of ways.

Other than gripping my butt, he made no further move. Waiting.

His cock hardened against my core, making me press

myself against him in need of more. Christ, that feeling was so good. He and I together. All of my blood and senses seemed to be rushing straight to the point of our almost connection. If not for his board shorts and my underwear, we'd be in a pretty good position right now.

"Maybe jumping in fully dressed wasn't such a good idea," I said.

"No?"

"Too late to worry about it now."

"Very true."

I kissed him hard, demanding, and he met my need with his own. Firm lips opening, tongue seeking. He made me so greedy. I wanted—no, *needed*—his mouth and his heat and his dick deep inside of me. Fingers dug into my ass, urging me closer. Our tongues tangled, a moan coming from my throat. Kissing him came so naturally, the give and take, the mutual need. It just got better each time, growing with each kiss. Like his mouth was made for mine, his body the perfect fit.

"Grind yourself on me," he said, teeth seeking out my neck, my shoulder. "Show me how bad you want it, Adele."

The head of his cock notched against me, making my insides tighten. Given enough time, I could come from this alone. Dry-humping him in the pool. Wet dry-humping, maybe. Whatever. It felt insanely good. There was no space here between us for worry or inhibitions. Just this raw lust.

"We could have been doing this all day." I sighed.

"I'm such an idiot."

He laughed, chest vibrating against me. "No you're not, beautiful. We had some things to sort out."

I arched my neck, giving him better access. The sting of his bites sent my need rocketing.

"It's good you got some sleep," he murmured. "You've got a busy night ahead of you."

"Oh?"

"But not in the pool or on the fucking floor. We're taking it slow and doing things right, this time."

"Sex in the pool doesn't count?"

"The bed is better," he said, moving toward the pool steps. "Out you go."

Sadly, horribly, he set me down. Wet material clung to my body, water dripping off of me as I climbed out. I dragged down the zipper, peeling the dress off. It went splat when it hit the pavement. Pete pulled off his board shorts, the heavy length of his hard-on bobbing in front of him. Cool water apparently didn't faze the man. Or, at least, it was no match for my grinding skills. Happily, trees, distance, the fading light, and a tall fence kept us safely out of the neighbor's sight. Though I'd keep my damp lingerie on for now just the same. He'd seen my thighs and belly before, but a little cover couldn't hurt my confidence.

"No wet clothes in the house," he said, voice rough and low. "Take it all off."

"I've worn my bikini inside before."

"It's a new rule." He picked up a towel, giving himself

a quick dry-off. Then he threw it aside, taking his dick in hand. "Now, please."

"Thought you wanted to take this inside?"

"I'm waiting."

Bossy jerk. I undid the back of my bra, peeling the wet straps and lace down my shoulders, away from my breasts and very hard nipples. All while he just watched. Next, I grabbed the waistband of my underwear, stripping the last of my cover away and dropping it on the ground. The man had already been inside of me, but standing naked in front of him still seemed an undertaking. Having his heated gaze roving over me, I ignored the urge to cover myself with my hands, to pick up a towel, maybe.

"Thank you," he said simply.

Then he stepped forward, taking my hand to lead me up into the house. We went straight to the French doors opening into his bedroom. Overhead, the fan spun in slow circles. The sheets on the bed were still disheveled from earlier. Pete's bed. It still felt like forbidden territory. A place of myth and legend. Though that might just be in my sex dreams. He stood at my back, hands slipping around my waist, his cock aligned with the crack of my ass.

"You okay?" he asked.

"Yes."

One hand slipped down to the crease of my sex, petting me gently, making me wet all over again. The other toyed with a nipple, rubbing his thumb over and around. I leaned back into him, reaching for the curve of his hips, the start of the smooth round of his ass. My body seemed to loosen and tense all at once. Like I wanted to simultaneously melt on the spot and climb him like a monkey. Instead, I widened my stance, giving his fingers room to slide between the lips of my labia. Given half a chance, the man would tease me into insanity. His arm banded around my middle, fingers plunging within, fucking me. The sensation drove me up onto my toes, the way his thumb played my clit.

"I've got you," he said, teeth grazing my earlobe.

I squirmed on his fingers, leg muscles tight as could be.

"You have no idea how badly I want to fuck you."

"So do it."

"First, you need to come."

How calm and in control he was annoyed me. I reached back, grasping his thick cock, stroking him. The growling noise he made stirred my blood. I wanted to take this man to his knees, own him in the same way he owned me. Whether he knew it or not. But most importantly, right then, I had to taste him.

"Wait," I said, trying to brush his hands away. "I want . . ."

"What do you want, beautiful? Tell me."

His hands pushed away, I turned in his hold and his mouth covered mine, kissing me hot, wet, and deep. Making it hard to think straight. But I was a woman on a mission. A very important one. I broke off the kiss and knelt, taking his cock in hand. The head was an angry purple, veins running along the heavy length. It was a nice-looking cock. An impressive one. Not so long that it headed into painful territory, but a good thickness. Wide enough that I might even need a little practice getting my lips around him. And he seemed to have gone awfully still all of a sudden. Guess I had his full attention.

Hand firm around him, I licked up the bead of pre-come. Salty. Then I dragged the flat of my tongue across and around him. Two could tease. I took the crown into my mouth, gently sucking at first, working my way up to more. Fingers swept my hair back from my face, holding it out of the way. He obviously liked to watch. His stance widened a little, chest rising and falling above. And I could feel his eyes on me, his absolute concentration.

My free hand stroked his thigh and his hip bone. The feel of his hot skin so perfect. Head bobbing, I worked him deeper before pulling back, gently dragging my teeth against the underside. My free hand cradled his balls, rolling them before tugging just a little.

"Fucking hell," he muttered.

The tip of my tongue dug into the sweet spot, where the rim of his crown met. All the while, I stroked him, keeping the rest of his dick occupied. There wasn't a trick I wouldn't use. Anything to get him as worked up and overwhelmed as he made me. Another bead of pre-come hit my tongue and I groaned. The vibration making his cock swell even more, pulsing against my tongue.

"Jesus," he said. "Adele, wait."

"Hm?" I blinked up at him, licking my lips. "I'm not

finished."

He grabbed my arms and drew me to my feet, backing me up against the mattress. "Beautiful, you're seriously fucking good at that and I'd really like to come in your mouth later. But right now, on the bed."

"You liked it?"

"I loved it," he corrected. "Now get on the bed."

I scrambled back, but apparently not fast enough. His hands grabbed my ankles, spreading them wide, making room for his body. Then he climbed on top of me, the heat of him intense. My hands slid up his arms, stroking his neck, messing up his hair. I couldn't get enough of touching him. Not in any amount of years.

"Look at me," he said, voice deep and demanding.

"I am. You're gorgeous."

He smiled and kissed me, a little messy, a lot hungry. And his dick rested against me, the silken-smooth, steel-hard length so close. Making my insides weep and clench with need. I wrapped my legs around him, urging him closer. I knew he'd talked about slow, but surely we were past that stage.

"Hey," he said. "I need to know if you want me to use a condom or not. I'm okay with whatever you want."

Oh. "We're both clean and I'm on the pill."

"Yeah. Definitely."

I nodded and rolled us, pushing him over onto his back. Of course, he let me. Highly doubtful I could move him anywhere without permission. I straddled him, leaning forward with one hand taking my weight and the other guiding him to my entrance. Slowly, I sank down, feeling the stretch of him deep inside. My breath caught, my eyelids squeezed closed. There was nothing beyond this bed. Nothing else mattered but feeling everything he had to give me. What I had to give him in return. When I was seated on his pelvis, I opened my eyes and squeezed my breasts. Almost over-aware of every part of my body. Every nerve ending seemed to hum with pleasure and expectation.

"That feels good." I smiled.

"And that's mine." He replaced my hands with his own, playing with my nipples. "Ride me."

Like I needed to be told. My hips rose and fell, gradually building up the pace. In no particular rush, however. Now that he was inside me, I just wanted to enjoy the feel of him. The slide of his dick in and out, the flawless friction. Pete lay back on the mattress, a thing of splendor on the white rumpled sheets. And I got to see him like this, to have him. His gaze darkened, his pupils dilating, the gray-blue of his iris almost gone.

Once there had been a lovesick girl flashing her breasts at an impossibly out-of-reach man in an ill-thought-through teenage folly that could only end in rejection and embarrassment. And now there was here, me riding him, owning him completely.

My orgasm built slowly, an awareness growing between my hips. A tightness intensifying my sensitivity until only coming mattered. His hands guided my hips, urging me faster, harder. Wet sounds filled the room, the musky scent of sex strong in the summer night air.

"That's it," he rumbled. "So fucking good."

Suddenly, the flat of his palm cracked across my ass cheek. A streak of pain flashing through me. Again and again. I cried out, driving myself onto him, coming impossibly hard. Everything inside me clenching tight before being swept away into a starless night. It was beautiful and terrifying and everything in between.

Strong hands gripped me, his body rising beneath me to drive his cock deep. He groaned, emptying himself into me. I just kind of collapsed on his chest like having bones had gone out of fashion. My skin coated in sweat, my lungs close to breaking. His arms wrapped around me, which was good. Someone had to hold me together before all of my pieces got lost.

Eventually, he raised his head, hand sliding over my behind. "Why, Adele, your ass is bright pink. Just the right cheek. My right, not yours."

"Thanks, I'm aware," I said, voice muffled against his chest. "I can feel it."

"Just checking."

"You're not funny."

"Sure I am."

He rolled us back over, reclaiming top position. Then he kissed me, soft, tender, sweet things, followed by deep, long kisses that made my head spin. I lost my breath all over again, gripping his shoulders tight. Then he pulled out of me. I didn't like him leaving my body, the loss of him. To be fair, though, my vagina could probably handle a short break. Last night had been intense, and tonight we hadn't really taken things any easier.

He lay on the bed beside me, smiling. Actually looking content. "Thank you for staying."

"You're very welcome."

Monday

I slept in until about noon the next day, obviously in full sexed-up holiday mode—much better than mere normal holiday mode. All of those happy hormones flooding my body. The flush of love and all that.

After the bed, he'd fucked me up against the shower wall. Then I'd woken at around daybreak with his hard-on poking me in the back. Spooning with Pete was nice and came with all sorts of benefits. His hand toying with my breast before traveling down my body to ensure my core was wet and ready. After we were done, he went to work and I went back to sleep. All in all, a thoroughly awesome day, and it was barely noon.

I was checking out the contents of the fridge when he walked in, the afternoon finally cooling a little as the sun dropped below the hills.

"Honey, you're home," I said, smiling.

"Hey." He gave me a brief smile and a quick kiss on the cheek. The scent of sweat and sawdust heavy on him.

"What are you doing?"

"I was thinking it must be my turn to make dinner."

"Huh."

"How was your day?"

"Fine." He filled a glass with water and downed it in one gulp. "Don't worry about dinner. I'll get something figured out in a while."

"It's not fair if you have to do all the work all the time."

He didn't look convinced, staring out at the back deck.

"By the way, your design for the kitchen was way better than my ideas," I said, refusing to be discouraged. "The big island counter really works."

"Thanks."

"I had been considering doing the 1950s housewife thing," I said. "Meeting you at the door in a fancy dress with your slippers and a martini in hand."

That got me another flicker of a smile. "The bikini's enough."

"I went swimming earlier. The water's lovely—did you want to go in?"

His brow descended. "Maybe later."

"Okay."

There was a weird vibe in the air. One I didn't trust. The way he avoided my eyes and the short tone of voice. Maybe his day had sucked and he needed time to decompress. Or maybe this was just another fucking mood swing and change of mind. *No. Don't jump to conclusions. Every-*

thing is fine.

"Can I get you a beer?" I asked.

He just shook his head.

Whatever. I headed over to the couch and turned on the TV. *The Castle* was showing on a movie channel. A classic film if ever there was one. A minute or so later, Pete slumped onto the other end of the couch. Head back and eyes closed.

"Mind turning it down a little?" he asked.

"Sure."

He exhaled, shoving his hands through his hair. "Can we check the cricket scores for a minute?"

"No problem."

I handed the remote over to him, not having a clue what channel it would be on. Cricket might be one of the nation's beloved sports, but it had never rocked my world. I shifted on the couch, cuddling up with a cushion. Meanwhile, he stared at the TV, a scowl still imprinted on his face.

"Is something wrong?" I asked finally.

The lines eased. "I just . . ."

I waited.

"Guess I'm used to having the place to myself when I get home."

"Oh."

"Normally, female guests only stay for a night," he said, gaze glued to the TV.

It was a fuck-and-go situation. *Right. Good to know.* Even after all of the carrying on about wanting me to stay.

Interesting how this came up now, when we'd just started sleeping together. And now, I did not feel welcome.

"I tell you what," I said. "I'm going to go out to the tavern for a while, have some dinner, and give you your space."

"What?" His head turned whiplash fast. "No . . . Adele."

"It's fine."

"You don't have to do that."

"We could both probably use some time to clear our heads." I smiled. "No big deal."

I rose, straightening my bikini to make sure it covered everything. Then I put one knee on the couch, reaching over to give him a kiss on the forehead.

"I'll just go get changed, then I'll head out for a couple of hours," I said. "Give you some peace."

Hands grabbed me, dragging me onto his lap. I sat straddling him, face-to-face. Lots of stuff was going on behind his pretty eyes. "You don't need to go."

"Then why do I feel like I do?"

His lips firmed. "I don't want you out on your own."

"You never did like that, did you?" I asked. "So you don't want me going out on my own, but you don't particularly want me here right now either."

Nothing.

"What's the answer, Pete?"

He just stared at me.

"Because I want to help you make good choices."

"You want to help me make good choices?" He sputtered. "How old am I, five?"

I shrugged. "You don't want your toy, but no one else can have it either. What does that sound like to you?"

"Adele, you're not a toy." His arms wrapped around me, pulling me in tight against his body. "I just . . ."

I rested my head on his shoulder, waiting.

"You're right, I'm not exactly making sense." His hands moved restlessly over my back, up and down my spine, soothing. "Seeing you so comfortable in my home, it just kind of caught me off guard. It threw me for a minute, that's all."

I kept quiet.

"What's worse, you looked like you belong here," he said, voice subdued. "In a way, it's your house too. You came up with the idea and everything. I've still got your sketches in my office. Do you remember all those hours we spent together, thinking of how things would be?"

"We dreamed this place together."

"Yeah, we did."

Silence.

He stroked my arms, my shoulders. Callused fingers trailing lightly over my skin, comforting both me and him. "I do keep the women I'm involved with at a certain distance. That's how I like it."

"Hm."

"Problem is, you suck at boundaries."

"Only when it comes to you."

"And every time I even think about you leaving, I swear I just about have a fucking heart attack," he said. "I hate it."

"So what's the answer?"

"You stay right where you are, give me a chance to get used to this." His fingers moved up to my neck, massaging. Against my chest, his heart was beating hard. "I want to get used to this."

"Are you sure?"

"Yes," he said, the word definite, confident. "Though I should probably go shower. I probably smell awful, running around all day."

"I don't think we're ready for a separation yet." I kissed his neck. "Besides, I like you how you are."

His hold on me tightened in response. It was more than enough. We sat there for hours, cuddling and watching TV. Normal couple stuff. After our chat, his occasional channel changing to check in on the cricket scores didn't even bother me that much anymore. And as the night wore on and *The Castle* moved toward its climax, he checked in less and less.

Tuesday

The call came just before four, the shrill ring of the phone startling in the early-morning darkness. Pete fumbled for his cell on the bedside table.

"Hello ... Jesus, is she alright?" The voice on the other

end continued, each word increasing the worry in Pete's gaze. "Of course. If there's anything we can do, please let me know . . . Alright. Thank you for letting me know."

I sat up and flicked on a lamp, wide awake. "What's wrong?"

"Helga's had a heart attack," he said, sitting back against the headboard. "Jesus."

My insides squeezed in shock. Helga had been working for Dad so long she felt like an irremovable part of the world up here. The fact that something might happen to her defied the natural order. "Is she going to be okay?"

"They think so," Pete continued. "She's out of immediate danger, at least. But it must have been really serious. Her daughter sounded devastated." I put my hand on his knee, trying to be comforting. His normally tanned face looked pale in the dim lamplight. "Talk about out of the blue. She was her perfectly normal self in the office this morning—yesterday morning, I mean." He looked like he was in shock. "Busy getting all the paperwork from the Toohey job sorted."

Even for me, it was hard to get my head around the idea. "Helga's been with Dad since he started."

"It kills me to interrupt him on his honeymoon," Pete grumbled, and then sighed in resignation. "But I'd better call him. Helga's basically family."

"He'd definitely want to know," I said, climbing off the bed, getting my thoughts in order. "Did you want to head to the hospital?"

"Sounds like her whole family's there." He shook his

head. "And she's isolated in recovery. We'd probably just be in the way."

"Okay. Coffee?"

"Please."

"How about I hop online and organize some flowers to go to the hospital as soon as possible?" I asked, needing to be doing more. "She's at Nambour?"

He nodded, as if relieved that there at least something we could do. "That'd be great. Thanks." He frowned. "She's going to need recovery time and everything. It sucks to have to think about it, but she's always been such a powerhouse at work, and it's doubtful she'll be returning anytime soon."

"I can help out in the office for a few days," I said. "At least until you get a temp in and get them settled."

With a small smile, he slid a hand around the back of my neck, pulling me in for a kiss. "Thank you, beautiful."

The gentle look in his eyes and sweet curve of his smile made me silly. I almost blurted out that I loved him. Just about went ahead and exposed my messy stupid heart to him. The tip of my tongue needed to take more care.

Instead I smiled back at him and said, "Of course. No big deal."

Chapter Eleven

Seven Years Ago

"You know, Pete, I've never been a huge fan of any of your girlfriends."

"This is really taking me by surprise," he said flatly. "Yet I always sensed there was something behind all the adulation and fawning you heaped on them."

I ignored his sarcasm. "But this one . . . what's her name again?"

Pete smiled, his face in perfect profile as the sun set over the ocean. "Serena."

"Right, Serena." And I totally committed that to memory. "She seriously has the most amazing resting bitch face I've ever seen."

He laughed, kicking a little sand my way. We were walking on the beach at Mooloolaba with our shoes in our hands. The sand warm under our feet and a breeze blowing in off the water. It was beautiful. Pete's date, meanwhile, sat up in one of the trendy beachside bars with a vodka and tonic, reading *Vogue* magazine and messaging someone on her phone. She didn't want to get her pedicure scuffed. Apparently sand could do that.

"Be nice," he said.

I shrugged. "It's a simple statement of fact. The minute it's declared an Olympic sport, the woman has that shit locked down. Gold medals, all the way."

"Language."

"Eighteen." I rolled my eyes. "Did it not occur to you to ask if she liked the beach before bringing her on a date to the beach?"

"Who doesn't like drinks by the water and a walk along the beach?"

"Serena, apparently."

"I thought it would be romantic."

I laughed.

"What?" And he had the gall to look affronted.

"Oh, please. The lies you tell. If you actually wanted to get romantic with her, you wouldn't have brought me." I shook my head. "You're over her; admit it. I won't be seeing Serena again."

One shoulder lifted. "She's a little high maintenance. But I mean, she is nice."

"She's not nice. She's hot. There's a difference."

He didn't respond.

"Has it ever occurred to you to date someone whose company you actually enjoy outside of the bedroom?

Someone you can have clothed fun with?" I headed for the shoreline, looking for seashells. Little waves rippled in, wetting my feet. "Ooh, the water is lovely. Dare you to go in."

"What?" The line appeared between his brows. "I'm in jeans and a shirt. I'm not going in."

"It's a dare, Pete. You can't turn down a dare."

"Sure I can."

"Seven years' bad sex."

"Don't talk about sex," he grouched. "I'm barely dealing with you being legal to drink."

"*Double dare.*"

"Kid."

I walked in farther, kicking water at him. It proved to be insufficient. So I bent over, cupping my hands to splash him good and proper. "Stop being so shallow, Pete. Come into the depths."

"Your dress is getting wet and there's a wave coming."

"I don't care. I'm having fun."

"Adele." He took a few steps forward, enough to wet the bottom of his jeans. Then he gestured me to him with his hand. But he was also smiling, enjoying himself. "Come on, don't be crazy."

I splashed him some more and sure enough, a wave surged up behind me, plastering the knee-length skirt of my yellow cotton dress to my ass and legs. What the hell. I fell backwards, ever so elegantly drowning myself. When I came up sputtering, he was laughing, his smile wide. The best sight on earth.

"Are you happy now?" he asked, standing in the water up to his knees.

"Almost." Hair hanging around my face like a sea monster and water pouring off me, I gave him a full-body hug, wrapping my arms around him. "Aw. Isn't this nice?"

"That's great," he said. "Thanks."

To my everlasting delight, he then pulled his dark-blue T-shirt off over his head. Christ, his body was something else. Sculpted muscles. Seriously ogle-worthy stuff.

"Come here," he said. "Kid, your dress . . . put this on."

"Oops." I laughed. Water had indeed made the material a wee bit see-through.

He just shook his head.

"But now you're all wet too. You may as well just come in."

And he did, dumping me into the next wave before diving in himself.

Tuesday . . . Now

"How's it going?"

"You want the honest answer or the easy one?" I asked.

Pete didn't even blink. "Honest. Always."

"Well, so far as I can tell, Helga's files are somehow

based on some sort of mystical numerological system dating back to much earlier times," I said, gaze on the computer screen. It was about midday, the early start and too many cups of caffeine possibly catching up with me. "We may need to crack open copies of *The Key of Solomon* to figure it out. Either that or the Dead Sea Scrolls, maybe. I'm just not sure yet. I mean, it's all here; I know it is. I just can't find half of it."

He said nothing.

"I will figure this out," I said, determined.

"I know you will."

I flashed him a smile. "Your messages are on your desk and I have about a billion questions when you've got a minute."

"Okay." He leaned his elbows on the taller front-counter part of the reception desk. "Anyone given you any shit?"

"What?" It took me a moment to work out what he was talking about. "Regarding the booby-trap incident of long ago?"

"Yeah."

I raised one shoulder. "No, just a couple of funny looks. About what you'd expect."

"Let me know if that changes."

"Alright."

God only knows the amount of crap that would circulate if people knew we were together. If we *were* together. We were something; I just wasn't sure what. One problem at a time.

"I'll make a couple of calls, then we'll deal with your questions," he said, heading into his office.

It was probably wrong to ogle the boss, but he did all sorts of good things for the company polo shirt, cargo pants, and steel-tipped boots. Seriously.

"Adele!" he yelled, almost as soon as he had entered the room. "Come in here, please."

I switched the phone to go to voicemail and smoothed down my plain black cotton fit-and-flare retro-style dress. Business wear hadn't really been on my mind when I'd packed. Plus, I needed to do some laundry. It might have been a bit casual, but with the sandals, a silver cuff bracelet, and slick ponytail I daresay I looked alright. Competent, even. I mean, I didn't particularly feel that way confronted with Helga's indecipherable kingdom of information, but it was nice to at least appear as if I had a clue.

When I stood in the doorway, he looked up from behind his desk. "Leona called?"

"Yes."

He just stared at me.

"I wasn't rude or anything, if that's what you're worried about," I said. "I don't even think she realized it was me. Guess she wasn't expecting me to be answering the phone."

"What'd she say?"

"Just that she wanted to talk to you."

He'd dumped his sunglasses, tablet, and other assorted crap to the side of his desk. The man was actually quite neat and organized. His office had simple, solid furniture and a bookcase full of files and such. And right now, he was sitting back in his executive-type chair, watching me.

"What?" I asked.

"Close the door."

I frowned, but did as asked.

"Lock it."

"We're both busy," I said. "If we need to talk about this, can we please do so later?"

He pushed out of his chair, coming around the desk. "You're stressed."

"I've got a lot to do." I crossed my arms. "And getting everything organized and ready for the temp is important to me."

Reaching around me, he flipped the lock. "Are you upset that she called?"

I shrugged. "Are you going to call her back?"

"Answer the question."

"*You* answer the question," I said, my voice hardening.

He stared into my eyes like he could read my mind or something. God, I hoped he couldn't.

"At the wedding, she said she'd call you after a few days," I said. "I expected this."

"That doesn't tell me how you feel."

"And none of this tells me if you intend to call her back or not."

"Such attitude from my newest employee," he said, face blank. Unreadable.

"Answer the question, Pete." Frustration boiled over, my hands curling into fists. "Well?"

He said nothing.

"Why are you being such an ass about this?"

He tipped his chin. "You talk to your boss with that mouth?"

"I suck his cock with this mouth."

For a moment, he closed his eyes, licked his lips. "Fucking hell, you're a handful."

"Not up to the job? That's a pity."

"Oh, beautiful," he said, getting in my space, a dark sort of warning in his gaze. "You have no idea."

His mouth slammed down on mine, tongue demanding entrance. And I gave; I'd always give to him. I couldn't do anything but give. Despite all the distractions of Leona's call, and Helga's numerology, and every other stressor that should have been battering around my mind, there was only space for him. Teeth smashed and tongues tangled, heads angling to get closer and closer still. He kissed me breathless, crushing all of the doubts and fears I hadn't even wanted to acknowledge. His hands held my face, slid down my neck, his hot mouth following. One hand held the back of my neck while the other pulled down the strap of my dress, clearing the way for his hot kisses. Fingers kneaded my breast through the fabric of my dress, mouth sucking. I tugged on his hair, holding him to me. As making out in a workplace went, it was my first time and a clear winner.

Right up until someone knocked at the door. We

both froze.

"Boss, you in there?" a voice called.

"What's up?"

"Question about the Meriel site."

"Be there in five, Neil," said Pete. "Just need to finish going over some things with Adele."

"Got it." Heavy boots clomped away.

Hands on my waist, he walked me farther into the room. "Bend over my desk. This is going to have to be quick."

"W-what?"

"Now, please." He turned me around, urging me to lean over the table with a hand to my back. Then the back of my skirt was flipped up, my panties pulled down to my knees. He wasn't messing around.

"You're not serious."

"Is that a no?" he asked, pausing.

"Of course not." I widened my stance. "Hurry up before someone else comes."

"Just checking. Remember, you've got to keep quiet."

Then the palm of his hand struck my butt cheek and holy shit. I had to bite my lip to keep in the yelp. My breasts pushed against the desk surface, lungs fighting for air. All of the muscles in my legs tensed, ass tipping up for more. He smacked the other side, warming my whole ass. No doubt turning it pink. Him and the spanking thing. I'd complain if only I didn't enjoy it so much.

"I like this view, Adele."

I'd have given him a sarcastic reply, but my thoughts

had scattered. Words lost.

"Are you wet, beautiful?"

"Mm-hm." I nodded.

He reached around under my stomach, feeling for my clit, the lips of my sex. The tips of his fingers stroking and caressing, turning me on even more. And all the while, his hard-on, still bound by his clothing, rubbed against my ass. Gently, he eased two fingers into me, pumping them slowly. But there was no time for foreplay. Once he'd satisfied himself as to my readiness, he drew back. Next came the sounds of belt buckle and zipper.

I trembled with anticipation. Impossible not to, knowing what I knew. The man had serious talents. Though it did annoy the crap out of me, not being able to see much. Pete looked extremely good even partially naked. But bent over at the angle I was, there was no hope of twisting around far enough to get an eyeful. I was missing out big-time. Still, facing the desk, not being able to watch, to know what he was up to, provided its own thrill.

The broad head of his cock prodded at my entrance. I raised my hips, pushing back. With one hard thrust, he filled me.

"Fuck," he muttered. "You feel even more amazing every time. No wonder I can't get enough."

He drew back, slamming in harder, giving me no time to catch my breath. With my ponytail wrapped around his fist, the man fucked me in earnest. I was pummeled with sensation. His cock rubbed amazing things deep inside me, hitting some sublime spot at this angle. My breasts bumped against the table, time and again. Everything in my core blazing and bright. His hips smacked into my ass and my teeth sunk into my lip, keeping all of my moans and groans inside. We really did need to discuss some things. But in the meantime, hard sex, this pounding, made for a wonderful method of communication. I rose up on tippy-toes, pushing back, taking all that he had to give.

"That's it," he growled.

When he reached under, searching out my clit again, I was done for. One stroke, two . . .

"Pete!" I cried out. Softly I hope.

Eyelids squeezed shut, a plethora of stars exploded inside me. My body, my mind. All of me was awash with fucking euphoria. An endless swell of bliss, rising inside me. My orgasm triggered his, hips crashing into me. He buried his cock as deep as he could, the grip on me vice-like. It was perfect.

He stroked my back, my bare thighs. Then he pulled out and I heard the sounds of him getting dressed. It took me a minute to find the energy to get off his desk. By the time I did, he was already tugging up my panties, smoothing down my skirt.

"I've never had sex in a workplace before," I said, voice still a little rough. "I hear that sort of thing is generally frowned upon."

Arms went around my middle, drawing me back against him. "It was important."

"Hm."

He kissed my neck, my cheek. "Tell me, Adele. Do you think I'm calling other women?"

"I'm guessing the answer is no."

"Damn right it is," his voice rumbled in my ear, his hold tightening. "She and I are through. Told her everything I had to say the other night. Okay?"

"Okay."

"I wouldn't disrespect you that way."

I swallowed. "Got it."

"Good," he said. Then he frowned. "Did you bite my financial reports?"

"You said to be quiet."

He turned me around, inspecting me. The pad of his thumb rubbed over my bottom lip, his knuckles swept down my cheek. I took the opportunity to finger-comb his hair back into place, more than a little pleased with his disheveled appearance. Inside my head, his words went round and round. He wouldn't be calling her. He wouldn't disrespect me that way. It had to be important, significant. Surely it meant he was mine.

"Hey, I heard from Helga's family," he said quietly. "She's stable, doing better."

"That's good. I've been worried."

"You look much less stressed." He smiled, kissing me lightly on the lips. A certain sort of male satisfaction filled his gaze. "In fact, you look distinctly well fucked."

"Ego, Pete."

"Not at all. It's important to take pride in a job done well."

I just smiled.

"And tonight, I'll do you again," he said, voice a low rumble "Only, slower and louder this time."

I licked my swollen lips. "You will, huh? I'll look forward to that."

"I think we should trade bad sex stories."

Pete looked up from his steak and salad, brow raised.

"You know, as part of our adult getting-to-know-each-other stage," I said, pausing to take a sip of wine. So I may have had a few glasses. It'd been a hard day in all the ways.

"That's honestly the worst idea I've ever heard."

"What? Why?"

He just went back to chewing.

"I've been walked in on by a roommate. Broken a bed. Accidentally bit a guy, and one dude pulled his back really bad when we were trying to bang against a wall," I said. "Had to drive him to the hospital, the poor thing."

Pete dropped his cutlery, staring off at nothing. Such a pained face.

"Your turn." I grinned.

"No, absolutely not."

"Why not?" I asked. Whined. Whatever.

He held up a finger. "Firstly, I fucking hate the thought of someone else touching you."

"You're jealous? That's so sweet."

His expression said he did not agree.

"What are the other reasons?"

"Secondly." Another finger joined the first. "You're my woman. I'm supposed to impress you so you think I'm perfect and can do no wrong. That's my job, here. Not making myself look like an incompetent fool."

"Yeah . . . problem is, I know you too well for that," I said. "Will you settle for me thinking you're near perfect and insanely hot?"

He thought about it, then nodded. "Sure. That'll work."

"I still want to hear your stories, though."

"Not going to happen." He picked the cutlery back up, finishing the last of the food on his plate. "Do you talk about this stuff with other men?"

"No, of course not," I said, scrunching up my nose. "These stories are embarrassing."

"So I'm just lucky, basically."

"I trust you." I shrugged. "And I'm used to talking with you about pretty much everything."

He shook his head. "I never did know what to say when you used to complain about your period."

"You would get this expression in your eyes. Raw panic, I think?" I laughed. "Those were good times."

He gave me a dour look.

"You do realize, I just used to do that to mess with you."

"I do now," he said.

"Oh, please. You loved it when I visited and shook up

your dull, staid, organized little world."

"Yeah, I did." One side of his mouth drew up in a hint of a smile. "Okay. How did you break the bed?"

"Well, this was during university," I said. "It was one of those single pine beds and I guess there was too much activity going on for the old thing. Some of the slats in the bottom gave way and the mattress just fell straight through. Made quite the clatter."

His smile grew.

"Your turn!"

"No."

"Come on, just one."

"Give up, Adele. It's not going to happen."

I smiled at him and he smiled at me, and shit. I was lost all over again. Feelings were the worst. "I bought you birthday cards every year and never sent them. Isn't that weird?"

His gaze softened. "No, not really."

"I still have them all in a box in my room back home."

"Did you write on them?"

"Yes." I exhaled. "That's where the bad poetry is hidden."

"Maybe you could give them to me sometime?"

I nodded slightly. "Maybe."

Silence.

"How did you accidentally bite someone?" he asked, the tone of voice similar to if I'd just confessed to murder.

"Ah, well . . ."

"On the dick, right?"

"Of course. Anywhere else is just playing."

His gaze turned hooded.

"We were messing around after dinner at his place," I said. "I crawled under the table to give him a blow job. Only there was not as much room as I was thinking. He got excited and his knee jerked and hit me, and . . ."

"Ouch."

"It honestly wasn't that bad." I sighed. "No blood or anything. We put ice on it and the swelling went straight down."

"Funny that," he said drily.

"Ha-ha." My alcohol buzz had morphed into a lovely full-body warmth. Between it and the company, there was probably little I wouldn't say or do. He always had been dangerous for me to be around in all the ways.

"What are you thinking?" he asked.

"Would you prefer me more socially acceptable? All polite and filtered?"

He shook his head just once. "Absolutely not."

I said nothing.

Without a word, he rose from his seat and walked around the table. Out in the dark, an owl hooted from the shadows of a nearby tree. On the ground, the citrus lamps smoked, casting shadows across the decking. Another perfect summer night. Yet something inside me felt unsettled, uneasy. Like amongst all of the silliness I'd exposed too much somehow. Nothing worse than accidentally letting all your insecurities hang out. How unsightly.

Pete knelt beside my chair, face serious. "Look at me,

Adele."

I did so.

"I want you. Nothing watered down or held back," he said. "Every crazy thought in your head, every bizarre story you've got to tell . . . I want to hear them all."

"I want you too." I trailed my fingers down the side of his face, along the smooth skin beside his eye and over his cheekbones. The rough of his stubble. He turned his head, pressing his mouth to the palm of my hand.

"Come inside, beautiful."

Chapter Twelve

Seven Years Ago

"Come with me," I said, dragging him down the empty hallway.

All around us were the sounds of the party. Loud talking and louder music. The vibrations of many feet thumping across the floor. Dad had said the party was for me. Most of the people, however, were his friends from work and assorted neighbors. The cake had been a nice touch, but all of them were really just celebrating New Year's.

"What's going on?" asked Pete.

"Let's get somewhere quiet where we can talk." The minute my hand touched the doorknob, he dragged us both to a halt.

"Hold up—we don't need to go in your room. Tell me whatever it is here."

"But—"

"Adele, what is it?"

I frowned, the whole world sort of hazy, care of the amount of alcohol I'd consumed. Rum was maybe not my friend after all. But I'd needed the liquid courage to finally make my move. To stake my claim. God knows, I'd spent hours on my hair and makeup. Birthday money had paid for the blue halter-neck dress and heels. For once, Pete hadn't brought a date. Everything was as perfect as it would ever be. The timing was right. Tonight would most definitely be the night.

This was right. You couldn't feel so much for someone and have it not be right.

"Kid?" He leaned closer, his own grin warm and easy, scotch on his breath. "They're going to count down to midnight soon. Don't you want to be out on the deck for that with everyone else?"

This was harder than I'd thought it would be.

"Hey," he said, voice heartbreakingly gentle. "You okay?"

I smashed my mouth against his. No holding back. No hesitation. For a moment, Pete just froze. Then he grabbed my upper arms, pushing me back.

"What the fuck?" he said, face confused, startled.

"I love you," I blurted out. "I want us to be together. Think about it, Pete, I mean . . . doesn't that make sense?"

"Fucking hell."

"Who knows you better than me?" I carried on, refusing to be deterred. It was do or die. "We couldn't before, but I'm old enough—"

His brows descended, forehead filled with lines. "You're just a child."

"No, I'm not."

"Yes. You are."

"How many times do I have to tell you? I am not!" And to prove it, I tugged at the tie on my dress. Material fell down, exposing my more than adequate rack. Tada, breasts!

The expression on Pete's face . . . the whites of his eyes. Holy shit, they were huge. And maybe not in a good way. Crap.

"What the hell is going on here?" Dad's voice thundered down the hallway, almost shaking the whole damn house.

My mouth fell open, my hands covering myself. "Dad. No!"

But too late. Dad rushed at Pete, his fist flying. Bone crunched, blood sprayed, and Pete howled. Jesus! Yelling filled the hallway. In a flash, partygoers were crowding in to see the source of all the excitement—workers, family members, and all. My fingers fumbled at the tie on my dress, desperately trying to claw back some shreds of dignity as shocked voices and eyes clamored in on me. But some knots, once untied, are not so easy to make whole again.

My party had turned into a nightmare.

Wednesday Night . . . Now

The Spirit House was twenty minutes up the coast in the hinterland at Yandina. Lush tropical gardens surrounded the restaurant built over a pond. It was wonderful. Ornate Asian lanterns and dark wood furniture, plus the most amazing smells coming from the kitchen.

"What do you think?" asked Pete, sitting across from me.

"I think I'm going to like this date."

"You've been working hard; you deserve it." The candle on the table flickered, casting shadows on the sharp cut of his cheekbones and jaw. "And you look spectacular. That dress is something else."

"Thank you. You clean up pretty well yourself."

And he really did. Dark dress pants and a white button-down shirt with the top couple of buttons undone. There was something seriously sexy about his neck. I'd have to investigate it later. Meanwhile, I'd worn my chambray fitted midi dress. Since the last time I'd been wearing it we'd been on the outs (the Friday-night barbeque before the wedding), he probably hadn't appreciated it properly. The way his gaze kept straying to the vee neckline, low without heading into dubious territory, told me he was now. It was lined and tailored, fancy enough for a night out at a nice restaurant. I'd worn my wavy hair down and taken care with my makeup. Tonight was important. Our first public outing as a couple.

I lifted my Thai basil daiquiri. Sounded strange, tasted amazing. "Here's to my victory over Helga's filing system."

"You cracked it?"

"Block numbers," I said. "So obvious when you think about it. But then when the files went to you and Dad, you saved them under client names. So you had two systems going on at once. I'm working on creating a second collection on the main computer of all current and upcoming projects saved under the name to make it easier to access information when people call."

"Well done."

"I didn't realize updates were being inputted manually."

He tipped his head. "We've always just emailed the file back to her. You don't agree with that?"

"I think you need to talk to a tech company about updating," I said. "Really, your devices should link and update automatically when in range. It would be far more efficient. Less chance for any human error."

"Can't say that your dad's a huge fan of change."

"True, but I think it would benefit the business. And that's what he really wants."

He sat back in his chair, looking at me like he was seeing me for the first time, or witnessing something new. Lately, he'd been doing that a lot. "He was right about you being good for the position."

"That's kind of you to say."

"It's just the truth," he said. "Have you thought about

it some more?"

I exhaled, turning to look out at the water, the lights reflecting on the surface. "There's a lot to consider."

Slowly, he nodded. "Yes, there is."

We were so fragile and new. I wanted answers, but I knew better than to push. Mostly. "You asked me to stay for a while longer, not to move here."

"Adele, I don't know how it would affect things between us, if that's what you're asking. I'm just taking this day by day." He reached out and took my hand, our fingers intertwining. His bigger, darker fingers against my more delicate pale skin. Maybe if I moved here, I could actually attempt a tan. Or at least a greater collection of freckles.

"Moving here, taking on the job, it needs to be your decision," he said, thumb rubbing over the back of my hand.

"I know." I picked up my drink, putting my dreams back on hold. Having patience when what you've always wanted was within reach was hard. I wanted him to say he wanted me here. All the time, not just for now. I wanted a lot of things. Everything I felt for him made it hard to set it all aside and just enjoy the moment. And Dad's reaction to this thing between us had to be on his mind. I know it was on mine. But fuck it, I was an adult. Dad would have to deal.

"Anything else of interest happen today?" he asked, changing the subject.

"Matthew asked me out for a drink."

"He fucking what?"

"Yeah, we're good mates now." I smiled. "Relax, would you? I think it was his way of trying to apologize for giving me crap at the Buck's Party."

"Tomorrow, Fitzy and I are going to talk."

"That's not necessary."

Pete did not look convinced. "I told him to stay away from you."

"I'm currently working there," I said. "Interacting with me to some degree is probably necessary, don't you think?"

He grumbled something I couldn't hear.

It had been a busy couple of days. Every private moment we got, we were either talking or fucking. We were insatiable. Both of us more than a little sleep deprived, running on lust and other good feelings. All of the excitement and nerves that come with something new. I always knew he had an appetite, but I'd never had so much sex in my life. The way he looked when he reached for me sometimes made me wonder if the same was true for him. If we were both a little out of control, then that would be okay. But the need had to go both ways. That I knew for sure.

Our food got delivered, green duck curry for me and a beef dish for him with some sides. It smelled amazing, but sadly necessitated the separation of our hands.

Everything tasted delicious. My taste buds had never had it this good. When I moaned in pleasure, he looked at me with such heat in his eyes, it was as if he preferred me on the menu. Later, I had a feeling I just might be.

"Pete," a familiar voice said, standing beside the table. "Lovely to see you."

He stiffened. "Leona."

"And you're here with Adele. How nice." She looked between us, a faint frown on her face. But she covered it quickly with a smile. "I was hoping to hear from you today. We need to talk."

"Said everything I have to say."

At that, she stared down at him, gaze tight with anger. Guess people didn't say no to her often.

"We won't hold you up," he said. A clear dismissal.

Movements jerky, she walked away.

I felt bad for her. Though no one had made her invade his privacy. With our lust fest in full swing, however, I'd forgotten how efficient Pete could be at cutting people from his life. It was just a little chilling. God knows, I'd been on the receiving end of it. Seven long years of silence. Perhaps he'd gotten the ability from his father. Secretly, I had a theory that abandonment issues and rejection, his mom's death followed by his father's uselessness and complete lack of care, had formed this part of the man I loved. But then, it's not like I was great at relationships either. My longest was four months and I'm reasonably certain he just hung around for the sex and because he was too polite to ghost. Both Pete and I were a bit of a mess. Maybe, just maybe, we'd make a whole together. Something good.

"How's your food?" he asked, giving me a smile. But

the mood was broken.

The one I gave him in return came less easily than earlier. "Great."

Back in the car at the end of the night, he held my hand some more. All of the way home, then up the steps and into his house. We never did quite regain the mood. Maybe Leona hexed us. I'm certain I could feel her death glare from across the room at various points. Awkward as hell.

"That didn't go quite as I planned," he said, turning me in his arms. "Let's see what I can do to fix things. Come here, beautiful."

His mouth seduced me. His kiss took me over so easily it was embarrassing. I was a fool for him. Our tongues danced together, hands grabbing and greedy. The hunger never quite went away. It was always there, waiting for the next opportunity. Love, lust, and obsession were dangerously close.

I couldn't tell if sex was our way of exposing our real selves and truly communicating.

Or if sex was what we fled to in order to avoid doing exactly that.

"You looked fucking edible tonight," he whispered hoarsely, walking me backward. "On the counter, Adele."

"Right here?"

"Yes. I'm done waiting."

A stool was pushed aside and he lifted me up, placing

my ass on the edge of the kitchen counter.

"Lie back," he ordered.

The man was clearly on a mission. Hands slid up my legs, divesting me of my underwear in no time. My skirt was pushed up, legs spread open, and his mouth was on me. In me.

"Oh fuck. Pete."

One of my legs hung over his shoulder, the other lying to the side. Not the most elegant of positions. But I didn't care. Not when he was eating me like I was dessert. Like I was what he'd been craving. His tongue lapped at me, fingers holding me open. I was wet and swollen and crazed in no time. More than ready for him, but he wasn't giving me his cock. Instead, he fucked me with his tongue.

"That's it, beautiful," he murmured.

The vibration of his words against my core rattled my very bones. I fisted my hand in his hair, holding him to me. Not that he'd made any effort to get away. Quite the opposite. Tension coiled deep inside me. His mouth sucked at my swollen lips, teeth grazing the tender flesh. Before his tongue slid over my clit, over and over.

"I'm so close," I panted.

Pete groaned into me.

"What the hell?" The yell shattered the moment. A deep voice. Not Pete's.

"Dad!"

Pete froze, his head buried between my legs. *Shit.* If only we'd made it to the bedroom, we might have actually had some warning we were about to have visitors. Shit.

Shit, shit, *shit*.

"I don't fucking believe this!" Dad bellowed.

"Really?" asked Shanti. "I must say, Andrew, I'm not surprised at all."

Pete wiped his hand over his face, gently lifting my leg off his shoulder and drawing down my skirt. My heart was absolutely pounding. For all the wrong reasons now, however.

"Can we have a minute, please?" asked Pete, voice strained.

Dad swore some more and Pete looked at me. Dad and Shanti turned their backs, I guess to give us some privacy. What a clusterfuck. Still, they had to find out about us sometime. The strain showing on Pete's face, however, was really not good.

"Easy," he said, lifting me down.

My legs were trembling, dammit. God only knows where my underwear had gone. We'd been in a rush. Pete just stood there, watching me. And his eyes were cold, distant. My stomach sank through the floor.

"I thought I could trust you," said Dad. "That's why I asked you to partner in the business."

"Of course you can trust him," chided Shanti. "Calm down."

"Then why the hell did we just find him doing that to my daughter?"

"Lower your voice, please, dear."

Dad grunted.

"She's twenty-five years old now, not eighteen." Shanti stood with her back to us, hands on hips. "More than old enough to decide for herself who she wants to be with."

"He's forty."

"And I'm eight years older than you. Does that matter?"

"Okay, we're decent," I said, crossing my arms. A purely defensive maneuver.

"So sorry for walking in unannounced, darling." Shanti smiled serenely. "Your father was so worried about Helga and what was happening back here, I decided we might as well have our honeymoon another time. The weather was also miserable. We'll go back to Bali when the sun is shining. It will be much nicer."

I nodded, tried to smile. It didn't work.

"Bali is not the issue right now." Dad glared at Pete.

And Pete looked guilty as sin. Like he'd definitely been caught. His hands curled into fists, the hard line of his jaw tightening.

"You said all of this nonsense was on her." Dad pointed the finger straight at me, his body rigid. "That nothing like that would ever happen again."

"Your daughter's feelings are not nonsense," said Shanti. "They're both adults, Andrew. If they want to screw on the kitchen counter then that's their business. Not ours."

Dad's nostrils flared. "Honey, can you please stay out of this?"

"I will not."

"Shanti—"

"You're being absolutely ridiculous and you're going to damage your relationship with your daughter, and your best friend and business partner, if you're not careful." Shanti opened her arms, walking toward me.

I met her halfway.

"Sorry about this, darling."

I hugged her back, saying nothing. Everything inside me was in a state of upheaval. Shanti's arm slid around my waist, her presence at my side solid and strong. I needed it; going from ecstasy to agony in under two minutes was a lot to take.

"I didn't mean for anything to happen," Pete finally spoke.

"Then why did it?" asked Dad.

Pete didn't answer. Just shoved his hand through his thick dark hair, mouth a thin white line.

"Jesus, Pete," said Dad. "Could you not keep it in your pants at least when it came to my daughter?"

"I'm sorry."

"You're sorry?" I asked, turning to Pete, my voice suddenly tight. "Seriously?"

"Adele. Sweetheart." Dad sighed. "I know you've had feelings for him for a long time. I'm not mad at you."

I held up my hand. "Stop. Jesus, Dad, just stop. I'm not a child. This time, this is most definitely nothing to do with you and I need you to respect that and stay out of it."

Dad just blinked. Then frowned. "But—"

"No."

He sputtered, but held his silence.

Whatever. My quota of idiot males to deal with was already full. I stepped away from Shanti, needing to face Pete on my own. As an adult.

"You said you wanted to figure this out together," I said. "That you hated the thought of me leaving. That I was important to you and you wanted to get used to this, me being here. What are you saying now, Pete? That you're sorry?"

He stared back at me in silence.

"Talk to me. Help me understand this."

"I meant all of that." He took a breath, then swallowed hard. "But you were only planning on staying a few days. You weren't sure about anything more, so I thought we could enjoy our time together. I thought that's what you wanted."

I said nothing.

Color infused his face. "Come on, Adele. You know it's complicated. Your dad was always going to come back."

"Yes," I said. "And now he's back, and he knows, so the most dramatic part is over. The question is, what are you going to do next?"

"This is my life here. Not just some vacation."

"You honestly think you were just a fling for me?"

He looked at the ground. Asshole.

"You wanted us to get to know each other as adults? Well, this is who I am," I said. "And I would never allow my job, friends, family, or even distance to dictate who I was involved with. Not if I really wanted to be with some-one."

He didn't respond.

"I'm going to get my things," I said, heading for the bedroom.

"I'll help you pack." Shanti followed.

I had no idea what Pete and Dad did or didn't say to one another. I was past caring. My sole focus was on get-ting my shit and getting out before I burst into tears or did something equally stupid. I didn't let loose. I couldn't. Not until I was safely ensconced in my childhood bed-room across the street. In the quiet and dark, with a pil-low over my head to muffle the noise. Then I'd let the tears flow.

Thursday

Getting a temp in for the business at that time of year wasn't as easy as I'd hoped it would be. Every business in the region had people on vacation who needed covering. Either that, or the temps were off on vacation themselves. So I spent another day of my holidays at Helga's desk, putting lists of information and instructions together for my eventual replacement. I also started talking to the lo-cal employment agencies, putting the job listing together in search of a permanent person. Since that obviously wouldn't be me.

Truth be told, with every fiber of my heart, I wanted to get out of the place. Out of the house, out of the town, out of this entire world. Build me a rocket ship and send me into outer space already. But I wouldn't run away. Not this time, scurrying away with my tail between my legs. There was a job here that needed doing. I was still here for Dad and Helga, and just because I'd said that I would do it. And damned if anything as trivial as a broken heart was going to stop me. Then, once the business was all sorted out, I would pack my bags and leave on my own terms and in my own time.

Dad had been quiet since last night. Restrained. I think Shanti had talked to him long into the night about what was and wasn't acceptable for the father of an adult child. He'd told me I didn't need to come into the office. How they'd figure something out. But that was bullshit—I knew the mess they were in. Helga had kept the place running. This side of the business was her sole domain and I was beginning to strongly suspect she'd hoarded information like candy. Not in a bad way. Just in a "don't step on my toes or I'll beat you with pictures of my grandchildren" kind of way.

Meanwhile, Pete had been out working at a site all day. This was good. The less we saw of one another the better. Like, forever and ever. How many times could you get your heart broken by the same person before you finally wised up? That was the question. And if he thought sending me flowers would smooth shit over, the man was sadly mistaken.

When he did come in, it was late. Later than I'd actually intended to be there. He strode past my desk, giving me side eyes. Cowardly fuck. I ignored him entirely. This tactic worked awesomely right up until he yelled at me from his office. I took my time, wandering on over to the doorway. Sometimes, petty victories were the way to go.

"What are these flowers doing in here?" he asked, glaring at the offending vase full of red roses and tropical blooms. They were spectacular, really.

"Well, I didn't want them."

"And you think I do?"

I crossed my arms, shrugged. "Give them to Leona if you like. I don't really care."

His gaze narrowed on me.

"Was that all?" I asked.

"Wait. You think I had something to do with these?"

Now I was confused. "You didn't?"

Frown in place, he tore the little envelope off, ripping it open to read the card. Must have been a hard day. Smears of dust covered his face, his mood obviously every bit as good as mine.

"'Dear Adele,'" he read. "'I hear you're still in town. Call me. Jeremy.'"

"Really? Huh."

He held the card out to me, but I just waved it away.

"Shanti's obviously been busy," I said. "I mean, you can see how I would just assume they were some lame suck-up attempt from you."

His tongue played behind his cheek. "I thought about sending some. Figured you'd just throw them at me."

"That vase looks heavy too. It would hurt."

"Yes, it would."

"Let me guess," I said, tapping a finger against my lips. "Were you going to run with the always golden 'I hope we can still be friends' line?"

"Had a bit more to say than that, actually." He sat back in his chair, watching me. Bastard.

"'Sorry I stuck my dick in you and then changed my mind?'" I rested my head against the door frame, getting comfortable. "That could look pretty on a card if you used the right font. A bit of calligraphy, maybe."

"You think?"

"Oh, yeah. It's quite poetic, really."

He raised his brows. "I admit, I panicked last night. But I think calling it off is best for both of us."

Wow. What fuckery. I honestly had nothing.

"I can see that now's maybe not the best time to try to talk to you about this," he continued. "What with us being at work, plus you apparently wanting to cut off my balls and wear them as earrings or something. Can you get these flowers out of here, please?"

"Pete, Pete, Pete. Give them to Leona or whoever is next on your fuck-friend list. Even better, take them to Helga and brighten up her day. I care not." I sighed. "Or you could just watch them wither and die as you contemplate the fragility of life. I mean, what does it all mean? Though maybe you've already got it figured out and being alone is best. In the end, don't we all just die alone, anyway?"

"Adele," he said through gritted teeth.

I wiggled my fingers goodbye at him. Only to turn and find Dad waiting for me. Not so subtly listening to the entire conversation would be my bet.

"You ready to go, sweetheart?" he asked, apparently ignoring Pete. Their relationship was their business.

And our relationship was our business—and I was done. "Sounds good."

Chapter Thirteen

Thursday Night

"Why are there four place settings?"

"Because I invited someone to dinner," said Shanti, putting the finishing touches on the plates of salmon, baby potatoes, and asparagus. "You can start serving these please, dear."

"Who did you invite?" I asked, highly suspicious.

Dad, meanwhile, just did as told. Marriage had mellowed him. Though I daresay Shanti had tamed him years ago.

The night had been so clammy and still, we'd retreated inside and turned on the air-conditioning. It gave me a chance to experience the new formal dining room. Shanti had gone for the same fusion of antiques with a modern edge. A beautiful old mahogany sideboard and matching dining table and chairs, with the walls painted a peacock blue. The pop of color was in-your-face stunning.

"Ah, Pete," said Shanti with her usual serene smile. "Right on time."

He carried a bouquet of native flowers in one hand, a bottle of wine in the other. Good to see his expression was wildly fucking uncomfortable. As it should be.

"Are you sure this was a good idea?" asked Dad, not even bothering with discreet.

"We are a family. Albeit, the family we have made for ourselves." Shanti pulled out a chair and gracefully sank into it. "We will behave like a family regardless of who is currently angry and disappointed in whom right now."

Nobody argued. Nobody dared.

"Who are those flowers for, Peter?" she asked, gaze curious. "They're very beautiful."

The grim smile returned. "I thought you might like them."

What a suck-up.

"How sweet. Just put them on the sideboard," said Shanti. "Thank you."

Dad sat down and got busy drinking his beer. "How was the Meriel place today?"

"Coming along well." Pete nodded, taking his place beside me. Dammit. "Adele, would you like to try the wine? You like Sémillon, right?"

Shanti beamed. "That was a very nice gesture, Peter. I'm sure Adele would love a glass."

"Or I could just stick a straw in the bottle," I whispered.

"What was that, darling?"

"A glass sounds great."

Pete poured the alcoholic offering into the wineglass in front of me, filling it up nice and tall. Wise of him.

"Dinner looks wonderful," I said, raising the glass in my new stepmother's direction. "Thank you for cooking."

She beamed. "My pleasure. It's lovely to get to spend some more time with you."

"About that—I'll be heading back to Sydney tomorrow," I said. "The temp agency called this afternoon with good news. They've found someone who can cover Helga's position, starting in the morning. I've left plenty of instructions and advice for her; I'm sure she'll be fine."

Dad frowned. "Thought you might stay at least until the weekend."

"I'd rather avoid the weekend traffic." I gave him a small smile.

"Have you thought some more about the job?" asked Shanti, eyes wide and innocent. Not. "Your father tells me you've been doing a brilliant job this week and I'm sure we'd all love to have you here permanently. Wouldn't we, Andrew? Peter?"

"Damn right," said Dad.

Pete forced a smile. "Of course. You've proven yourself without a doubt this week. I mean that. The job's yours if you want it."

"Thanks," I said, studying my plate.

"What do you think?" Dad watched me from across the table. "Sweetheart?"

Everyone's gaze was on me. Talk about being put on the spot. I picked up my wine, downing a couple of mouthfuls. Given recent emotional upheavals, the level of scrutiny was extreme. Hopefully my concealer hid the worst of the bruising beneath my eyes. A broken heart was a bitch on the complexion. But it'd been my own dumb fault, getting all wrapped up in him. Thinking we actually had a chance. We were both messed-up people in our own sweet way. I guess two wrongs really didn't make a right.

"You could go, give your two weeks' notice straight away," he said. "Be back here in no time."

I took a deep breath. "Thank you, Dad. But no. I—"

"This is about Pete, isn't it?" Dad's voice was flat. Dark.

"We talked about this," said Shanti, placing her hand on Dad's arm. "Andrew, we have to let them work it out for themselves. If that is the reason, and she can't see herself being happy here right now, then that's the way it is. Maybe things will change sometime in the future."

Dad scowled and drank his beer. I drank my wine. And Pete sat beside me, rigid. So dinner was turning out to not have the most festive mood. What a surprise.

Shanti picked up her glass of red wine. "For now, we let Adele go back to Sydney, where she will no doubt find someone who sees exactly how beautiful and wonderful she is, sweeps her off her feet, and makes her forget that our Peter ever even existed. Why, he'll be nothing but a dim, sad memory to her in no time. Meanwhile, Peter can go back to having meaningless relationships based on almost casual sex with women he barely even likes."

At that point, Pete started drinking too. Couldn't really blame him.

Dad wore the mightiest smirk I'd ever seen. He really did have excellent taste in women. Shanti was the best. Also, I was beginning to strongly suspect that I wasn't necessarily the alluded-to angry and disappointed-in person present tonight. My new stepmother having my back was all kinds of awesome.

"To Adele and her very bright future," Shanti toasted.

"Thank you." I wasn't sure whether to cry or to laugh. "That was really . . . thank you."

"Anytime, my darling."

"What are you doing here, Adele?"

It was around midnight when I banged on his door. Little wonder he answered in sleeping bottoms and nothing else. Hazel and I had had a long chat on the phone. But getting it all out and going over it, trying to sort out the pieces, hadn't helped. I'd lain in bed wide awake, staring at the ceiling for hours. However, storming Castle Pete in pajama shorts, a tank top, and bare feet might not have been the wisest idea.

"I realized I have some things I need to say to you before I leave," I said.

He stepped back, swinging an arm wide. "By all

means, come on in. I haven't been insulted nearly enough today."

"In the my-broken-heart-versus-your-mild-inconvenience-and-a-few-insults contest, I'm the clear winner," I said. "So suck it up."

The door shut behind me, Pete's eyes full of regret. It pissed me off even more than the poor-me expression he'd been laying on the moment before. Best just not to look at him directly. Anyway, his bare-naked chest was a distraction I could do without. The rounds of his pecs and his sexy brown nipples. A dusting of chest hair above and the happy trail disappearing into the waistband of his pajamas below.

"I left a pair of underwear here too, last night," I said. "Where are they?"

"I don't know."

"Find them. Send them to me. You don't get to have souvenirs."

His lips thinned to nothing.

I scowled, but asked the question I had come to ask, planting my hands on my hips. "If you knew you were just going to break it off as soon as it was convenient, why did you even start with me?"

"Because I didn't know."

"Oh, please."

"Yeah, it was likely, but . . ."

"But what?"

His jaw tensed. "I don't know, okay? I wasn't thinking long term or consequences, I just—"

"Wanted to fuck me."

"Wanted to be with you." He started pacing. "Jesus, Adele. You turn up back here with your wise-ass mouth, getting in my face like you always did, all grown up and looking hot as fuck. What was I supposed to do?"

"How about not think with your dick for a change?"

"This isn't all on me. You wanted into my bed."

"Because I thought there was a chance you'd finally see me. That you'd get real with me. But you knew you never would. Real isn't even on your radar," I said, hands shoving into his chest, forcing him back a step. "Why have you not sorted out your issues, huh? Still running scared like a little boy from any sort of emotional vulnerability at forty. What the fuck, Pete?"

"Maybe I didn't want my life upended based on only three days of being together," he said. "Maybe I don't make major decisions based on a whim, like you do."

"Firstly, I agreed to take it day by day. But when it came down to it you didn't have my back about that. And a whim?" I asked, incredulous. "Are you serious?"

"What if I'm not the person you think I am and you decide this isn't what you want after all?"

"You think I don't know you?"

"I think you've got some idea in your head of who I am. Like a teenage fucking crush."

"Oh, Pete. I do not have you on a pedestal, rest assured," I said.

"Adele—"

"I love you, you idiot."

He paused, face going pale. "You don't love me."

"Yes. I do. Unfortunately for me."

He just stared at me.

"And you're not some vague notion or dream-date ideal to me," I said, pushing him back another step. "I know who you are. I know where you come from. Hell, I even know what your problems are, not that I can solve them for you. I know that losing your mother and having your dad neglect you hurt something inside of you that hasn't healed. You act all nice and easygoing, but underneath you're all hard surfaces. No one can break through. You hardly trust anyone, forget letting someone near enough to hurt you again."

He blinked, mouth a flat line.

"I know your flaws and your virtues; I've heard just about all of your stories and told you mine too. I opened up to you like I never have to anyone else." I shoved him again, getting in his face just like he'd accused me of doing. "Give me a better answer than 'it seemed like a good idea at the time,' Pete. Tell me you felt something for me."

"I . . ."

"Tell me."

But he had nothing. *Jesus.*

The disappointment was beyond bitter. A lead weight I'd carry with me all of my days, but I would not cry. He didn't deserve my tears and emotions. Not ever again. Without saying a word, I slipped out the door, heading back to Dad and Shanti's. Maybe there was a murmur behind me as I left the room, but I scarcely heard it. Outside, bare feet meant taking it easy on the asphalt. I'd had enough pain for pretty much forever.

"Wait," he called out behind me. "Adele."

I ignored him, picking my way through the front garden and around to the side of the house. Nothing remained to be said. We were done. And what a beautiful night to have everything come crashing down, shining moon and twinkling stars.

"Hey," he hissed, keeping his voice down. "You don't just leave like that."

"You want to shake hands? Hug it out? What?"

"Would you . . ." He grabbed my arm, drawing me to a halt.

I shook him off. "It's over, Pete. Now we go our separate ways. That's how this works."

"You climbed down the tree?"

I shrugged, lifting myself up onto the first handy foothold of the trunk. Inside, I felt so foolish and empty. "If they knew I'd gone crawling back to you after everything . . ."

"You didn't come crawling back. You damn near kicked my ass."

"Maybe the two things aren't so different. And keep your voice down."

Fortunately, the house wasn't too far off the ground. Just high enough to ensure that a ninja-style jump and roll out of my bedroom window would be really unadvised.

"I hope you're being careful," he said.

"I hope you're fucking off."

He snorted.

"Dickhead," I muttered, trying to hang onto my anger. It was much better than the all-consuming sadness threatening to sink me.

Despite my years of not climbing backyard trees, it wasn't too hard to reach the branch running alongside the open window. I inched along carefully, taking it slow.

"This is fucking ridiculous," he whispered. "You're sneaking back into your dad's house in the middle of the night again like you're a teenager."

"And this is the last time I'll ever do it too. Poignant, really."

Nothing from him.

"In the future, we will not be friends," I said, stating the facts. "We will not be anything."

"Don't say that."

"Give me an alternative."

More nothing.

I sat on the branch beside my window, trying to think of any last words. Any final thing I had to say to him. He stood below, hands on hips, looking up at me. That's when I heard the cracking sound and suddenly everything, me included, plummeted toward the ground.

The emergency room was pretty quiet at two in the morning. They'd already glued up Pete's cut and diagnosed him with a mild concussion. He lay on the hospital bed alongside mine, resting. Most of his face was white as the bed-sheets, but one side of his forehead had started turning spectacular shades of purple and gray. The wound neatly dissected his left eyebrow. When it healed, it would give him a dashing, roguish air.

"You'll probably look like a pirate," I told him. Because irritating the crap out of the jerk remained its own reward. What a night. "Women dig scars. This is going to bring your game up to a whole other level. You should probably be thanking me."

He didn't even open his eyes. "Shut up, Adele."

"Shut up, the both of you," said Dad, sitting in a chair to the side. There was much thunder and ire upon his tired face even several hours later.

Shanti just gave me a weary smile. She'd run out of laughter about an hour back. Not that she hadn't been concerned for our various injuries. But the whole situation seemed to have left her mostly amused. Guess we were better than reality TV.

"You're free to go," the male nurse said, giving me a friendly nod. At least someone was still talking to me.

You'd have thought I'd made Pete stand directly underneath the branch, then cunningly orchestrated it breaking, the way people were carrying on. Like I'd made the poor innocent man try to catch me along with a decent-sized part of a tree. Such a dumb idea. And it wasn't like I'd come out of the accident unscathed either. My ulna was fractured, meaning I'd be wearing a cast over my forearm for quite a while. At least it was a nice blue color.

Mom had always encouraged me to find a positive even in the most messed up of situations.

"I guess driving back to Sydney is out," I said, carefully hopping down off the bed.

Dad grunted. "You're flying. I'm buying you a ticket."

"Thanks, Dad," I said, moved by the display of parental affection.

"I don't care if you have to go first class," he continued. "You're leaving today. I can't take any more. The sooner you two are separated, the better and safer for everyone."

Pete just hummed in agreement.

"What about my car?" I asked.

"You're not going to be able to drive it for at least six weeks, anyway," said Dad.

"We'll sort it out later," said Shanti. Even she seemed to agree that running me out of the state was for the best, patting me on the shoulder. "Alright, darling, let's get you home. Enough adventures for one night, I think."

We drove home in silence. Pete was either asleep or determinedly ignoring me, or a mixture of both. I tried to snooze. God knows I was tired and the painkillers had made me drowsy. But this was it. Again. The end. And what an end it was. We all climbed out of the car, yawning and weary.

"I'll sleep on Pete's couch in case he needs anything," said Dad.

"Yes, dear." Shanti kissed him on the cheek. "See you at breakfast. A late one, I think."

Dad just nodded.

I turned to Pete to say something, but he just slowly stumbled off into the night. Nothing I could do. Apparently, I'd already done it all. It wasn't even my fault. Not really.

"Come on, darling," said Shanti, taking my unbroken arm.

"He didn't even say goodbye."

Her brows rose. "Maybe that means it's not the end? Who knows?"

"I think maybe it means he blames me for everything and hates me," I said glumly. "That seems the most likely answer."

Her arm went around my shoulders, squeezing me tight, her sigh soft in the darkness. "Perhaps walking away right now is for the best. It's sad, but sometimes loving someone isn't enough. One day, if the stars are aligned, you might be ready for each other and come together for the right reasons."

"A pretty thought." I gave her a small smile and we headed in.

Not so surprisingly, I didn't see Pete again before I left.

Chapter Fourteen

Eight Weeks Later

"We have Indian."

"What'd you get?" asked Hazel.

She and Maddie were cuddling on the couch, the very picture of happiness and love in the late afternoon. Ah, togetherness. It barely even hurt anymore to see. Them, random couples on the street . . . none of it really bothered me anymore. Sure, living with people who were in love had been a drag at first. But now I was over him. So over him. After all, life was a glorious thing full of opportunities and experiences, not to be wasted fretting over some penis-wielding moron.

I slid the bag full of spicy awesomeness onto the kitchen counter. "Chicken tikka masala, lamb rogan josh, something vegetarian with paneer, raita, pickles, and cheese and spinach naan breads. Everything we need for a feast to celebrate the removal of my gruesome cast."

Maddie smiled. "Nice. We have something for you too."

A brown paper bag sat on the table, waiting. Curious. "What is it?" I asked.

"Open it," instructed Hazel, rising to her feet.

Maddie watched, eyes guarded.

"Alright." I picked up the package. "I applied for another position today; this one's at the offices of a plumbing imports company. Italian toilets are cool, right?"

"Funny you should mention toilets," said Maddie.

"Why?" I opened the paper bag and immediately dropped it with a gasp. A brown snake appearing in my hands would be less shocking. "What the hell!"

"Just breathe," said Hazel, using her counselor voice. It kind of made you want to confess your darkest sins or cry about your childhood. Sometimes both.

"It's not funny," I said. "Why on earth would you buy me that?"

"It's not a joke."

Maddie picked up the pregnancy test, holding it out to me with a determined sort of smile. "The symptoms are all there. It's time you found out for sure."

"No."

"Yes," they both said.

"It was just a stomach bug."

"For six weeks?" Maddie raised her brows.

"You made puking look like your new hobby," added Hazel, not helpfully.

"And then there's the tits." Maddie blew out a breath, tucking a strand of curly blond hair behind her ear. "You've gone up a size, haven't you?"

"I'd say two," said Hazel.

"Stop ganging up on me," I cried. "Oh my God."

"Adele, be honest. When was the last time you had your period?"

"It's been a very stressful time," I said. "Stress can affect the body like that. You're studying medicine, Maddie—you know these things. Tell her."

Hazel tilted her head. "It was Maddie's idea to get the test."

"Why don't you just quickly go pee on the stick and then we'll know for sure?" asked Maddie, henceforth known as the betrayer.

"Because it's pointless. It's going to be negative." I was surrounded, encircled by two completely wrong best friends. The wrongest best friends in all of time and space.

"Then it's not a big deal, right?" Hazel smiled. "We'll have a glass of wine and eat all of that yummy curry you bought to celebrate."

"Wanting spicy food is a big indicator, by the way," said Maddie.

"No, it's not, I was just craving . . ."

Oh shit. No.

Maddie pressed the test into my hand. My numb fingers closed around it, my brain in the process of shutting down completely. It couldn't be. I couldn't be. This was all a horrible, terrible mistake. The bigger boobs were a gift from God and the puking thing had just been a virus. Any sudden sensitivity regarding my middle was just a weird anomaly. Skinny jeans were sure to go out of fashion eventually anyway.

"No need to panic," said Hazel, using the irritatingly soothing voice again. "But it's best to know for certain, right?"

Not really.

Sweat broke out across my back, my heart beating double time. I swallowed hard, my throat and everything below or above it feeling god-awful for some reason. More stress. It was just more stress. This time inflicted on me by my soon-to-be ex-best friends. Next time, I'd be sure to find people who neither cared about my physical well-being nor noticed the size of my breasts or any persistent puking I happened to partake in. Much simpler.

"Okay," I said, eventually finding my voice.

They nodded, giving me encouraging smiles.

"Right." The pregnancy test was clutched tight in my hands. "I'm going to go and do it now."

"We love you," said Maddie. "Good luck."

"Whatever the result is, we'll work it out," promised Hazel. "Everything will be fine."

Bathrooms were surprisingly comfortable for both short- and long-term stays. You had water. Facilities should your bladder or bowels require attention. Why, you could even have a nice, long hot soak in the bath should you be so inclined.

Right then, I wasn't so inclined.

I just sat on the cool terra-cotta tile floor with my arms looped around my knees. Balanced on the edge of the sink above my head was the dreaded test. It didn't count, however, if I refused to look at it. There was no possible way it could turn my life upside down if I just continued to ignore the damn thing. I was safe. Quietly terrified, but still.

"Are you ready to come out yet?" asked Hazel through the door.

"No."

"It's been almost two hours."

"I'm fine," I lied.

"Okay." She sighed. "Whenever you're ready."

Truth was, my stomach had been grumbling for a while now. All of the wonderful Indian food was just sitting out there going cold while I had to be stuck in here with that thing. People were talking farther back in the apartment; I heard a deeper voice than either Hazel or Maddie could attempt. *Shit.* They'd called for backup. I wondered who it was. The pregnancy test police maybe. I couldn't hear what they said, but it couldn't be good.

Knuckles rapped on the door. "Adele?"

I sat up, startled. "Pete?"

"Ah, yeah," he said in his usual low, rough tone. "Want to let me in?"

I nodded yes, but said, "No."

"Hazel and Mat—"

"Maddie," corrected Maddie.

"Sorry." He cleared his throat. "Hazel and Maddie said you're doing a pregnancy test? That's a bit of a surprise."

"You told him?" I yelled. "Holy shit, guys!"

"I'm sorry," said Maddie. "He saw the box on the table."

That made no sense. "What? How? I've got it in here with me."

Hazel sighed. "We got extras in case you had a positive result and needed to do another to be sure. You freaked out enough at the sight of one; imagine what two would have done to you."

"Okay," said Pete. "Do you really think you're pregnant?"

I just frowned. "Why are you here?"

"I brought your car down. Figured you might need it since your cast was due to come off."

"She just got it off today," confirmed Maddie.

"Great," he said. "Had some business to see to down here anyway, so . . ."

Of course he wasn't here for any romantic dying-without-me-type reason. Damn my stupid heart for hoping otherwise. After all of the countless lectures I'd given myself about giving up on him, some idiot part of me still held on. It had to just be a bad habit. There should be wrong-man rehab. Counseling, hand holding, and maybe a little waterboarding for the extreme cases like me.

Whatever it took to get the him in question out of your head.

"Will you come out, please?" he asked.

I said nothing.

"Come on, beautiful. I feel like an idiot talking to you through a door."

"Yeah, well, I feel like an idiot sitting on the bathroom floor too scared to look at the test results," I said, wiping away a tear. "But here we are."

Nothing.

"And don't call me that."

"Ladies, would you mind giving us some privacy?" he asked.

I heard shuffling, a whispered threat from Hazel to cut off his dick if he upset me. Then silence.

"A baby? Hell," he said, voice coming from closer and lower, like he'd sat down next to the door. "I don't know what to say."

"We don't know for sure that there is one."

"Hm."

"We never talked about kids seriously. For no reason in particular—just wondering—how would you feel about having one?"

"Honestly, my own experience being one was so shit I never saw a good reason to inflict that on someone else," he said. "Plus, I didn't have the best example for parenting. What if I fucked it up?"

"But you wouldn't. You'd care. Besides, look how good you were with the kid who you got stuck with during the summers all those years. Practically your finest moments."

He was silent for a moment, then he asked, "What about you? And kids, I mean."

"Sure, someday maybe. Not now."

One of the taps was dripping. I'd never realized they could be so loud. The tiny sound echoing in the small room until it seemed like thunder.

"What do you want to do if you're pregnant, Adele?"

"I don't know." I covered my head with my hands, pinching my eyes shut. "I just . . . I don't know."

Silence.

"Truth is, you're the business I've got in town," he said. "I drove down because I missed you."

I frowned in disbelief.

"After you left, well . . . I was pissed at you for a while about the tree."

"That wasn't my fault."

"It wouldn't have happened if you hadn't been climbing trees in the middle of the night like a crazy woman," he said. "You realize people don't generally do that sort of thing. You do realize that, right?"

I rolled my eyes. A sophisticated and superior gesture that was lost on him, courtesy of the wall of wood standing between us.

Silence.

"I was late taking the pill when I was on holidays," I confessed, just getting it out. "I took it as soon as I remembered. I thought it would be okay. But if I'm pregnant, this is my fault."

"Pretty sure it would have taken both of us to make a baby," he said. "I could have used condoms with you, but I didn't want to. Never done that before, but I liked being bare in you too much."

I had nothing.

"Have you looked at it yet?" he asked, voice softer.

"No."

"You're going to have to sometime."

"I know."

"Adele, whatever you want to do, I'll support you."

"Thanks," I said. Then stopped. "How do I take care of a baby? There isn't room in my life for a child, not right now."

He said nothing. Probably busy doing his own panicking on his side of the door. Which would be fair enough, really.

"Hazel and Maddie are great, but I'm pretty sure they weren't planning on me having a baby here anytime soon," I said. "Babies are loud and they need stuff. Lots of stuff. I'll have to find someplace else to live. I guess there's maternity leave, so work should be okay . . ."

"You'd stay in Sydney?"

I just concentrated on breathing for a moment, needing to calm the fuck down. "I honestly don't know what I'd do."

"If you are pregnant," he said, "I want you to know, we could raise the baby together. I don't want to be some absentee asshole that just sends money. You and a baby would need more than that and you'd deserve more than that."

"You'd want me to move north."

"I'd want my child near me, of course." He made a noise in his throat. "I mean, I'd want both of you near me so I could help. Fuck, I'm just . . . I'm trying to figure out what the right thing to do here is."

"Me too."

Nothing.

"You missed me?"

"Yeah."

"Want to expand on that?" I asked. "You seemed pretty sure about the whole me-not-turning-your-life-upside-down thing and now you're here?"

This time, the sigh was closer to a groan. "I was. Or I thought I was. I like my life how it is, Adele. Worked hard at my job to get Andrew to raise me to management. It took me years to build my house, get everything exactly how I wanted, how I always imagined it. I've finally got my own space, a home I can be proud of, the money to do some things, and a couple of good friends. Then you come back."

I kept quiet.

"I thought everything would go back to being the same after you left, but I couldn't move on," he said. "Didn't want to. Kept thinking about you and . . ."

"And what?"

"Come back up north with me now."

My eyes popped open in surprise.

"Regardless of if you're pregnant or not. I've been thinking about it and I think you should move north and take the job," he said. "That's what I came down here to tell you. The car was just an excuse."

Huh.

"I think that if things hadn't gone to shit with us, that's what you would have done."

I shrugged. He was probably right.

"Maybe things would work out between us, maybe not," he continued. "I don't know. But either way, I didn't come all this way not to be involved in your life. Whatever else has happened, we were always friends. I want that back. I've always wanted that back."

Huh.

"I'm asking for your patience, I guess."

Interesting. Though he had said something eerily similar about seeing how things worked out between us before and it hadn't ended well. Maybe we hadn't had enough time for him to figure out how he felt about me and the offer was genuine. It had only been a few days, after all. Or maybe this was him keeping me close, yet at a safe distance. The same as every other woman he got vaguely involved with. Hard to tell. Though given current circumstances, we probably had more pressing issues.

"Say something," he said.

I reached up for the test. Two pink lines. My insides flipped up and over.

I was going to be a mother. Holy shit.

A collection of cells was happening in my uterus right

now, made up of me and the man I'd loved, right or wrong, since time immemorial. This was big, so incredibly huge, my brain could barely wrap itself around it. Consequences from this event went on forever and ever.

"Adele?"

"I looked." A small voice.

"Okay."

"I'm pregnant."

A pause. "Okay."

"I think I want to keep it." The two pink lines wavered, my eyes filling with tears. Shock and fear and I don't know what else. "I can't . . . it's us, you know?"

"Open the door, please."

I walked over on my knees, flicked the lock, and then scooted backwards.

Carefully, the door eased inward and Pete appeared. Hair all messy and in disarray like he'd been shoving his fingers through it, as he was wont to do when stressed. Eyes a little tired and stubble on his cheeks. Clothes distinctly crushed.

"You didn't go to a hotel or something? You came straight here?" I asked.

He looked down at me and nodded. "I needed to see you."

"I missed you too."

Pete didn't go to a motel, but he did sleep on the couch.

Maddie and Hazel were great about having a guest. I don't know that Pete was happy about the couch situation. But we'd been back and forth in this maybe relationship so many times, I was too nervous to consider anything more right now. Perhaps in the future things would work out between us. Perhaps not.

Meanwhile, he of course stepped up, doing the good-guy responsible thing. Once I'd decided that I was returning up north with him, he took charge of the worst of packing up my room and assorted shit. Heavy things were lifted, high items were reached, and jars were opened. All of the manly stuff covered. But it was a strange sort of friendship now.

Another round of pee on a stick and a test at the doctor's the following day confirmed I was indeed carrying our child. My stomach a riot, I nearly threw up on the poor doctor's desk from nerves. Pete packed and kept busy while I worked my two weeks' notice. Well, week and a half. Given the circumstances, my boss was kind enough to let me off a few days early.

"What's this?" I asked, standing outside the apartment building the following Friday afternoon. This time, holding a bag of Chinese food. If the fetus wanted fortune cookies for our very small going-away party, who was I to deny her/him/they?

"Hey, how'd your last day of work go?" Pete grinned.

"Good. Thanks." I cocked my head, taking in the shiny new Subaru Forester parked in the street. The one he was standing proudly beside, swinging a set of keys. "You bought a new car?"

"You know how we were talking about how your car isn't exactly suitable for a baby seat and everything?"

"When you called it a small unsafe piece of shit that you were tempted to run into a ditch on the drive down?" I asked. "Yes. I recall that conversation."

"I might have been a bit harsh, I'll admit."

He patted the side of the SUV. "But this car, on the other hand, has excellent safety standards and a good amount of space."

"Okay."

"And all of the stuff from your room fits in, just fine."

"Great," I said. "Thank you for taking care of the moving and happy new car."

"It's not mine." He pressed the keys into my hand with a smile. "It's yours."

"I *have* a car."

"No, you have a small unsafe piece of shit that Maddie's willing to buy due to its fuel economy," he said. "Sorry to be harsh. Again."

"You bought me a car?" I asked, tone less than delighted.

"Blue is your favorite color, right?"

"You can't just buy me a car, Pete."

"Already did." He kissed my cheek. "You're welcome."

"No, I—"

"Adele, you need something suitable for you and the baby," he said. "This is a really good vehicle. Not too big that it'll be a hassle to park, but it's got all the features you'd want. Here, let me take that bag. It looks heavy."

"Thanks." Face tight, I looked at the key-fob thing. "I'm not comfortable with you spending this amount of money on me."

"It's not a big deal."

"It is and we didn't even talk about it," I said. "You can't just make decisions for both of us."

"I wanted it to be a surprise. Think of it as an accumulation of all the birthday presents you missed from me over the last seven years."

"Don't bullshit me," I said, frustration mounting. "You knew I'd have a problem with this, so you just went ahead and did it instead of talking to me about it so we could reach a decision together."

He gave me a pained, somewhat irritated look. "I want to look after you."

"And I want you to love me—we don't always get what we want." Then I stopped, thought about what the hell I'd just let out of my mouth. Dammit. "Pretend I didn't say that."

"Beautiful . . ."

Jesus. I hung my head. "It was just hormones. I know we're not there. I know that's not . . ."

He said nothing.

It was just like the Stones said. You really can't always get what you want. Also, I needed to get better at locking down my emotions for everyone's sake. Ever since he'd found out about the pregnancy, Pete had been doing everything he could, doting on me. Although the baby meant we'd always have this connection, it felt more like an ending instead of a beginning. I knew he'd love our child and by default, maybe me. Just not in the way I wanted. As he'd said, he'd come to Sydney willing to settle for friendship. To make amends for scaring me off from moving north to take the job. Yes, he'd missed me. It wasn't enough, however. Not really. We were right on track to wind up like my own parents, bound together by a child instead of mutual love and affection. And their marriage had been a slow-motion explosion, excruciating to be a part of.

I had to put aside my own wants and put the baby first. It was the smart thing to do.

"The car is great, thank you," I said. "In the future, though, please talk to me about any large purchases first."

"I'll do that." His arm slipped around my shoulders and he kissed me on the forehead. "You're doing great. I know you're tired and you haven't been feeling so good. I think you're amazing, okay?"

My eyes felt itchy, my throat tight. Hormones were the worst.

"It's been a long time since I had someone I wanted to look after," he said. "When you were young, you just needed to be entertained, fed, and watered. It was easy. Things are more complicated now."

"Fed and watered. You make me sound like cattle."

He laughed. "No more surprises, I promise."

"Thank you. I've also been thinking about moving into the guest room at your place," I said. "It was good of you to offer, but I'm going to have to decline. I need to get my own place, have a space of my own. I've made up my mind."

His face creased, unhappy.

"Let's go eat," I said. "The food will be getting cold."

And that was my last night living in Sydney.

We'd called Shanti and told her about the baby. It was easier that way. She then told Dad. Dad yelled for a while. Shanti talked him down. And once he'd had time to get used to the news, everyone was officially delighted.

When Pete and I had taken my mother out to dinner, she was also thrilled. She then told Pete he had a striking physique and asked if he'd model for her beginner life drawing class. He declined upon finding out that he'd be expected to pose nude. Perhaps I got the touch of crazy from Mom's side.

Hazel and Maddie were ready to have the apartment to themselves, I think. At the very least, they were ready to hand over the management of my hormonal mood swings to someone else. Though we'd all miss hanging out together and having wine and takeout nights. Pete and I made the twelve-hour drive north the next day in my new car.

While Pete might have gotten his way about the car, he didn't get his way about where I'd be living. I wasn't changing my mind about that.

"I wish you'd rethink this," he said as we pulled into Dad and Shanti's driveway.

I pushed open the car door. "We've talked about it already."

"Yeah, but I think you're wrong."

"So you mentioned. Multiple times, even. Hi, Dad. Hi, Shanti."

Dad hugged me gently, a somewhat judgey look in his eyes. "Pregnant?"

"I know, right? Who knew that could happen?" I grinned. "Boy, did you not explain some things."

"Your mother had that talk with you when you were twelve," he said. "I checked with her at the time."

"Huh. Guess I zoned out."

"Should I just call you Dad now?" asked Pete with a wry smile.

"I don't know," said Dad. "Should I just hit you now?"

"There will be no violence," scolded Shanti. "Andrew, be nice. Peter, don't poke the bear when you just knocked up his daughter. That's not wise. Now, how was the drive, darling?"

"Long." I accepted my hug and kiss on the cheek. "Good to see you again, Shanti."

"Come and have a nice cold drink. What's this about you living here for a while?" she said as she ushered me up the stairs. "Not that you're not welcome, of course. I was just surprised. I thought for sure you'd be over at Peter's."

This was going to be a very long night. And I couldn't

even have alcohol. "We're taking things slowly, concentrating on the baby."

"Isn't that closing the gate *long* after the horse has bolted?"

"Being with someone just because you're having a child has a bad history of not working out in this family," I said. "As I'm sure Dad has mentioned. I think it's best if I get my own place."

"Hmm." Shanti looked back over her shoulder. "Careful, Peter, it looks like you might be losing your touch."

Yeah, no. "And I for one am really looking forward to us all being overinvolved in one another's lives and having such open and honest opinions about each other's relationships."

"That's her way of saying butt out," said Dad.

"Thank you," I said. "Pete and I are just friends who happen to be unexpectedly having a baby together."

Dad pulled a face. "Friends, huh? I'd rather see a ring on your finger, but whatever you say, sweetheart. I told you after the tree incident, I'm staying out of it. You two can sort yourselves out."

Pete just scratched his head, giving me a vague smile.

"Alright, I'll stop prying. I'm sure you know what you're doing." Shanti gave me a squeeze. "What do you think, Adele? A boy or a girl?"

"I have no idea."

"Not a problem. I'll just shop for both," she said. "I'm very excited about becoming a grandmother. Are you excited about your impending motherhood?"

"Um, I'm getting there."

"Everything will be wonderful, darling. Just wait and see."

"Hey, what's up? Are you alright?"

"Talk about déjà vu, huh?" I stood on Pete's doorstep at around midnight the same night.

Yes to the sexy pajama bottoms but no to the bare chest this time, however. He was wearing a plain gray T-shirt. So sad. At least my sleep-shorts-and-tank-top combo were slightly different from last time. With the pregnancy-enhanced boobs, I'd taken to wearing a top with a shelf bra. Much more comfortable than having mammaries all over the place.

"Come in here," he said, closing the door behind me with a frown. "You didn't climb that fucking tree again, did you?"

"The branch is broken; I couldn't if I wanted to. And in my current condition, I don't."

"Thank God for that."

"I'm sorry to wake you, but I'm so tired," I whined, shoulders slumping. "And I can't sleep because Dad and Shanti's room is next to mine and they keep having loud sex."

At this, he laughed his very fine ass off.

"Pete, it's not funny."

"Saturday night." He shrugged. "They're newlyweds."

"But he's my father," I said. "That makes it officially eww. I'm dying of sleep deprivation and their bed is banging against the wall like they're filming a porno. It's not okay."

"Come on." He took my hand, leading me toward his bedroom.

Whoa. Warning signs, red lights. "I was just going to crash in the guest room."

"Bed's not made up and it's the middle of the night," he said, flicking off lights as we went. "We're both dead on our feet. This is faster and easier."

"I'll just take the couch."

"You're not sleeping on the couch." He shot me a smile. "Relax. We're sleeping together, not *sleeping* together."

And it was tempting, but no. I pulled to a halt. "Pete, stop. I'm not going into your bedroom with you. That's . . ." I shook my head at the thought. "Let's just stick with being respectful friends who don't share a bed, okay?"

"Alright." His lips firmed. "Let me grab some sheets for the spare room."

"Thank you."

He stuck his head in a hallway cupboard, rustling up some linen. The air of discontent around him was thick indeed. Much awkward. Previously, I would have been more than happy to jump into bed with him and seen where things went. New baby, new rules.

And anyway, that prior policy of drifting into sex hadn't really delivered results for me. Apart from the type of results you get from peeing on a stick.

"Sorry to be such a bother," I said.

"You're not a bother, Adele. I want you to come to me if you need something."

"Dinner went well."

He headed into the guest room and I followed. "Andrew was pretty calm, I thought. Come on, I'll help you make the bed."

"Thanks. Have you told your father about the baby?" I asked, changing the topic neatly from my dad to his.

"No," he said, dumping the sheets on a chair before picking out the fitted sheet and sending it flying across the bed. I tucked in one side and he did the other. "Not yet. I will, though."

"I think you're really supposed to wait until the first trimester is finished to go announcing things anyway." I lifted one shoulder. "Miscarriage is pretty common in the first three months."

"Hey, don't worry about that. Everything will be fine."

Next came the top sheet, followed by a light blanket. We each wrestled with a pillow and cover. Silence was interspersed with the humming of bugs and the occasional scurrying and chittering of a possum. It was peaceful. At least, it should have been.

"I'm all set," I said, climbing onto the bed, sitting with my back against the headboard.

"Good, good. I should let you sleep." But he didn't leave.

"I'm kind of awake again now. You probably are too.

Sorry."

"Mind if I sit for a minute?" he asked, pointing at the other side of the bed.

"It's your house."

He settled in, in the same position as me, only one of his feet stayed on the floor. "I never really expected to settle down with anyone. So I'm probably going to suck at this at times. And I know we've got a lot going on right now with the baby and everything. But there's got to be a little room in there for you and me to work on things too, don't you think?"

Way to lay it on me. I said nothing.

"You've been putting off talking about it since we found out about the baby," he continued.

"I know."

He just waited.

"If you really wanted, we could date, I guess." That didn't sound too dangerous. Surely no one's heart could be mortally wounded yet again over dinner. Not without some concerted effort at least. "Casually."

"Or you could move in with me," he said. "You know, just while you're looking for a place of your own."

"Actually, I checked out some real estate sites earlier. Seems I'm in luck. There's a couple of places available close by." I smiled. "Shouldn't be hard to find something reasonably quickly."

"It's got to take a week or two at least, right? It'd just be practical if you were here."

I made a humming noise. "I should be fine at Dad

and Shanti's."

"I'll repeat, newlyweds."

I grimaced.

"You're pregnant," he said. "You need a decent full night's sleep. Not to be walking over here at midnight all the time."

"I don't know."

"You didn't even last one night over there. What if you walk in on them doing something on the dining room table?" he asked. "Because, as history shows, that obviously happens."

"Oh, God. I'd probably have to gouge my eyes out."

"Exactly. It'd be such a shame. You have beautiful brown eyes."

I exhaled. "I hope the baby has eyes like yours. A little boy with blue-gray eyes and dark hair."

He fell silent. Talk of the baby as an actual eventual living-and-breathing being still had the capability to freak him out at times. Which was kind of my point. The man was all sorts of temperamental. No wonder I had trust issues.

"And we'll call him Neville," I continued.

A grunt. "You're not naming my child Neville. Not a chance. And don't think I don't realize you're just doing this to change the subject."

"I mean, sure, Harry and Ron kept stealing the show," I said, on a roll now, and not all just changing the subject. "But Neville was always the true hero, right?"

"Adele . . ."

"Plus he grew up to be smoking hot. A total bonus."

"Fuck's sake."

"If she's a girl, we'll call her Minerva," I said. "I always loved Professor McGonagall. She could turn into a cat—how cool is that?"

"You're not naming our child after Harry Potter characters."

"You know, Pete, talk like that will get you thrown straight out of Pottermore."

"What the hell is that?"

"You're not a Harry Potter Fan Club member?" I gasped. "I can't believe I had sex with a nonbeliever. I feel so dirty."

Oh, his sly grin. "I could make you feel dirtier."

"Forget it. Neville and I need our sleep."

"Neville." He laughed. "Jesus. You know, this is why you should just move in with me. Who else would happily listen to you babble this insane stuff?"

"You're *happily* listening?" I scoffed. "I'd hate to imagine what grumpy listening would look like."

And all of a sudden he turned serious, very much so. "Adele, I'm sorry. I know I hurt you and let you down before."

"You change your mind, Pete. A lot."

"I know." He exhaled, gaze sober. "But I also now know that I'm a pitiful useless sack of shit without you."

I frowned. "That sounds oddly specific."

"Your father may have called me that a time or two over the last couple of months."

"Huh." I smiled grimly. "So Dad calls you names when you're getting with me, and also when you're not with me. Seems harsh."

"Doesn't mean he's not right both times." He sighed. "If dating is all you're willing to give me right now, then I'll take it. Thank you."

He reached out, taking hold of my hand. Our fingers curled around each other out of pure instinct. It was like drawing lines in the sand by the shoreline; waves just kept washing them away. Only my messy heart couldn't take any more hits. We were staying friends for the foreseeable future whether Pete liked it or not. No matter how good his dating game was.

"Just know, you're always welcome here," he said, voice quiet. "You can have whatever you want, beautiful."

But that wasn't the truth. Not really.

Chapter Fifteen

The temp had done a great job. I returned to no backlog, everything up-to-date and reasonably organized. Neither me nor the office looked all that different since the last time I'd been there. Though my sensitive and expanding waistline sadly ruled out some of my wardrobe. Lucky I had a few looser summer dresses. Today's was a green jersey number with knee-length skirt, no sleeves, and a scoop neck that didn't show too much hormone-enhanced cleavage.

Comfort was everything.

But the outfit also looked pretty cute with an amber colored resin bangle and sandals. Maybe I could rock this pregnancy thing. Or at least survive it with some small amount of dignity intact. There were a few half-hidden whispers and looks from the workers, but nothing too bad, given I had doubtless underlined my status as all-time town scandal.

I'd spent Sunday night in Pete's spare bedroom again. Shanti did her best to look innocent, but I'm pretty sure she knew exactly what effect their nightly sex-fest would have on me. Disgusting people. Driving me out of the house with their vulgar and loud copulating. They should be ashamed of themselves. All I knew was if I had to listen to her shout "yes, my lion, yes" one more time, my ears would probably start bleeding. Parents having sex was plainly unnatural and should be outlawed at once. Where this new law would leave me once the baby was born, I'd contemplate another time.

Meanwhile, Pete loved having me back in his house and I secretly loved being there. No major lines were being crossed so long as I slept in my own room. And it was only temporary.

An older gentleman marched into the office wearing a pinstriped suit, his face set in grim lines as he checked out the place. Apparently nothing pleased him, since the pissy expression remained. It took me a moment to recognize him. He was Pete's dad, and the years hadn't altered him any. "Peter Gallagher in?"

"He's out on site, but I expect him back shortly."

His gaze fixed on me, even more lines digging in beside his mouth. They weren't from smiling. "You're the girl, aren't you?"

"Yes, I am 'the girl.'" I swiveled in my office chair to face him directly, speaking with an excess of politeness. "Anytime, anywhere in the world, when someone is talking about a girl, they are in fact talking about me. Amazing, huh?"

He scowled at my words, and I smiled up at him. A smart mouth rarely gets you out of trouble. But it does make trouble a lot more fun to be in.

"I remember you." His lip curled in distaste. If only he had a villainous mustache to twirl, it really would have completed the picture. "He brought you to the house that time."

"That's right."

"And now you've—"

"Dad." Pete strode in, depositing his tablet and sunglasses on the top of my desk. "I didn't know you were planning on stopping by."

"Your sister called me."

His voice dropped. "Right."

"I should have heard it from you," said his dad.

Pete faced him, hands on hips. "And you would have, when I was ready to tell you."

"How could you be so stupid?"

"The baby might be unexpected, but Adele and I are both happy about the news."

"You'll be paying for this mistake for eighteen years." He jabbed his finger into Pete's chest.

"Dad—"

"That girl has her hooks in you now. Soon enough there'll be an ungrateful brat just draining you dry."

"That's enough."

Spittle flew from the old man's lips. "Getting had by some young piece of ass. I thought you were smarter."

My whole body went rigid, but I stayed put. Kept quiet.

"I said, that's enough!" Pete grabbed his father's arm, hustling him over to the door. "How dare you come here and insult her? This shit, Dad, is exactly why I didn't tell you. It's also why you won't be a part of either my or my child's life ever again."

Mr. Gallagher's eyes were big as moons. "W-what?"

"As if I would allow you near my child," said Pete, hands trembling and jaw set. "I'm sorry Mum died, but we all lost her. We all went through that. And instead of being a decent father and being there for Chrissie and me, instead of showing us just an ounce of love now and then, you turned into the sort of unmitigated asshole I wouldn't even inflict on my worst enemy."

His dad sputtered in outrage.

"We're done—I mean it. You just managed to blow any tiny chance you ever had of knowing your grandchild. Now get out of here and don't come back."

The old man drew himself up tall and then charged out the door. My ears rang at the sudden all-consuming quiet. Though my thundering heart soon filled the space. Holy shit.

"Jesus, what a prick," said Fitzy, standing in the hallway beside my father.

Damn, there'd been a full audience. I hadn't even noticed they were there. When he turned, Pete's face was tight, gaze grim. It was like he'd shut down completely. Everything locked and bolted tight.

"Are you alright?" I asked, not daring to reach for him.

"Fine," said Pete, grabbing his sunglasses but leaving the tablet. "Sorry about that. Are you . . . you're good?"

"Yes."

A nod. "Good. Okay. I—ah, I'm heading out for a while."

Fitzy, my father, and I all nodded, but said nothing. We watched in silence as Pete followed his father out the door. Though I highly doubted there'd be any tearful forgiveness in the parking lot. I was more concerned he might take a swing at the bastard. That would be a bloody disaster. I dashed over to the glass door. All clear. There was no sign of Pete's dad, who seemed to have had the good sense to make a quick exit, at least. Pete got into his truck, slammed the door, and backed out of the lot. I kept right on watching until he disappeared from view.

Dad's hands rested lightly on my shoulders. "He'll be okay, sweetheart. Just give him some time to cool down. Glad he finally kicked the asshole to the curb. That's been overdue a long time."

I nodded. "Yeah. He'll be alright."

"Of course he will."

But I wasn't quite convinced.

"He does not sound like a nice man," said Shanti after dinner that night.

"That's an understatement."

Dad had already gone to bed with a hardcover thriller in hand. Maybe they were giving the orgy a break for the night. Or maybe my new law prohibiting parental sex had finally been passed. Thank God. Shanti and I sat on the front deck so I could keep an eye on Pete's place. There'd been no sign of him all afternoon and now at nearly ten o'clock, his house lay in darkness. I'd tried calling him but gotten no answer. Who knew where he was, what he was doing, where his head was at? It had to hurt, shutting his father down like that, after all these years. Even if it probably was the right thing to do, the man was still his father.

"Some people shouldn't be allowed to be parents." Shanti swirled the contents of her wineglass. "It sounds like Peter's sister should have known better than to leak the news to the man in such a fashion."

"Mm."

Earlier, there'd been rain, leaving the air smelling alive and clean. Underneath were the scents of earth and growth, a faint trace of the frangipani, eucalyptus, and other things in bloom. Frogs croaked from out in the garden. It was hard to miss the lights of the city when you were surrounded with so much beauty.

I yawned, my jaw cracking.

"Why don't you go to bed, talk to him in the morning?"

"No, I'm going to go wait over there," I said, rising out of the wicker chair.

"What if he doesn't want to talk?"

"That's up to him. I just want him to have the option, and to know he's okay."

"What if he brings someone home with him?" Her dark eyes gleamed in the low light. "When he's in a mood, he tends to drink, and when he drinks —well, it's not always so easy for people to break their habits, darling."

I swallowed. "Then I'll come back, I guess. I don't own him; I mean we're not . . . together."

"I don't mean to be hurtful," she said, voice low.

"I know. But he's spent enough of his life alone."

"Mostly that's been his choice."

"Yeah," I said, searching for some clarity. "If he doesn't want me there, then I'll leave. But he's always been my friend first. Anyone else, if they'd gone through what he did today, I'd want them to know I was there for them if they wanted to talk."

She just nodded. "Our door's always open to you, darling."

"Thank you. 'Night."

I wandered across the road in pajamas and Birkenstock sandals. My hair tied back in a messy ponytail. On the off-chance Pete did bring some hot piece home, I'd be looking real good. Not. He didn't have any chairs on his small front porch. Really should have thought to bring a cushion with me. Instead, I sat down on the dry top step, leaning against the railing to try and get comfy. Maybe this was stupid. My life was so full of wonder. Mostly wondering what the hell I was doing. I guess, in the end, you could only do what felt right. What you'd hope someone would do for you.

Eventually, the lights inside Dad and Shanti's place went out. Only the dim porch light was left shining for me. It was just me and the night and my good intentions. That would have to be enough.

Hours later, I startled awake in the process of being lifted by strong arms.

"Easy, beautiful. It's just me."

"Pete?"

"I should have thought to give you keys to the place," he said, carrying me inside. My limbs ached from my slumped sleeping position on the front stairs, but the familiar scent of him, the heat of his body, all felt far too good. The only light was a lamp on the side table glowing softly, casting shadows on his handsome face.

"What time is it?" I asked, my sluggish mind slowly waking.

"A bit after eleven." His voice was low, rumbling through his chest. But it was clear, and his hold on me was firm. He hadn't been drinking after all, despite my and Shanti's worries. "I'm sorry I left you out there waiting."

"Not your fault. I wanted to make sure you were okay."

"You did?" He actually sounded surprised. "You didn't have to do that. I'm fine. Everything's good."

"He's your father."

"Yeah, well, he's a shit one. It was about time for me to cut ties," he said, depositing me carefully on the spare bed.

I shuffled up into a sitting position, keeping a hand on his arm. He sat on the edge of the bed beside me, his gaze weary. A young boy's hurt seemed to linger in his eyes, coupled with a man's regret. My heart ached for him. For a long time, he looked at me. And the world felt very small right then, with just me and him alone in the night.

"Had some thinking to do," he said at last. "Went to the beach and walked for a while, trying to clear my head."

I just nodded, trying to hold back a yawn.

"I called Chrissie and told her what happened. She apologized." He rubbed at his mouth. "My sister still thinks she's going to break through all the ice one day and finally have a father worth knowing. She thought he'd be happy to hear we were having a kid."

"Ah."

"Yeah." His gaze dropped to my middle. "You have a small belly, Adele."

"It could be cake, but I prefer to believe it's baby."

His smile was brief. No more than a flicker. "You're exhausted. I should let you sleep."

"It's fine." I picked up his hand, toying with his fingers. "I'm here for you if that's what you want, Pete. I mean, not sex. I don't . . . we're not there yet. But, you know . . ."

"I know." His hand curved around the back of my neck, drawing me in for a quick kiss. "I'm glad you're here. At the end of a very shitty day, seeing your face is exactly what I need."

I smiled.

"Not sex, but would you mind if I slept in here with you tonight?"

"Sure." I wriggled down in the bed, getting comfortable.

Meanwhile, he went and closed the front door, turned out the light. In an unparalleled act of strength, I didn't watch while he pulled off his boots and undressed, stripping down to just his boxer briefs.

They were gray. Alright, so I might have peeked.

The mattress dipped and he settled beside me. I reached for his hand, slipping it under the hem of my tank, against my middle. With his skin on mine, things seemed more settled. He was here. He was okay. Or he would be.

"It's funny," he said, voice low in the dark. "You think you've dealt with stuff, that you're fine with it. But it's like it sits in the back of your head, affecting how you see things, the way you live your life."

I stroked the back of his hand in silent support.

"Thought I was smarter than that, stronger. I fucking hate that I let that happen."

"Relationships with parents are complicated."

He snorted. "Yeah, they are."

"Relying on someone so much, needing them when you're small and helpless," I said. "I mean, everyone's bound to drop the ball occasionally. We're only human. But some people, like your father, it's as if they don't even try. They don't want to."

His thumb stroked across my skin. "That's not going to happen with our child, beautiful."

"I know."

"Time to let it go," he said, rolling onto his side, replacing one hand with the other. "I'm just . . . I'm so through with it. With him being any part of my life. Our lives. Did a lot of thinking today."

"Yeah?"

"I know I haven't exactly been down with your plan, you getting your own place, us just dating." He smiled. "But if that's how you want to play it for now, then I'm good with that. Us figuring things out, moving toward something."

I smiled. "Okay. That's great."

The white of his teeth as he smiled back at me was just visible in the low light. And I hoped he wouldn't crush my heart again. That he knew what he was doing now, what he wanted. But only time would tell.

"I really like that color on you, darling. It's a very nice dress."

"Thanks."

"There we go. Perfect." Shanti stepped back, examining my updo. Because of course the woman was crazy great with hair along with everything else.

It was Saturday night and I'd done the getting ready

at her and Dad's house. It was all part of the official dating plan. Despite my nerves, my hands weren't shaking and I wasn't sweating too badly. Thank God.

"You're amazing," I said. "I love it."

She smiled. "You're going to knock Peter on his ass."

I smoothed down the front of my blue bodycon dress in a mostly forgiving soft fabric. My slight middle didn't throw things out too much and the rounds of my breasts were sort of spectacular. Since pregnancy was giving me extra curves, I was down with putting them on show. Silver drop earrings, a fancy hairdo compliments of my stepmom, red lips, and nicely emphasized eyes. I was good to go.

"Peter's arrived," she said. "He's sitting with your father in the living room."

"Dad must be loving this."

"I asked him to behave himself. But it is the first time he's ever gotten to send his daughter off on a date. Allowances must be made."

"Hmm."

She followed me out to the living room, where Pete was indeed wearing a somewhat pained expression, his foot tapping manically against the floor. Dad meanwhile sat back in his chair, his gaze more than moderately hostile. Lovely.

"Told him to have you back by ten," he said. "And no funny business."

"Dad."

"Alright, eleven," he amended. "He can have a good-night kiss, but should keep his hands to himself. I'll be watching."

I shook my head.

Pete rose to his feet, resplendent in a black suit with a white shirt, open at the neck. Dark hair done in the slight pompadour style that made him look shit hot. I might have swooned a little.

"Hey," he said. "Feel like I should have brought a corsage."

"Just you is fine." I smiled.

"God, you look beautiful." He stepped closer, his gaze roving over me. Ever so gently, he slid a hand around my waist to the small of my back, bringing us closer. He even smelled like heaven, himself and a hint of cologne. "I'm a very lucky man."

"Yes, you are," said Dad. "Don't forget it."

The urge to reach up and kiss him, to call off the date and go straight to his bedroom, was strong. But we needed to take these small steps. To do it slow and right so it stuck this time. See if it would work, which I really hoped it would. But I'd been here a time or two before. Not exactly like this, though close enough. My heart on my sleeve, and everything I wanted just within reach. Maybe this time he'd reach back for me.

"If you keep staring at my mouth like that, this is going to be a very short date," he mumbled, soft enough not to have his words carry to Dad.

I blinked. "Right. Sorry."

Less carnal thoughts. I could do it. Probably. With

the way my hormones were and how good he looked, it wouldn't be easy. Self-restraint rarely was my thing.

Meanwhile, Shanti gave a happy sigh, hand resting on my father's shoulder. Her gaze was all soft and shiny, as if she were about to cry. "You look wonderful together."

"You ready to go?" asked Pete.

I nodded, letting him slide his fingers between mine, holding on tight.

"Don't wait up," I said. "And thank you!"

Dad grumbled something, but Pete just raised his free hand to wave goodbye, keeping us moving. Down the front steps, and out to the driveway where his truck waited. The night was perfect and full of promise. Carefully, he lifted me into the passenger seat.

"I can manage," I said.

"You shouldn't have to." He leaned in, licking his lips. Something about his gaze seemed off. Whatever lay beyond intense, that's what was in his eyes. "We're doing this right, yeah?"

I nodded somewhat hesitantly.

"So instead of the local pub, we're going to go have a nice dinner. I booked us into a fancy restaurant with beach views," he said. "Best steak you've ever eaten, I promise."

"Sounds great."

"Okay. How are you feeling?"

"Fine."

"Good."

He carefully closed the door, walking around the

front of the vehicle. The engine rumbled to life, his hands gripping the steering wheel tight. Seemed the man was even more nervous about this than I was. Which was nice. His taking it all so seriously, thinking it was as important as I did. Yay for slow and steady winning the race. My hopes were sky-high.

"Your father said you went to check out an apartment at Woombye today?"

"Yes. It was nice."

His chin jerked.

"I think I'm going to take it."

"Great. That's great," he said, pulling out onto the road and driving at a sedate pace down the street. "You found a place fast."

"Yeah."

His fingers flexed around the steering wheel, knuckles showing white. Next a muscle jumped in his jaw.

"Are you okay?" I asked.

"Yep. Great."

At the corner, he stopped, checking traffic both ways. It was clear. Not another headlight in sight. Yet for some reason, we still weren't moving.

"Pete?"

No response.

"Hey..."

"This is fucked." His Adam's apple bobbed. "I'm sorry. I can't do this."

My stomach dropped. "What? What do you mean?"

"No," was all he said.

Without further ado, he shifted the car into reverse, turning us around. Back toward home we went at a much faster rate than we'd left. The sharp angles of his cheekbones stood out in his face, lips a flat line. This couldn't be happening.

"I don't, I don't understand." My throat ached, eyes blinking back tears. As if it would help.

We pulled into the driveway and he jumped out of the vehicle. Leaving the engine running for a quick getaway no doubt. I'd been so stupid. Again. When would I learn? I didn't even bother fighting him when he came around to my door, undid my seat belt, and lifted me out. Evicted me from his fucking vehicle. Fingers wrapped around my wrist, he dragged me back into the house. Bright lights dazzled my eyes, blurred in my watery vision. Dad and Shanti had moved into the kitchen, preparing dinner. Shanti froze and Dad frowned as Pete hauled me into the room. It was like something out of a nightmare. Everything inside of me was breaking. Shattering.

"I'm not dating your daughter," he said, hand like a manacle around my wrist. Not tight, but not moving either. I tried to shake him off, but he wouldn't let go.

No one said anything.

"I'm sorry, Adele," he continued. "I know that's what you wanted, but it's bullshit."

Dad just sort of growled.

"Explain yourself, Peter," said Shanti, holding a very large chopping knife.

Pete, however, missed the clear threat on account of

being busy flicking a tear off my cheek. His brows lowered, lips thinning. "Don't do that, beautiful."

I stared at him, dumbfounded.

"I'm not dating the woman I love who's carrying my baby, because that's messed up," he said. "We're getting married."

"W-we're what?" I asked.

He nodded, all enthused. "Yeah. We're getting married. You're living with me. No more of this nonsense, okay?"

I blinked.

"I just don't think it's good for either of us." He gently wiped another tear off my face. "Seriously, beautiful, you've got to stop crying. You're supposed to be staying calm. It's not okay for you to get all upset."

I swallowed. "Why is this all happening now?"

"Because it can't wait. Don't you see?" His eyes looked at me pleadingly. "Because if we wait long enough, then you'll have the baby. And I'm good with kids. I open up around them. You know that. Either by your side, or in the house down the road, I will be the best dad for our child."

"I know."

"And that terrifies me."

I blinked. "What? Why?"

"Because it would be so easy for both of us to settle for that." He shook his head in determination. "But I don't think that either of us deserves to settle. Not for one moment of the rest of our lives."

Shanti cleared her throat. "Am I to understand, Peter, that you're asking Adele to marry you now?"

"That's right," said Pete. "Well, I'm not asking. She might say no and want to try the going-slow thing again. Honest to God, I tried it—doesn't work."

"You're asking her to marry you because you love her?"

"Yes."

"I see," said Shanti. "I'm not entirely certain she's aware of that fact."

Pete turned back to me, licked his lips. "I love you."

"You do?"

He nodded just once. "Like crazy. You wanted me to see you. But, Adele, you're all I see."

"Wow. Okay. This is, um, it's kind of new." I swallowed hard, trying to pull myself together. "Are you sure about this? When did you decide exactly?"

"After you went back to Sydney."

"That was months ago."

"Yeah. Sorry about that," he said. "Just took me a while to get it straight in my head."

I had nothing.

Dad crossed his arms. "Are you asking for my daughter's hand in marriage?"

"No," said Pete. "I'm telling you that I love her and we're getting married. She's everything to me. Took me a while to figure out, but I know it now."

"And you're definitely sure about that?"

"Yes. Positive. So we're good?" he asked, turning back

to me. "Don't get me wrong, beautiful. More than happy to take you out to dinner or the movies or whatever whenever you want. But I'm not dating you, because this isn't casual or temporary or whatever. This is you and me together forever now, okay?"

"Huh," I said, still catching up. "This isn't just a reaction to me finding an apartment, is it?"

"No, though I fucking hate that idea too."

I just stared.

"I need a yes, Adele."

"You love me and you're mine?"

"Completely," he answered without a moment's hesitation.

I bit back a smile. Suddenly, I could breathe again. All of the angst and heartache were falling away. "You really do need to ask me to marry you, not tell me. That's not cool."

"Yeah." He scratched his head. "Sorry about that. I got a bit freaked out that maybe I'd waited too long and messed things up."

"No, you haven't."

He smiled. And it was the most beautiful thing I'd ever seen. "Good to hear."

"Say it again."

He leaned in, pressing his lips against the corner of my mouth, my cheek, my earlobe. "I love you, Adele. I'll buy you a big-ass ring and get down on one knee. Do whatever you want . . . I just need a yes from you."

"You do, huh?" I relaxed against the hard length of

his body, grinning. How completely insane this all was. No way could I get my mind around it. But my heart was hammering, my head spinning, and all I could see was me and him together. Me and him having a family. Amazing. There was so much goodness laid out in front of me for years to come. "Yes. I-I'll marry you. I will."

"Thank you," was all he said.

Epilogue

"What are you doing creeping in here?"

"Like a ninja," I added. "Creeping in here like a total ninja. That's what you meant to say, right?"

Pete laughed. Light dazzled my eyes, my man strolling toward me with a smile on his face. "What are you doing creeping in here like a totally pregnant ninja with a key to the front door?"

"Don't diminish my accomplishment," I huffed. "And we ninjas are always well prepared."

"Sorry," he said, hands sliding around my waist. "Decided against the not-seeing-each-other-the-night-before thing, huh?"

I shrugged. "I got bored and then I got nervous, so then I just decided I may as well come home."

Despite Shanti's protests, we'd organized our wedding on the fly. Only a little over a month after he'd proposed, we were going to tie the knot. Shanti had been keen on organizing a marital extravaganza, possibly after the baby was born. But Pete and I just wanted a simple ceremony on the beach. I wanted to take things easy and just enjoy where we were at.

"Good idea," he said. "I missed you."

"You did, huh?"

Instead of answering, he showed me, kissing me sweet and soft. Seducing me with his lips. Of course, as nice as it was, it wasn't remotely enough. Nothing was ever enough when it came to him. Next his tongue was in my mouth and oh God . . . the taste of him. I fisted my fingers in his sleep shirt while his hands slid into my hair, holding me fast. Before I knew it, he had me cornered, backed against the front door. Not that I was trying to escape. Hell no. I was actively trying to climb him like a tree, wanting to wrap my legs around him and never let go. He grabbed hold of my ass, lifting me into position.

"Bedroom?" he asked, breathing heavy. Every bit as excited as I was.

"Here. Against the door."

"You sure?"

"Yeah. Hurry."

He clucked his tongue. "Always in such a rush . . . We have to go easy—precious cargo."

"Neville's fast asleep." I moaned. "We're good to go. Last chance ever for sex outside of wedlock. And besides, there's every chance the entirety of tomorrow night will be taken up with you patiently extricating a thousand bobby pins from my hair while I sit there exhausted. I recommend you get some while the getting's good."

He just laughed some more. God, I loved that sound.

Very soon the baby belly would be too big for this position. Best to make the most of it while we still could. And I was situated in the perfect place so his hardness rubbed against me. Our mouths fused together the whole while, he shoved his pants down, getting his dick in hand. There was no time or need to take off my baggy sleeping shorts. He pushed the fabric aside, lined himself up with my core, and plunged his cock in deep.

"Pete," I whispered, holding onto him for all I was worth.

Face buried in my neck, he fucked me slow and easy. The rolling motion of his pelvis, burying his hard length inside me—it was perfect. The way his body cradled mine, holding me against the door, made for a maddeningly delicious climb to orgasm. My clit pounded with my own heartbeat, all of my insides awakening and aching with need. When he rubbed his pelvis against mine, I swear my blood turned to lava, hotter than the sun. Gradually he gathered speed, increasing his momentum. The door started rattling with each thrust, grunts sounding deep in his throat. We were like soon-to-be-married animals in some sort of mating frenzy rutting on each other. My fingernails dug into his neck and back, urging him on as he pounded into me. Sensation built and built, my lungs burning and heart thrashing.

Everything in me centered on him, on what he did to

me. Nothing else mattered.

When it came, it tore through me, sending my mind floating free. My body was a useless, trembling thing. Pete shouted, hips shoving his cock deeper and deeper until he finally slowed. My floaty mind was free.

Carefully, he set me back on my feet, pushing my mussed hair out of my face. His chest rose and fell furiously as he tried to regain his breath. "You okay, beautiful?"

"Mm-hmm."

"Coming over here and using me for sex the night before our wedding." He tutted. "You should be ashamed of yourself."

And I totes would have been, had I not been busy yawning.

"Come on. Bedtime for you, my blushing bride."

He picked me up, carrying me into the bedroom in full romance mode. Our bedroom. My clothes hung in half the armoire; my makeup cluttered up part of the bathroom. And Pete didn't mind at all. He'd moved his office to the other end of the house so the room closest to ours could be turned into a nursery. Everything was as it should be. Because this was where we were at our best, together.

"I love you," he whispered, placing me in the middle of the bed before climbing on after me.

"I love you too."

"Thank goodness for that," he said. "Could have been awkward otherwise."

I snorted.

"Want to get married tomorrow?" he asked, a smile in his voice.

"Hmm, why not?" I grinned, overflowing with happiness, overwhelmed with that feeling you have when everything in the universe seems to be exactly how it should be. That feeling was as rare as it was beautiful.

"Alright then," he said. "Sounds like a plan."

Find Kylie at:

www.kyliescott.com

Facebook: www.facebook.com/kyliescottwriter

Twitter: @kyliescottbooks

Instagram: kylie_scott_books

Pinterest: @kyliescottbooks

BookBub: www.bookbub.com/authors/kylie-scott

To learn about exclusive content, my upcoming releases
and giveaways, join my newsletter:

https://kyliescott.com/subscribe

Purchase Kylie's Other Books:

Trust

THE DIVE BAR SERIES
Dirty
Twist
Chaser

THE STAGE DIVE SERIES
Lick
Play
Lead
Deep

THE FLESH SERIES
Flesh
Skin
Flesh Series: Shorts

NOVELLAS
Heart's a Mess
Colonist's Wife

Keep reading for a free sample of

trust

NEW YORK TIMES BESTSELLING AUTHOR
KYLIE SCOTT

chapter
one

"**D**on't forget the corn chips!" yelled Georgia, hanging out of her car window.

"Got it."

"And hot salsa, Edie. None of that mild crap, you coward."

I flipped her off and kept walking, watching the ground.

Rain had turned every pothole in the Drop Stop's parking lot into a mini-swamp. We were finally out of a drought, so yay for rain. Bottle caps and cigarette stubs were floating like tiny boats on murky waters. The Northern California wind made waves, blurring the yellow light reflecting off the Open sign. Everything else was dark. Things were quiet in Auburn around midnight. Georgia and I were forced to drive across town to meet our movie marathon snacking needs. Watching all eight Harry Potter films in a row being our contribution as citizens of the Endurance Capital of the world.

"Oh, Oreos!"

As if I'd forget the Oreos, I said to myself, entering the shitty little store.

What you're most likely to drop at the Drop Stop are your standards. And I had. It had been my black yoga pants, a sports bra, and a baggy old blue T-shirt versus Georgia's satin unicorn-print slip. In the jammies most likely to be mistaken for normal clothing competition, I was the clear winner. I don't think it occurred to either of us to actually bother getting dressed. Too much effort for summer break.

Inside, the fluorescent lights were dazzling, the air-conditioning cold enough to give me goose bumps. But there it was. An aisle's worth of every bad food choice you could possibly make and as my ass could testify, I'd made them all. Happily and repeatedly.

I grabbed a plastic shopping basket and got busy.

There were only a couple of other customers. A tall guy in a black hoodie and some other kid, talking in low voices, over by the beer fridge. I highly doubted either one of them was of legal age to be drinking. One of the local college students manned the shop counter, identifiable by the textbook he'd chosen to hide behind. Note to self: Study like crazy all through senior year if you want an offer from Berkeley.

Hershey bars, Reese's Pieces, Oreos, Gummy Bears, Milk Duds, Skittles, Twinkies, Doritos, and a jar of salsa. The bottle proclaimed it to be hotter than hell; there was even a demon dancing on the side. It all went into the basket, each and every major processed food group represented. Still, there was a little room left and it'd be silly not to go all in since we'd driven to the other side of town. Why, it'd take a good ten to fifteen minutes at least just to get back to Georgia's parents' place. Sustenance for the journey alone would be required.

A tube of Pringles for good luck and prosperity, and we were done.

I dumped my basket on the counter, making college boy jump. Guess he'd been seriously engrossed in his studies. Startled brown eyes gawked at me from behind wire-rimmed glasses.

Shit, he was cute.

Immediately, I turned away, only to be facing an entire stand of titty magazines. Wow. I sincerely hoped a percentage of sales went toward helping women with lower-back problems. Some of those breasts were scarily big. Nothing much could be seen through the filthy window, but it might have started raining again. So wearing flip-flops had probably been a mistake.

Beep, beep, beep went the sales register, adding up my purchases. Excellent. Cute clerk guy and I were ignoring each other. No further eye contact was made. This was the best of all possible outcomes. Human interactions in general were a trial, but attractive people were far and away the worst. They unnerved me. I always started sweating and turning red, my brain an empty, useless place.

All of my loot got shoved into a thin white plastic bag, guaranteed to tear halfway across the parking lot.

Never mind. I'd hold it against my front, stretch the bottom of my T-shirt out to bolster it or something. Easier than asking him to double-bag it.

I shoved the money in his vague direction, mumbled thank you, and got moving. Mission accomplished.

Except a scrawny guy entering the store was in an even bigger hurry than me. We collided and I lost, my flip-flops sliding out from under me, thanks to the wet floor. I stumbled back into the shelving before dropping, hitting the cold, hard ground. The plastic bag broke and shit went everywhere. *Fother mucker.*

"Awesome," I muttered sarcastically. Followed up fast with a sarcastic, "I'm fine. No problem."

How embarrassing. Not that anyone was paying me any attention. Must have caught a metal edge on the way down because I had a scratch on my waist. It stung like a bitch, both it and my bruised ass.

College boy gasped. Fair enough. I'd be pissed too if some fat chick in pajamas started throwing her stuff everywhere. But the douche canoe who'd sent me reeling slammed his hand onto the counter, snarling something, as college boy stuttered, "P-please. D-d-don't."

I froze, realizing this wasn't about me crashing into the shelf.

Not even a little bit.

College boy fumbled with the register, panic written all over his face. This was wrong. All of it. Time slowed as the kid punched register buttons, tears flowing down his face because it wouldn't open for some reason. Skinny guy was shouting and waving something in the air like he'd lost his mind.

Suddenly the drawer flew open with a discordant little jingle.

College boy grabbed a wad of cash, shoving it into a plastic bag as the skinny guy slammed a hand down on the counter again, full of frustration and anger. Then the scream of a police siren split the air and I heard tires screech. I watched in horror as a battered car careened out of the parking lot, knocking over a garbage can and spilling trash across the pavement. A cop car followed it over the curb as another came to a halt in front of the store, lights blazing.

The man at the counter spun toward the parking lot, yelling something indecipherable as he twitched, his eyes messed up, pupils swollen and huge. Red patches—sores—covered his face, and his teeth were nothing more than rotting stumps. Then I saw the gun in his hand and my heart stopped.

There was a gun. *A gun.* This was happening, right here. Right now.

Red and blue lights flashed through the filthy windows and I sat stunned, my eyes wide, nothing computing. It was all moving so fast. I saw the instant the gunman realized he'd been left behind, because his whole body jerked. The gun wavered and then he turned on the college guy.

For one second they stood frozen, one shaking in terror as the other pointed his weapon. Then a loud cracking noise filled the air. College boy fell. It looked like someone had thrown a bucket of crimson paint across the rack of cigarettes.

The sound of sirens grew louder as more cars surrounded the building.

"You bitch!" the man screamed, even louder than the siren and the ringing in my ears. "*Joanna, you fucking bitch!* You weren't supposed to leave! *Get back here!*"

I couldn't breathe. Throat shut tight, I stayed cowering on the floor.

He turned back to the mess of blood behind the counter and swore long and hard.

"Put down the weapon," said a woman's voice through a loudspeaker. "Put it down slowly and come out with your hands in the air where we can see them."

Heavy, mud-splattered brown boots smacked against the floor, coming at me. *Oh, no.* I had to reason with him, talk him down somehow. But my brain remained stalled, my body shaking. He might've been skinny, but he easily dragged me to my feet, the grip on my arm strong enough to break me in two.

"Get up." A hand fisted painfully in my hair, the hot muzzle of the gun shoved beneath my chin. "Get to the door."

Step by shuffling step we moved forward as he used me as a human shield. I almost tripped on my Pringles, the tube rolling beneath my foot, messing with my balance. His grip tore at my long blond hair, ripping a chunk free. Tears of agony flowed down my cheeks.

"We can end this without any more violence," said the policewoman, voice crackling. "Let her go."

The headlights were blinding, lighting up the rain. I could make out the shadow of a head, one of the cops half-crouched behind a car door, arms extended with a gun in hand. Georgia was out there somewhere. God, I hoped she was safe.

"We've got both exits covered. Let her go and put down the weapon," she repeated. "We can still end this peacefully."

Pain tore at my scalp again as he pulled my hair, shoving the gun into my mouth. My teeth chinked against the hard metal, the muzzle scratching the roof of my mouth. The stink of gunpowder filled my head.

I was going to die, here, tonight, in the Drop Stop in my fucking pajamas. This was it. Out in the parking lot, someone screamed.

"I'll kill her!" he yelled, foul breath hot against the side of my face, holding the door ajar with his body.

"Don't." The cop sounded panicky now. "Don't. Let's talk."

The gunman didn't respond. Instead, the hand that had been in my hair grabbed the store door handle, pulling it closed. Next he locked it, dirty fingers pushing the deadbolt home. No escape. Not with the gun in my mouth, trembling just like his hand. All of the things I'd never do if he pulled the trigger filled my mind. I'd never get to go home again, never say good-bye to Mom, never become a teacher.

"Back up," he said. "Move!"

The gun pressed deeper, making me gag. I dry-heaved. It did no good. Slowly, I put one foot back, then another, panting as we took baby steps. Racks full of magazines filled the front glass wall; nothing could be seen of us below chest height. Above that line, the world was red, white, and blue. It looked like some messed-up disco, colors flashing between the posters advertising drinks and other stuff. In the distance, I could hear the blare of a fire engine getting closer.

Then he pulled the gun from my mouth, pushing me to the floor. I lay there, sucking in air, trying to keep calm, to make myself small, invisible. High above me chrome flashed, his arm swung in a mighty arc, and *bam*. The pistol's butt slammed into me, pain exploding inside my skull.

"Stupid whore," he muttered. "Stay there."

Then nothing.

He did nothing else. For now.

Honestly, I couldn't have moved if I tried. When I was eight, I'd broken my arm falling off the top bunk at camp. That had sucked. This, however, was on a whole different level. Agony crashed through me in waves, flowing through me from my head to my toes, turning my mind to mush. Staying aware of him wasn't easy between the hurt and the blood flowing from my forehead, dripping in my eye. I peered out from behind my hair, the world a blur.

No movement, no noise at all. I tensed at the sound

of footsteps, but they were moving away from me this time. I breathed as shallow as I could, crying silently.

Everything turned to shadows as he switched off the overhead lighting. There was still enough light coming in from outside to see, though. Guess the policewoman had run out of things to say. The rain on the roof was the only sound.

"Don't shoot," said a male voice. Muffled footsteps. "We've got our hands up. You're Chris, right?"

"Who the fuck are you?" spat the gunman.

"Dillon Cole's little brother, John," said the same voice.

"Dillon..."

"Yeah." Footsteps moved closer, toward the front of the store. "Remember me, Chris? You came around to see Dillon a few times at our house. You two used to hang together, back in school. You were both on the football team, right? I'm his brother."

"Dillon." The gunman rocked on his feet, voice slurred. "Yeah. How the fuck is he?"

"Good, real good. Keeping busy."

"Shit. Great. Dillon." The muddy boots moved back, both coming into view. I could see bits and pieces, my face mostly shielded from view by my hair. The gunman leaned against the blood-spattered counter. "What are you doing here, ah..."

"John," he repeated his name. One of the guys who'd been standing by the beer fridge. It had to be. "Just re-upping. You know how it goes."

"I know, I know," said Chris. "I was just...I was picking up supplies too."

"Right." John, the guy in the hoodie, sounded friend-ly, relaxed. Probably drugged to the gills like Chris, our friendly neighborhood psycho. I didn't know how else you could be calm at a time like this. "You should try the back door."

"Yeah," slurred Chris. Straight away, he headed for the door in question, disappearing out of sight with a wave of the gun in our general direction. "None of you three fucking move."

It was so quiet. The click of the lock on the back door and the slamming of the same door a second later came through clear as day. Chris swore bitterly, striding back to the counter. "No good."

"Damn," said John.

"Not a bad idea, though...you know. Shit. Forgot this was open." Out of the topmost corner of my eye I could see Chris reaching over the counter, pulling cash out of the register. "You need any?"

"Twenty never hurts, right?"

"Right," laughed Chris, handing a couple of bills over. "Go around and grab me some cigarettes, would you?"

"Sure. What do you smoke?"

Chris huffed out a breath. "Marlboro."

"No worries," said John, moving around behind the counter. "Man. What a mess."

Squelching noises came from back there, the kind you get when a rubber-soled shoe meets something wet.

My stomach turned, bile burning the back of my throat. I swallowed it down, trying once again to calm my breathing, trying to stay still.

"What's your problem?" asked Chris.

"Slippery back here," said John. "Never been great with blood."

"Pussy." Chris giggled like a lunatic. "You've gone gray, man. You going to puke?"

A grunt. "Go easy, I'm still in high school. I got a few years to get hard like you. Mind if I grab a pack?"

"Sure, kid. Help yourself."

"Thanks."

I stayed still, taking it all in. And wasn't it beautiful that John and his hero Chris the meth-head could spend this quality time together? Fucking hell.

Chris cleared his throat. "Who's your friend? Grab some for him too."

"Ah, that's Isaac," said John. "A friend from school. He's on the football team."

"No shit?" said Chris. "What position?"

"Receiver," came a quieter, less assured voice.

"I was fullback, Dillon was quarterback," said Chris proudly. "Those were the days."

Isaac mumbled something agreeable-sounding. A match flared and the acrid scent of tobacco smoke drifted through the air.

"Want me to get us something to drink?" asked John, like he was helping to host a damn party.

"Mm."

Squelch, squelch, came the footsteps toward me. Faded green Converse, the soles stained red with blood. I stayed still, sprawled on the ground, blood puddled around my face. At least the cool floor eased the ache in my head a little. A very little.

Chris's friend, John, stopped beside me, watching for a moment. Without a word, he about-faced, leaving a trail of bloody shoe prints behind him.

"Better not go past the door," he muttered.

"No," said Chris, giggling again. "That'd be bad."

Bottles clinked against one another. Outside I could hear car doors slamming and lots of different voices. The flashing red, white, and blue were brighter than before, as if a whole squadron of cars had joined in with the light show. *Please, God, let one of them do something constructive to get me out of here.* I'd go to church; I'd do anything. I was only seventeen, still a virgin, for fuck's sake. And while I knew I'd probably never make prom queen, I'd at least like to live long enough to attend the damn thing.

"Nice," said John. "They've got Corona."

More noises. The pop of beer bottles being opened as the boys settled in to celebrate the whole hostage situation. I couldn't see the other kid, Isaac, just Chris the tweaker and John. They were sitting on the ground with their backs to the counter, hanging out. It was ridiculous. And they might've known each other, but I don't think John did drugs. At least, not seriously. His shoulder-length hair wasn't patchy and greasy like Chris's. Scruff covered his jaw, framed his mouth. But his lean, angular face didn't have the same sores or emaciated appearance.

"What's your name?" he asked when he caught me looking.

I licked my lips, trying to summon up some moisture. "Edie."

"Eddie?"

"No. Ee-dee."

A nod. "Eee-dee allowed to have a drink too, Chris?"

"Whatever," the guy mumbled, staring off at nothing.

John rose, carefully approaching me like I held the gun. You'd have thought the meth-head would be the bigger concern. Then the nutter—John, that is—winked at me. Not a come-on kind of wink, but a play-along sort of thing.

Huh. I'd read him all wrong. He wasn't trying to be like Chris. He was trying to *manage* him.

"Sit up," he said quietly, crouching down at my side.

God, it hurt. Moving, thinking, breathing, everything. I set myself right, leaning back against the edge of a shelf. Gray fuzz filled my vision, the world tilting this way and that. He popped the cap on another Corona, putting it into my hand, closing my fingers tight around the cold, wet bottle. The way he touched me might have been the only thing that didn't hurt.

"Drink up, Edie," he said. "We're being social, right, Chris?"

Chris huffed out a laugh. "Sure. Social."

"That's right," said John. "It's all good."

I only just stopped myself from snorting.

"Maybe hold it to your head," he said, a little quieter. "Okay?"

"Yeah."

Beer had never been my thing. Georgia and I were prone to liberating the occasional bottle from her mom's wine collection. All of it cheap and nasty crap. It wasn't much like she'd notice, let alone care. The beer slid down my sore throat, joining the churning and nausea going on in my belly. I willed it to stay put, taking deep breaths, swallowing it back down.

John nodded.

I nodded back, still alive and all that. "Thanks."

His eyes were intense, gaze heavy. In a pretty-boy contest, he'd have beaten the now-dead cute clerk guy easily. What a screwed-up thought. Who knew whose blood would wind up decorating the walls next?

"What school you from?" John asked.

"Greenhaven."

"Poor little rich girl," said Chris, words slurred. "Bitches, all of them."

I kept my mouth shut.

"Dillon always liked the Green girls." John joined Chris back over by the counter.

"Liked fucking them."

"That too," said John with a false smile. "Said it was easier, going with a Green girl. They couldn't hassle him at school. Less maintenance."

Chris chuckled.

"What do you think, Edie, want to go out sometime?"

asked John. He couldn't be serious. The boy had to be crazy.

"Sure," I said, keeping the WTF off my face.

"What do you want with *her*?" Chris scratched at this chin, lips set in a sneer.

"I like blondes." John just smiled. "And Edie here seems cool with drinking stolen beers. My kind of girl."

Chris shook his head.

No words were safe, so I sipped my drink.

Drawing back his arm, Chris let his empty bottle fly, glass smashing against the rear wall. My shoulders jumped, the sound was so startlingly loud.

"Another?" asked John, calm as can be. Like he saw this kind of thing every day. Maybe he did.

"You." Chris jerked his chin at the silent friend.

"I'll get some more," said Isaac, voice shaking.

"Wish I hadn't left my stash in the car," said John. "Be good to pay you back, Chris."

Chris coughed out a laugh. "'nother time."

With a nod, John smiled.

A sudden obscenely loud trilling broke the silence, making my breath hitch. It was the phone. Just the phone. At this rate, I'd die of a heart attack long before the head wound could do its damage.

"Don't answer it," said Chris, body snapping to attention, glaring at all of us. As if we'd dare.

The ringing stopped, a moment later starting up once more.

"Bastards!" Chris struggled to his feet, keeping low as

he took aim. Crack went the gun, again and again. It took him three tries, but he finally managed to score a hit. At least, the ringing stopped. "I'm just...just going to wait. Joanna, she'll come back. She'll have a plan. She's always got a plan. Probably have to ram a window or something, I don't know."

Isaac returned, handing out more beers.

"Cool," said John, lighting up another cigarette and exhaling a ring of smoke.

"You can go then." Chris smiled, flashing a mouthful of black and broken teeth. "We just have to wait."

John licked his lips. "You didn't want to get rid of Edie now?"

Frown in place, Chris turned his head. "Why the fuck would I do that?"

"Like you said, useless Green girl. We don't need her," said John, voice smooth, compelling. "Bet you she'll panic and mess things up, make shit difficult for you. Might as well send her out, right?"

"Wrong!" Faster than I'd thought possible, Chris grabbed the younger boy. "What the fuck you playing at? You think I'm stupid?"

"No, no. Wha—"

"Shut your fucking mouth," Chris snarled, his fingers tightening around the gun. "She's the only real hostage I've got. You think the cops would give a shit if I killed your drugged-up ass right now?"

"I won't panic," I said, not stopping to think. "I promise."

Face lined, gaze angry and a little confused, Chris turned my way.

"We just have to wait for Joanna," I continued, my breath coming fast. "Thank you...thanks for the beer."

Slowly, Chris eased back, the fury falling from his face. "That's right. We just have to wait for Joanna."

I didn't risk looking directly at John, to thank him for trying to help, to see if he was all right. Eyes down and mouth shut, that was safest.

"Won't be long now," Chris mumbled as if to himself. "It'll all be over."

To keep reading, purchase

TRUST

at your favorite online retailer today!

CPSIA information can be obtained
at www.ICGtesting.com
Printed in the USA
LVHW04s1318300918
591920LV00002B/382/P